THE FATAL VENGEANCE

AN ABSOLUTELY GRIPPING THRILLER

A SERGEANT EVELYN "MAC" MCGREGOR THRILLER

BOOK 4

JULIE BERGMAN

I dedicate this book to my amazing husband and family. They have shown me unwavering support. They always believed in me, agreed to be my sounding board, lent me their creative minds, and read my work when it was still in the beginning stages. To my talented editor, who taught me so much. Thank you to all my brothers and sisters in the military who have served and are currently serving our country.

"Vengeance is in my heart, death in my hand, Blood and revenge are hammering in my head." ~ William Shakespeare

JOIN JULIE BERGMAN'S NEWSLETTER

Thank you for supporting a Disabled-Veteran-Owned business by purchasing this book.

Receive a Free Short Story

Join Julie Bergman's newsletter and get your free short story, updates about future books and get to know the author only at: https://juliebergman-author.com/my-books.

PROLOGUE

IF ANIKA SUSPECTED a killer was living in her home, she would have planned her day differently. She stretched her long, elegant limbs to the left as she centered her body into a warrior's stance. Her movements were fluid and precise. She'd been practicing yoga at the same studio for over a year. Her favorite teacher was at the front, and she always stayed in the back. Starting her morning with a yoga session put her in the right mindset to take on the day. So many clients needed her undivided attention that she couldn't afford to neglect taking care of herself.

As a defense attorney, she had to be on her game, and the case she was working on was one with a lot of moving parts. A decorated officer's daughter had died. A tragic case, and it was her job to prove it was an accident. The prosecution was trying to railroad the young man who was with her. They had both passed out drunk, and at some point she stumbled outside and froze to death in the cold Washington winter. Despite the high visibility of the case and the pressure on the local police force, she was determined to ensure that her client wouldn't be convicted. More than enough reasonable doubt surrounded this one, but no one would listen.

It had taken Anika a long time to be this good. As a small German woman with a mixed background, she had a hell of a time breaking into the good ol' boys' club. She started her career in prosecution but found it unfulfilling. Most of her prosecution cases involved young airmen who made stupid choices. Some of them weren't old enough to drink, but they were old enough to fight for their country. The problem with the Uniform Code of Military Justice and the military was it allowed little room for error in almost every area, but with drugs, there was zero tolerance.

She tired of prosecuting young men and women for something that would have been a misdemeanor in the outside world. Sending them out of the military with a conviction, jail time, and discharge because of drugs was too much for her to handle. Stupid, yes, but it left them out in the big, imperfect world with little in the way of a future. Most of the time, they couldn't even land a job at a fast-food joint, let alone anything that would pay the bills.

She dropped into a plank and stretched into a cobra pose, glancing out the window at the snow, wondering about the same vehicle that sat there day after day. Light music played in the background as she took a deep breath and let it out. This was the place she did her best thinking before she dug into a nasty case, and this one was going to be a bugger. The rumor mill in the military ran at a fast pace, and her young client was already being convicted by popular opinion. She had a lot to overcome with this one. Everyone loved the father of the girl who had died. He was a popular commander and beloved leader on the base, and they wanted to be supportive after his loss. They wanted to be angry with someone, and her young client was it.

Several threats to his safety and well-being surfaced after the incident. She put in a request to have him moved out of his squadron, but few wanted to listen and said the other airmen were just blowing off steam. Anika knew too well how things could get out of hand when people grouped against a common cause. If they all decided it was a good idea, then they might beat her client, or worse.

She stretched her hands over her head and tilted back, allowing her thoughts to run through the case. Her days were always busy, but this was her time. She needed it to stay focused, and it was one of the main reasons she was so good at her job. She didn't have time for anything else except for this one form of self-care. It was something she wasn't willing to give up, no matter how busy she was. Maybe one day she would make time for a love life, but not today. The teacher at the front of the class was done. "Namaste."

———

Gennavie sat in a stolen old green Jeep Grand Cherokee as the snowflakes fell, watching and waiting. The defense attorney came so well recommended, but now her husband, Vincent, was rotting in prison facing the death penalty all because of Anika. Her incompetence had to be punished. Punishment awaited them all, but she would be the first to face it.

As Anika stretched her slender arms over her head, Gennavie fantasized. She thought about how nice it'd be to have her partner-in-crime back. She and Vincent played together so well, but since they'd thrown him in jail, things weren't right. Playing with him made her alive and whole. Hunting by herself wasn't as fun without someone watching, except for this one. She couldn't wait to make this one pay. Now, for the first time, she needed someone in her life. Her world was upside down without Vincent.

Watching the class end, excitement flooded through her. It was time. She flipped a U-turn and headed back. She had been watching Anika for almost three weeks and things couldn't have come together any easier. The attorney lived in a tiny house on the outskirts of Seattle that was perfect for Gennavie's purposes. Her target went between Joint Base Lewis-McChord and Fairchild Air Force Base to work cases, so her little home sat close to Seattle but allowed for a simple drive to Spokane. She followed Anika home one day; otherwise, she would never have found it.

Most people thought they were safe if they tucked themselves away in the woods, but in reality, it allowed people like Gennavie unfettered access. No nosey neighbors, no one to drive by a quiet place for her to work and do as she pleased. She drove past the house, slipping her Jeep down an old path she found weeks prior, covered it with branches, and hiked back.

For a smart woman, Anika was clueless. One night, Gennavie

posed as a parking attendant at the Davenport Hotel when Anika was coming for dinner. Gennavie couldn't believe her luck when Anika showed up dressed in a little strappy silver cocktail dress. Her slender shoulders were back, her head held high like the world owed her something.

For the evening's events, Gennavie wore a wig and applied heavy makeup just in case. She held her breath as Anika handed her keys over, hoping the attorney wouldn't recognize her. They had never met in person, but Anika knew who she was. Gennavie was all over Vincent's evidence and case file as his accomplice. They didn't know the half of it.

Anika didn't give her the time of day. She didn't look as she handed her keys over, muttered a "thank you," and walked away. It was almost too easy. It had only taken Gennavie less than a minute to copy her target's key and hang it up on the board where it belonged, disappearing into the night, and dropping her borrowed uniform into a nearby trash bin.

Things were almost meant to be for this one. When she went hunting, she expected to run into problems, but with the defense attorney, it all came together without an issue. She was almost waiting for something to go wrong, anything, but so far nothing. While Anika had been TDY for court defending poor airmen, Gennavie made herself comfortable. It was quite genius if she said so herself. She installed a tracking device on Anika's phone to give her access to her calendar. It notified her when Anika would be in or out of town and where the defense attorney was—or at least where her phone was—at all times.

Gennavie had been meticulous about leaving the place the way she found it every time she stayed. Most of the time she would waltz through the front door, and no one had a clue. This was one of those occasions. Gennavie entered the house, knowing Anika wouldn't be far behind. Her slender body fit with ease under the queen-size bed. The room held Anika's scent, and Gennavie took a deep breath, inhaling when she heard the lock on the door turn.

The amazing amount of space under the four-poster bed allowed Gennavie's smaller-than-average frame to tuck in undetected. The hardwood floors were uncomfortable under her back, but she didn't mind. It had been a while since she'd played, and she was itching for a little fun.

She had to admit she kind of liked this woman. With sex and domination, Gennavie was an equal-opportunity employer. She was one of the rare creatures who enjoyed men and women on an equal playing field. There was something to be said for the softness a woman brought to the bedroom. The anticipation ran through her body like electricity coursing through her veins.

She settled in and waited. Her favorite part was about to start.

———

Anika entered her front door and dropped her keys on the kitchen counter. The same strange scent greeted her. She'd cleaned her entire house and couldn't figure out where it came from. It wasn't a nasty odor like a dead animal, but foreign, like the faint scent left behind after company came to visit. She opened her refrigerator door and pulled out a small bottle of water. *I guess it's time to go to the store,* she thought. Maybe she was losing her mind but could have sworn she had more food than that.

She shook her head, thinking she must be mistaken. Who else was going to eat her food? She lived alone and mostly liked it that way. Her life was too busy to fit another person into it, and it always complicated things. She tried a few times, but they always gave up when they found out she was married to her job. Not by choice, but the JAG Corp expected it. After only four years in the service, she thought she might get out soon and go back to the civilian sector. At least she wouldn't have to give up her entire existence.

Serving her country was rewarding, and overall fulfilling, but also all-consuming. At the young age of twenty-nine, she still had time to start a family and settle down, but if she stayed too long, that ship would sail. She knew a lot of military members who had later-in-life children, but she thought the generation gap might cause problems for kids. Her uncle had his child when he was in his forties, and now, when they went out, people would ask if he was her grandpa and not her dad.

She stripped off her workout clothes and threw them in the hamper, flipping on the exhaust fan and the shower as she went. Picking up her phone, she accessed the music and listened as the gray Bluetooth speaker came to life. "Dirty Deeds" from AC/DC filled the small bathroom as she stepped into the shower. Her music choices depended on her mood, but she liked classic rock in the morning to keep her blood pumping. She had a full day ahead of her. Today was the anniversary of the death of Amelia Churu, the victim in her case, and she needed to make sure she was at the service. It took a year for the slow-moving wheels of military justice to bring her client's case to court, and a year of hell for her client.

His squadron and leadership shunned him. She felt disappointed by how the military treated individuals who hadn't been found guilty. Most people figured the military wouldn't prosecute unless they had ironclad evidence. Boy, were they wrong. She ran her head under the warm water and closed her eyes to relax her mind.

Her short dark hair was easy to wash and style. Earlier in her career, she tried to keep it long and styled every day but found it hard to keep within regulations during her demanding schedule, so she chopped it off. The trial would be in a few short weeks, and she hoped her client would keep it together. She turned around and filled her puff with vanilla body wash. Her home was the one place where she relaxed. It wasn't fancy, but warm and inviting, with rich wood running throughout the house. They constructed the shower of stone with a glass door, creating a rustic yet elegant design.

Her young client kept creeping into her mind. If anyone could save him, it was her. Most other defense attorneys would have thrown in the towel by now, but she viewed things from a different angle. The government's case had only circumstantial evidence. Her guy was in the wrong place at the wrong time.

She thought about another case that was the same until she started digging. Vincent Wulf appeared good on paper. His superiors gave him stellar enlisted performance reports and recognized him on several occasions. He was what you would call a model airman, minus his extracurricular activities.

At first glance, she thought he was in the wrong place at the wrong time. She had even gotten his confession thrown out under duress, but the man couldn't keep his mouth shut. Of course, in that case the government had a bit more than circumstantial evidence. He'd taken an active-duty military member, Sergeant McGregor, at gunpoint. He abducted her and threatened to kill her until she drove their vehicle off the pier, giving her the advantage and allowing the authorities to bring Vincent into custody. Witnesses saw everything and were more accurate than most with their descriptions. Anika breathed in the vanilla scent, still angry with herself for not being able to get the death penalty off the table, but Vincent insisted on testifying.

———

Gennavie slipped out from under the bed and stood outside the bathroom door as her prey showered, trying not to become aroused. Anika hummed to the music. Gennavie pulled her body forward to get a better look, took a deep breath, and let it out. Anika walked out of the shower. Anika's beautiful naked body was perfect in every way. Muscular, tight, and firm, but still with soft curves. Gennavie tried her best not to become distracted as Anika dried herself and slipped on a pretty pink thong.

Gennavie squeezed the syringe in her hand, waiting for the right moment. Anika stepped out of the bathroom, still drying her hair with a towel, when Gennavie moved into her path. Watching the look of surprise in her eyes that turned to recognition and then absolute terror, Gennavie smiled. She threw her hand up, plunging the needle deep into Anika's neck, but Anika lunged, dodging to the left. Anika let out a primal scream, grabbing a lamp off the nightstand and smashing it over Gennavie's head. *The little bitch is stronger than I thought.* Gennavie sat stunned for a moment, watching Anika's shapely legs head for the door.

She reached out and grabbed Anika's ankle, pulling her to the ground. Blood was threatening to run into Gennavie's eyes. Anika looked back at the deranged woman coming at her with a trickle of blood seeping out of her red hair plastered under a see-through cap and down her beautiful face. Gennavie picked up the lamp and smashed Anika across the back of the head while she tried to squirm out of her grasp.

Anika lay crumpled on the ground and didn't move. A little blood seeped from a minor wound on Anika's head, but Gennavie didn't think she'd killed her. Gennavie slid her hands under Anika's arms and dragged her to the bed. It took all her effort to lift the attorney's dead weight. It pleased Gennavie to see Anika's chest move with the steady rhythm of her breathing. Touching her perfect skin sent electricity through Gennavie's body. She wanted to savor the moment, but a trickle of blood slid down her high cheekbone, past her eye, and tickled the corner of her mouth. She left Anika lying on the large poster bed to look at the damage in the bathroom.

The bathroom mirror was a large, ornate piece with a classic dark-mahogany double sink vanity pushed against the wall. She had to give the attorney credit: she had decorated the place tastefully. The image staring back at her looked foreign, even to her. She looked like a cross between a wild beast and an exotic animal that was slipping away from human. Bending near the toilet, she grabbed a handful of tissue, wetted it in the sink, and cleaned off the blood, touching it to the slight cut on her scalp. It stung like hell, but it would heal. She kept the blood contained, dropping the toilet paper into the toilet and flushing it, dropping her gloves in with it.

She returned to her bag and fished out a fresh pair of gloves. Gennavie had to be careful not to leave anything behind, but this was not her first rodeo. Before Anika returned home, she removed her clothing, no fibers, and she kept her body shaved clean, with no stray hairs. The only thing she had on was a pair of latex gloves. She picked up her bag, which had everything she needed inside, and checked Anika's pulse. It was strong under her fingers. She tied her victim's arms and her slender legs to the bedpost. This one was strong, at least as strong as Gennavie. They would be a pretty good match in a fight.

She sat on the side of the bed, waiting for her prey to wake up. It took more time than Gennavie expected, but there was always an acceptable margin of error with these things. She ran her fingers up and down Anika's legs, the arousal mounting between her thighs. She had been looking forward to this one.

Vincent had been the first and only person she had ever shared her true self with. Not that she loved her husband, but she needed him. He took her need to dominate to a different level. With him watching, things were more exciting and electrifying, with the added benefit that he was strong enough to dispose of the bodies for her. His only downside was his stupidity. Not only had he gotten caught, but he sang like a canary and landed on death row. Stupid man, and Anika hadn't been smart enough to get him released. Such a pity, she thought as she ran her fingers between Anika's legs, toying with the soft fabric of her little pink thong.

———

Anika's large, panic-stricken brown eyes shot open, looking around the room until they landed on Gennavie, who was stark naked at the foot of her bed. As Gennavie stood and walked around to her side, Anika let out a blood-curdling scream, but as she did, she knew no one would hear her. She'd chosen her home because it gave her complete privacy and silence to work on her cases. Anika saw the look in Gennavie's eyes and knew she was going to die. Her mother's sad eyes crossed through her mind and the suffering of her young client without her defending him.

CHAPTER
ONE

Fairchild Air Force Base, WA

EARLY ON MONDAY MORNING, Master Sergeant Evelyn "Mac" McGregor was running behind, hitting every traffic light on the way to the base. She slipped on the ice twice and had to slow it down so she wouldn't wreck another vehicle. This was the third time her insurance company had replaced one for her, and she didn't think they would give her another.

She was due at Public Affairs and had no time to waste. They'd turned her world upside down when she came back from Holloman Air Force Base in New Mexico. She remembered when Hudson said he couldn't wait to return to their daily lives, but nothing was normal. Someone had leaked the case surrounding her mother to the press, and now she couldn't go anywhere without having a microphone shoved in her face.

She maneuvered behind a long line of cars, all waiting to enter the base. "Shit," she said out loud. No way she was going to make it now. Her heart was pounding, her blood pressure rising. Little beads of sweat were forming on her forehead. "Why is it so hot in here?" And then she remembered the heated seats. She clicked them off and cooled down. The ABU uniforms were uncomfortable but fit much better than her blues. Whoever designed them was not a Latino woman. Nothing fit right and everything pinched in all the wrong places. She'd tailor them but she was trying to save some money. All these trips were setting her back. The military paid for some of it, but they didn't cover everything. The little getaway to Amsterdam with Hudson to hunt down information on Gennavie set her back. The one who got away.

This was never what she wanted. The notoriety and visibility left her exposed and unnerved. If she could go back and do it all over again, she would have left well enough alone. At first, she thought the case was about some missing airman. However, once she found out what her mother was doing, there was no turning back.

Telling her boss, "Sorry, sir, I think I'll pass on that one" was not an option for her. But the conversation never took place, and she'd walked right into the nightmare that was her family. Within a short month, her mother got arrested, her brothers died, and so much happened since then.

She thought about how things should have gone in a different direction, but every time she thought about it, she couldn't figure out how. Maybe if they sent someone else instead of her… No, it had to be her. No one else would have put in the extra effort to save her niece and soon-to-be brother-in-law. Her little SUV inched forward, and she picked up her cell to let them know she would be late. "Hi, this is Master Sergeant Evelyn McGregor," she said into the phone.

"Where the hell are you? The press conference starts in twenty minutes," Captain Boom yelled. It struck Mac as funny how much her name fit her personality. She pictured the small Asian woman with a round face and pretty features. She sounded like she had a permanent megaphone stuck to her mouth. The first time Mac met her, the loud voice that came out of the petite woman took her by surprise. Now she was getting used to it.

"Yes, ma'am. I'm sorry, but the gate is backed up all the way down Highway 2. Can you stall them?"

"What part of 'you can't be late' was confusing to you? Don't let all this attention go to your head. You're still in the United States Air Force, and you're expected to be prompt."

Mac stayed quiet, letting her finish. Arguing would just make it worse. There was nothing she could do about it now, other than to sit and wait for the traffic to move and let the captain get it off her chest.

"Are you still there?" Boom asked.

"Yes ma'am, still waiting in line at the gate."

"Don't be smart with me. Get your ass in here as soon as possible. Climb out and walk if you have to, but your ass better be here before this thing starts." Boom hung up the phone.

Sinking back into her leather seats, Mac took a deep breath, trying to calm her frayed nerves. Nothing had gone right since they returned home, except for maybe being with Hudson all the time. That part was nice. His warm embrace always made things better. The world would melt away when she got lost in his arms. She wasn't sure what their future looked like, but she loved him, and this crazy world was much better with him in it. Closing her eyes, she thought about his scent and warm body. Her mind got lost in thoughts about the rest of him—the strong jawline she liked, and when his stubble came in over the weekend. The little wicked grin that spread across his face when she wanted him. His broad shoulders that went down into his nice, trim waistline. And what lay below the washboard abs.

The car behind her honked.

"Yeah, yeah, I'm going," she said out loud to the other driver, who couldn't hear her. One of the Security Forces guards opened another lane, and the traffic moved. "About time," she said to no one. She had been talking to herself a lot and wondered if it should be something to worry about. One of her friends told her as long as she didn't start answering back, she would be okay.

She pulled into the Wing Headquarters building with less than three minutes to spare. Her tires slid on the ice as she came into the lot a little too fast. She blew the air out of her lungs when her SUV dropped into a parking spot without hitting the car next to her—a shiny, brand-new black Porsche she couldn't afford to hit. She was thankful for minor miracles. If she hurried, she might still make it. The ice in the parking lot was slick as an ice-skating ring, and she almost bit it but caught herself before going down.

Once inside, she took the stairs two at a time, almost colliding with the command chief of all people. "Hi, Mac, slow down. Where's the fire?" he asked.

"Sorry, Chief, I'm running late for the press conference thing."

"Stop by my office when you're done. We have some things to discuss."

"Will do, Chief." That was all she needed. Every time someone high on the food chain wanted to call her in, it was because she had done something they didn't like, or they had another case for her. She could handle the first but wasn't sure if she wanted the second.

CHAPTER
TWO

MAC WALKED around the corner to find Captain Boom waiting for her. For the first time, the captain stepped up to her and whispered, "Are you ready for this?"

"I might throw up, if that tells you anything."

"Sounds about right. Now stand tall. Don't let them fluster you and remember to take a deep breath before answering questions that might be adversarial," Boom advised.

"Okay." Mac took a deep breath in as the two women walked into the room together. The Wing Conference room was daunting, with large windows laid out overlooking the courtyard. The room was large, with seating on both sides and an enormous mahogany table in the center for the base leadership.

As soon as they entered, the entire room fell silent. She could see a little fly bouncing its body against the glass as all eyes stared at them. Sweat dripped down the back of her uniform. She was thankful she had her uniform shirt on and not the thin tan T-shirt underneath. She focused on the large windows behind the podium so she wouldn't have to look at the sea of reporters to the left of her.

Boom made her way to the podium, putting her back to the floor-to-ceiling windows. Mac stood to the side, doing her best not to fidget, placing her hands behind her back so the reporters wouldn't see. "Good morning, everyone," Boom began. "Thank you for coming out. Master Sergeant Evelyn McGregor agreed to answer some questions, but if anyone is disrespectful, we will end the press conference."

In the front, an attractive young man with thin blond hair and a green shirt raised his hand. "Is it true your mother is a drug lord from Mexico and the only reason you're here is because you were hiding from her?"

Mac took her place at the podium. Her camouflage uniform helped hide her figure and the nervous twitch underneath. "It is only true in part," she said in a shaky voice. "My mother is being held in a Texas penitentiary on drug-related charges, but I'm here on my accord because I chose to serve my country." Okay, that wasn't so bad, she thought.

"Is it true you were once involved in the queen's drug empire and were her successor?" green shirt in the front asked.

Where the hell were these people getting their information? Mac found it interesting the press had picked up that Reina, her mother's name, meant *queen* in Spanish. And that they referred to as the *queen of the drug trade*. "I was never involved in her business, and I left home when I was young. I had no dealings with her business."

A young blond woman in a red blouse stepped forward and pushed her mic toward Mac. "Isn't it true you had an arranged marriage with a man in the drug trade? While you were also in a romantic relationship with one of your coworkers?" She delivered the question the same way she would have asked Mac what she had for dinner the night before, instead of accusing her of having inappropriate relationships.

Boom put her hand on Mac's shoulder to remind her to stay calm. Mac took a deep breath. "That is inaccurate." Breath in, breathe out. "No arranged marriage existed. My mother requested for me to marry someone to advance her business." She prayed they would leave Hudson out of this, but that wasn't the case. "As far as my romantic relationship is concerned, he is not my coworker. We work in different squadrons with unconnected chains of command. It would be like you dating someone from KHQ and saying you're coworkers." The woman was from KHQ's competition, KREM News. She hoped it would shut them up about Hudson.

"Is it true you slept with the Security Forces First Sergeant in order to get out of a pending drug investigation?" the young blond man with the green shirt in the front asked.

"No, that is not true. Those were false allegations."

"Are you getting out to go back to Mexico and take over your mother's empire?" one of the young men in the back shouted. "With your brothers dead, does it make you the next in line? How much money will you inherit?"

Boom stepped forward. "I warned you against this line of questioning. Master Sergeant McGregor served her country and has no intentions of becoming the next queen of the drug cartel. Move on to another line of questioning."

"What can you tell us about your work with serial killers?" the same man in the back shot back. He wasn't tall but had on a bright blue button-down shirt that contrasted well with his dark skin and made him stand out.

"I'm not at liberty to discuss ongoing cases," Mac said.

"What about the man you killed? Can you tell us about him?"

Mac paused, not sure how to answer the question. She was struggling to come to terms with that part of her past, let alone telling strangers about it. "They deemed it self-defense," was all she could say.

"Was it the first time you had ever killed anyone? What was it like?" red blouse asked from the front row.

The blood drained from Mac's face. "Okay, that's it," Boom said, stepping in front of the podium again. "Press conference is over." She ushered Mac out the door and into her office, leaving a crowd of reporters shouting questions at their backs. "Stay here, I'll be right back." Boom walked out, locking the door behind her. Reporters were ruthless, and they wanted a juicy story.

Mac sat in the small office, waiting for Boom to return. She expected some of the questions and hoped they wouldn't attack Hudson, but she hadn't realized how unprepared she was for this. How does one explain you took another human being's life? The problem was Chief Deleon was her first, but she also had to kill while in Mexico. She didn't want to, but it came down to either her or him. The second man she killed was Gabriel. He was the son of the drug supplier her mother worked with who drove her sister to suicide and was trying to choke Mac when she gained the upper hand. She didn't feel remorseful about the world getting rid of both men, but she hadn't made peace with the fact that it was she who took their lives.

She'd never experienced something like this and never wanted to again. Maybe it would be a good idea to leave the military but not to take over her mother's cartel. She enjoyed the military and took pride in serving her country, but she couldn't deny how tired and stressed she had been. Her mental health was taking a back seat.

It took thirty minutes before Boom returned. "Are they gone?" Mac asked.

"Yeah."

"Sorry, you said they were going to ask some tough questions… but I froze," Mac tried to explain.

"You have nothing to apologize for. They were throwing heavy hitters right out the gate because they didn't know what kind of time they had. They can be vultures sometimes."

"How're you doing now that it's over?"

"I'm still sweating like a sinner in church, but I'll be okay." Mac smiled, trying to lighten her mood.

CHAPTER
THREE

MAC LEFT Boom's office and headed for the command chief. He was a nice man and always kind to Mac but being called into his office couldn't be good. His reputation made her think it wasn't pleasant. It wasn't the man; the position he was in dictated it. Part of what he did to assist the wing commander was to keep his finger on the pulse of good order and discipline on the base for enlisted members. This gave him a reputation as the one always involved in disciplinary matters. He did many other positive things, but people focused on the negative.

She walked into the Wing Headquarters suite of offices. They decorated it in all-dark wood, with large desks and plenty of natural lighting. The secretary stood up to greet Mac. She only stood five feet on a good day with long, jet-black hair. Coming around her desk, she shook Mac's hand. "Hi, I'm here to see Chief LeBannel. He requested my presence."

"Of course, Mac. How have you been?"

"I'm okay, Mara. How are things going up here?"

"Busier than you can imagine. Every time I think I'm about to get my head above water, they throw something else on top, and I sink again."

Mac liked her. The few times they'd met, she was nice and never appeared to have a bad day. She always took the time for a kind word, no matter how busy things were. "I'm not surprised. I couldn't fathom being the one to manage the wing commander and all the others under your purview."

"You give me too much credit."

"Only where it's due."

"Mac, thanks for coming by." Chief Master Sergeant LeBannel poked his head out of his office. He engulfed most of the door frame, standing at almost seven feet. As a prior semi-pro bodybuilder and wrestler, his stature was massive, with wide shoulders and thick arms that looked more like tree trunks. He held his hand out to Mac, and she shook it. Her smaller hand got lost in his. She thought she would be used to it after being around Hudson, but this man made Hudson look small, which was no easy feat.

"Not a problem, Chief. What can I do for you?"

"Come into my office so we can talk in private." Mac followed him in, shutting the door as she went. "Take a seat." She sat across from him in a small gray chair and waited. "I wanted to check on you. How are you doing?"

"Fine, thank you for asking," she said, looking at her hands. It was like she was in the principal's office, and this principal was intimidating.

"Okay, let's try a different question. Can you tell me about the bags under your eyes?"

"Chief?" she asked it as a question rather than an address.

"I haven't been here long, but I pride myself on being well-informed. And you are the talk of the day right now, which can come with a great deal of pressure and stress."

"Yes, Chief, but I'm fine. It's nothing I can't handle."

"Understood. We need to discuss containment and getting Fairchild out of the limelight. We don't mind a little media attention when it's positive, but your family is nothing we want to be known for. Where does the case sit right now?"

"I'm not sure." She wasn't lying; the FBI and others investigating her mother's case had kept her in the dark. "She's being held in Beaumont Federal Penitentiary in Texas pending arraignment, but many players are involved. The Feds are taking point, but several states and Mexico want a piece of my mother and her organization."

"How does that sit with you?" LeBannel asked.

"Um…" she wasn't used to sharing her feelings with her higher-ups. In the military, they taught you early on to "suck it up, butter-cup," and not complain. Without question, you weren't supposed to cry during your breakfast and share your feelings with your leadership.

"Look, Mac, I need to know you can handle what's going to come your way. If you don't want to talk to me about it, I need you to talk to someone else. I would recommend someone who doesn't have a dog in the fight."

"Copy that, Chief."

"I'll check up on you to make sure you're seeing someone. It's ther-apeutic to talk to someone even if they can't help fix it. Getting it off your chest can do wonders."

"Um, isn't it voluntary unless my commander orders a psych eval?" Mac asked, trying not to cause problems. She wasn't trying to pick a fight with this man because she respected him and it would be career suicide, but she also didn't like to be ordered into mental health.

"Yes, it's voluntary for now, but this is a lot to handle, and we're concerned about you. It's not every day you help put your mother behind bars and lose your brothers."

"I agree, Chief. It isn't every day, and I don't like what happened to my brothers, but other than the press attention, it's a bit of a relief. For the first time in my life, I'm not looking over my shoulder or wondering when they're going to find me. It's like I can plan for the future and make a life for myself without worrying about people I care for getting caught up in their mess."

"That's a healthy way to look at it, but what about when they want you to testify against your own mother? How is that going to go?" LeBannel pointed out.

"I'll have to cross that bridge when I get there. After surviving so much already, I can handle almost anything they throw at me."

"You've shown great strength in the past, but don't forget you're human; sometimes people need self-care. Like when I was powerlifting and threw out my back, didn't take a break, and kept pushing through, it ended my career. If I stepped back and took care of myself, I'd still be in the circuit. Mental health is no different. It's important you do that. Take some time now and take care of yourself. Not six months from now, right now."

"I understand, Chief. I'll find someone to talk to."

"I don't think you're hearing me, Master Sergeant McGregor." The change in the tone of his voice and his address by her proper rank and name got her attention. She'd thought this was a health and wellness check. "We've spoken with your boss, and until you're told otherwise, you are being taken off any major cases. We aren't benching you, but you will only assist with the low-level cases at the defense office for now."

"Chief, I don't understand. Did I do something wrong?"

"No. This isn't a punishment, but it's also not a discussion." He stood to his full height, indicating their meeting was over. He walked around the desk. Mac stood, tiny in his presence, as he opened the door.

"Yes," she said, and walked out.

MAC GOT BACK in her car, not sure what to do, so she called Hudson.

"Hi, hon. How'd the press conference go?"

The sound of his voice washed over her like a warm shower. "Not great, but it went further downhill from there."

"That doesn't sound good. How bad could it have been?" Hudson asked.

"Depends on how much time you have to talk."

"Well, about that, I'm headed into a meeting, but would love to talk about it tonight when we get home. Are you still up to going out?"

"Sure, I welcome the distraction, otherwise I'm likely to obsess over this. Go to your meeting, and I'll tell you all about it tonight."

"Sounds great, hon. Love you."

"Love you too," she said, hearing him disconnect. She needed to find someone to talk to who wasn't familiar with her family and didn't want something from her. Sometimes she held back with Hudson because she didn't want him to think she was crazy. It wasn't fair to always use him as the person she dumped all her stress on. He always took it well, but she didn't want it to affect their relationship.

She wondered if Chaplain Bastion would be available. He'd mentored and supported her when she'd faced being wrongfully accused of dealing drugs on base and had hunted down Chief Deleon. The chief was her confidant at the time, and the man who set her up on suspicion of drug charges. The betrayal still stung, and she already had trust issues. She wished she'd gone back to talk to Bastion after killing Deleon in self-defense. It could have helped with the nightmares.

It wasn't that simple. The nightmares were getting worse. She woke most nights with her head spinning and visions of either Deleon or one of her other cases. She would wake covered in sweat, not being able to breathe with her latest cases filling her brain. Her first major case was with Deleon, who was killing women. He kidnapped the sister of one of his victims, but there were others. Vincent and Gennavie crept into her dreams regularly. They were an interesting couple who hunted together. She thought she had almost gotten that case out of her mind when her latest case blew up and her brother tortured her on her mother's orders. She would pay good money to stop thinking about her family and shut her thoughts down or, at a minimum, compartmentalize.

It had crossed her mind to sit down with a doctor. Maybe a little medication to help her relax and soothe some of the anxiety. But she hated the zombie state her brain was in under medication, or the thought of becoming addicted to whatever they gave her. After seeing the poison her mother dealt and what it did to people, she was afraid of drugs, even over-the-counter kinds.

Her SAT phone rang from the bottom of her bag, pulling her out of her thoughts. She realized she hadn't moved. The phone was at the bottom of her black duffel bag. Searching, it took a moment to find it tucked under her gym clothes.

Her sister picked up on the first ring. "Hey, how're you holding up?"

"Good Lola, how are you? How's Jack?"

"He's doing a hell of a lot better. He sat down with a counselor and overall, he's in good shape. Olive has been asking about you."

"That's great news. How is her cuteness doing?" Mac asked, remembering when they found Jack in their mother's wine cellar. He was overall in good health, but after being held captive in a tiny room, well, that kind of thing could mess a guy up. "So, are you staying in the US until they go to court?"

Mac and her sister, along with a team of FBI, El Paso Police, and their dad helped take their mother's drug cartel down. Now, their mother was waiting to find out her fate. Lola's brilliant hacking skills brought in a ton of information on their mother's operation, leaving little doubt of a conviction.

"Nah, we have to head back overseas to button a few things up on our operations. We'll be back before they figure out the jurisdictional issues and go to court. There's no sense in us sitting around and waiting."

"Makes sense. When do you leave?"

"We fly out tomorrow afternoon," Lola said.

"That's a bummer; it'd have been nice to meet up before you take off."

"Sorry, but duty calls. We'll be back before you can miss us."

"How's our little princess doing?" Mac asked again.

"She's doing fantastic now that we're all back together. She still won't take off her pink cowboy boots except for her bath and asks for Ms. Nonnie. I'm not sure which she likes better...the boots or the bubbles in the bath," Lola said with a little giggle. Their mother had kidnapped Lola's daughter and her soon-to-be husband. Nonnie had taken care of and raised Olive. Ms. Nonnie had been a mother to them and treated Lola's little girl the same way.

Mac laughed out loud, thinking of the little redheaded girl refusing to take off the pink boots Ms. Nonnie bought for her. "I'm glad you guys are doing better. See you soon. Keep me posted when you arrive on the other side of the pond."

"You got it," Lola said and hung up.

She sat in her SUV for a few more minutes, the little hairs on the back of her neck standing on end. This had happened multiple times since she'd been home. It had to be paranoia, she told herself. Everywhere she went, it was like she was being followed. The sensation that eyes were upon her was back again. Trying to convince herself she was paranoid did nothing to help when her heart was pounding in her chest, and she couldn't breathe. She couldn't get enough air, and she felt strangled in the small space. She reached over, pushing the button to let her window down, but nothing happened until she realized the keys were not in the ignition.

Panic crept up her spine. She located the keys in her cup holder, but it took three tries to put them in the ignition and turn. The SUV started, and with her finger still on the button, the window came down, engulfing her face in the cold air. Gulping several times, she filled her lungs until she calmed down. Falling back in her seat, she closed her eyes, breathing in and out. It wasn't her first panic attack, but they were increasing not only in numbers but in length.

CHAPTER
FIVE

LISTENING to the purr of her little SUV helped her calm down. She had a choice: dive into busywork at the Area Defense Counsel's office or go to Chaplain Bastion for some overdue counseling. The thought of doing paperwork at the ADC office wasn't appealing, so she pulled out of the parking lot and headed to the chapel. If she was lucky, Bastion would fit her in. If not, maybe she could make an appointment with him.

She pulled into the parking lot and got out, almost slipping on the ice. One of these days, she would use the Yaktrax they issued her. The weird spikes that clung to her combat boots and kept her from slipping were effective, but weird to walk in. She hadn't gotten used to them and found it annoying to take them on and off every time she went in and out of buildings. Instead, she tried not to slip and bust her ass in the winter.

Last year, she had to sit on a donut for a week after bruising her tailbone. It happened not long after her incident with Deleon. She was already in awful shape, and the slip on the ice did nothing to help the situation and slowed her healing progress. She and Hudson made quite the pair. He was still recovering from totaling his truck after Deleon sabotaged it. He had visible bruises on his face and arms, and she took quite the beating herself. When they went out in public, people would look at them, wondering if they'd gone toe to toe in a fight and debating which one came out on top. What a nightmare, she thought.

The warm air hit her frozen face as she walked into the chapel, sending a prickly sensation across her skin. They always kept it warm and inviting, making it pleasant to visit. It was a little like a campfire, in a nice way. They had an old wood-burning stove in the kitchen that ran in the wintertime, making it like an old hunting lodge. She went about pulling off her heavy Gortex jacket and kicked the snow off her boots on the standard Air Force blue carpet before heading into the inter-offices.

"Hey Mac."

Benjamin Vigoren came out of his office to greet her. He had been at the chaplain's office for as long as she had been on the base. As a civilian employee, he didn't move or deploy unless he volunteered for it, so he was the continuity. "Hi Jammin, how have you been?"

"Oh, same, nothing new. We haven't seen you in a while."

"Yeah, I've been TDY. Just got back from Holloman on a case."

"I think everyone's heard about it. You doing, okay?"

"As good as expected, taking it day by day."

"You here looking for Bastion?"

"Yeah, the big dogs told me I needed some decompression time."

"I don't disagree, Mac. The universe threw some shit in your lap over the last couple of years. You're no good to anyone if you stop functioning."

"So they tell me. Is he in?"

"Yeah, he's back in his office."

"Thanks." Mac walked back to the corner office, where she found Chaplain Bastion sitting behind a desk covered in papers. It was comforting that some things never changed. His office looked the same way it had the last time. The man was messy, but efficient. He always knew where everything was, but she didn't know how. Stacks of paperwork in different piles covered every surface.

"Mac, as I live and breathe. How are you?" He held out his hand.

"Good, and you?" she asked, shaking his hand and taking a seat on the other side of his desk. The chairs were large and comfortable, covered in brown leather, and looked more like something you would find in someone's family room, not what sat in most military offices.

"Not much has changed for me. Living the dream, as they say." He started moving papers around his desk until he unearthed his calendar. "Did we have an appointment today?" He looked at the planner with knitted brows.

"No, sir, I'm stopping by to see if you can fit me in or if I can make an appointment. I'm sorry to drop in on you, but I was in the neighborhood," she said, smiling.

"Not to worry, you're always welcome here, Mac." He looked down at his planner again. "We can make it happen," he assured her. "How about we start now and then visit again tomorrow? I have forty-five minutes until my next appointment."

"Sounds great."

He came around and took the seat opposite her. She liked that about his style of counseling: he always walked around the desk to give her his undivided attention and let nothing on his desk distract him. Taking the time to mute his phone and close his door for privacy, he maintained his focus in one place.

He looked at her with his kind brown eyes. "So, Mac, I'm aware of bits and pieces of what's been happening to you, but I want you to tell me everything from the beginning."

"I'm not sure if we have enough time for all of it, but I'll give you the CliffsNotes version, and we can go from there."

"Fair enough," he said, settling back into the comfortable chair and folding his arms over his barrel chest.

She collected her thoughts and took a deep breath to help her relax. The stress melted, but not all the way. "So, let's start with the good stuff. Do you remember the last time we talked?"

"Yes, of course. You told me about a love interest you'd met and the case you were working on."

His memory always astounded her. She couldn't keep the facts straight about all the people she met. What impressed her the most was it happened a year ago. "Yes, the man in question is still here." For the first time since she had been home, she felt relaxed. She needed to figure out why her alarm bells were always going off at the weirdest times. Most of the time she was so jumpy, she was wondering if she was going crazy.

"You look surprised by that," he said, tilting his head to the side.

"Well, I guess it's because I kind of am. Most people find out about my past and go running, but so far, Hudson has stayed. For the first time in my life, I have someone I can trust."

"If memory serves me, the number has been small throughout your life. How are things going now that the cat is out of the bag?"

"People are treating me different from before. Like I have something to hide, and some of them are upset because I didn't tell them before, but they don't understand. Except for Hudson, he gets it."

"That's good. Everyone else will come around. Now tell me about this Hudson fella. Where do you see your future with him?"

"I want to spend the rest of my life with this man." She said it without hesitation. It was the one thing she was sure about.

CHAPTER SIX

GENNAVIE STRETCHED HER STRONG, slender legs out on her couch after a long day of following Mac and setting things in motion. She was enjoying watching Mac become paranoid. The sheer joy of fucking with her was invigorating. Leaving Mac with the impression that she was in control one moment and not the next was too much fun. Gennavie went as far as messing with the things in Mac's house, in her car, in her office. Everything was coming together with little effort. The time to execute was coming near, and she needed to plan.

The microwave dinged, telling her dinner was done. She missed her more lavish lifestyle, but this place was nice, too. The cream granite countertops and natural wood finishes left little to be desired. The owner had a comfortable king-size bed she sank into at night. Her host was kind enough to provide a high-end mattress and a stocked kitchen, even if he didn't have a clue she was using it. They'd deployed him for six months. He had been one of her playthings for a while until he left. She lifted his keys one night and copied them, letting herself into the large four-thousand-square-foot home as soon as he left. She couldn't stay at the defense attorney's place anymore once it became an active crime scene.

She grabbed her leftovers from the microwave and padded back to the couch wearing the man's robe and clicking the remote to make the television come to life. A huge seventy-inch screen covered most of the wall. Her manicured red fingernail clicked on the little buttons until she came across a local news channel. She stopped and stared at the screen when Mac's face came up.

"That bitch." Her face flushed red. How could Mac take the spotlight and have all the attention when *she* was the magnificent one? Mac was playing it up big, which made it worse. Mac had the audacity to look stressed as the reporters asked her uncomfortable questions. But Gennavie knew it was all a game, watching her big brown eyes go wide when one reporter accused her of sleeping with Hudson to get out of drug charges. "It would have been delicious gossip, but Mac is too much of a goodie-two-shoes for something like that," she said to the empty house. Now Mac was using her looks for attention when Gennavie and Vincent should have been the ones in the spotlight. Or maybe not in the spotlight, but still allowed to hunt and play as often as they wanted to.

Now Vincent was rotting in prison, and she was living in squalor. She looked around at the large, vaulted ceiling and planted her feet on the light-gray plush carpet. Okay, so maybe not squalor, but she had to live in the shadows. She laid her head back and closed her eyes, remembering the first time she met Vincent. They took away her promising military career at the Medical Group. Her excellent work earned her respect and awards. It allowed her to play at night with no one suspecting a thing.

The day Vincent came to her clinic was still fresh in her mind. He had been nothing to look at, maybe a five or six to her solid ten, but the look in his eyes caught her interest. The same look she had in hers—animalistic, primal hunters. After the first day in the clinic, he followed her and found her at one of her favorite hunting grounds. It took a little time to convince her to let him in, but once she did, there was no turning back.

While stationed at Joint Base Lewis-McChord in Tacoma, Washington she had the freedom to play. It was a big place that butted up against Seattle and allowed for all kinds of naughty business. She took him to a meeting with one of her clients. On their first outing together, she whipped and strangled the man not only because she enjoyed it but because her client asked her to. Having Vincent took the experience to a different level.

Her client paid her well for the treatment, and the entire time Vincent stayed quiet in the corner, not saying a word, admiring her work. Once the client left, they had the most mind-blowing sex she had ever experienced, which said a lot considering the business she was in.

After that night, they were inseparable. He fed her insatiable appetite to dominate and push boundaries until one night they pushed too far. Vincent was watching in the corner, stroking himself while she straddled a man on a cheap hotel bed. Every time metal scratched against metal, it brought back the memory of the old bedframe creaking as she did her worst. The man under her was gasping for air as she strangled him with her bullwhip, watching as he turned red and then purple. Her excitement mounted when Vincent walked up, placing his hands over hers, and helped her push harder, crushing the man's windpipe. The moment the bones gave way into fleshiness, his eyes widened and then went dark, looking vacant. She had never been so alive, watching life drain from his eyes.

Vincent took her at that moment, right on top of the dead man. After that day, she was ravenous. Nothing compared. All she wanted was to go out hunting with her husband. He enjoyed it as much as she did and helped to keep her grounded and focused on making sure they kept their cover. Until Mac showed up and ruined everything.

Her little boy toy, Hudson, went undercover with Mac and ruined one of Gennavie's favorite places to play. They had flown all the way to Amsterdam, where Gennavie had started and taken her first solo victim. She enjoyed that one, but killing with Vincent was on a different level. On top of the excitement, he was also willing to clean up her mess and dispose of the bodies.

That little seething bitch put Vincent behind bars, ruining all her fun. The worst part was she had to remain in hiding while Mac resumed her normal life.

But not for long.

CHAPTER
SEVEN

MAC'S DAY ENDED. If one more person asked her how she was
doing, she might lose it. They were only concerned, but it was like she
was the local freakshow people wanted to dissect. Once she sat down
and talked with Chaplain Bastion, things were better. It was time to get
help and clear her mind. The nightmares were taking their toll, and she
was having trouble staying focused now that she had little to focus on.
The command chief's decision to bench her for the moment didn't
help. Another case would provide a distraction, but it couldn't be good
for her mental health.

With her focus off, and the crazy year they had survived, it'd be
nice to go out with Hudson tonight and relax. He had something fun
planned for them, and she could use it to let her hair down and focus
on him for a while. She wondered if he thought she was neglecting
him because of all the distractions. Soon, they would go someplace
where the media wouldn't find them. She walked through the door of
his place and hung her Gortex jacket up on the hook, leaving her keys
on the little table in the doorway. "Hey hon, I'm home."

He didn't answer back. His truck was in the driveway.

She came around the corner and into what became their bedroom.
At first they'd been going back and forth between each other's houses,
but she had been staying at his. After her mother delivered a severed

head to her house, she had a hard time sleeping or cooking there. Every time she went into the kitchen to cook a meal, she would picture the severed head in the soggy box on her countertop and would lose her appetite.

The house needed to be put on the market. But it was a bold move when she and Hudson were still dating. She hoped with every fiber of her being things would work out for them. There were no guarantees in life, and he hadn't put a ring on her finger. Maybe now that her mother was behind bars and her brothers were deceased, they could move forward. She was confident he wanted the same things she did, but they hadn't discussed it since coming back from her family's saga.

Things had changed, or at least they were different for her. They had both killed people in self-defense, but no matter the reason, it still changed a person on the inside. It was no small thing to take another person's life. They needed to talk about it, but every time she tried to start the conversation, it ended up going in a different direction. Maybe tonight, she thought.

The lyrics to "Cherry Pie" by Warrant were playing in the bathroom. Over the shower, Hudson's deep baritone sang along to the song. She stood outside the door, smiling at the sound of his voice. He was a pretty decent singer, and she enjoyed listening when he got into a song. Slipping out of her boots and uniform, she left them in a pile in the corner and padded into the bathroom. The scent of his woodsy bodywash filled her nose. He was in the gray-tiled shower, dancing to the beat, wiggling his fine ass back and forth. She stifled a laugh as her body tingled with anticipation.

His sudsy hands were scrubbing his hair, showing off his beautiful broad back and strong shoulder muscles. She slipped out of her little red thong and dropped her lacy black bra on the cold bathroom tile and slid in behind him. He jumped when she put her chilly hands on his warm, wet backside. She wrapped her arms around his waist. "You're early. I wasn't expecting you," he said.

She pressed her soft breasts against his hard body as the water streamed down between them. "It's been a long day, and I thought a little stress relief was in order." She reached between his legs and started massaging him.

"Um"—he paused, not able to form words as he grew into her wet hand—"I'm here to please," he muttered.

He turned around to face her, bending forward to cover her mouth with his and wrapping his arms around her small waist. He left her mouth and worked his way down to her neck, causing her to let out a soft moan. It was one of her favorite spots. He grew more excited against her as he reached down and put her left nipple in his mouth and licked and sucked. This was what she needed.

He reached down, cupping her ass with his hands, scooping her into the air. She wrapped her legs around him, inviting him in as he pressed her into the corner of the shower, supporting her with his powerful arms. The steam engulfed their bodies as the pressure mounted. He pressed deeper inside as she coiled around him, wrapping her legs tighter and pulling him in. Letting out a deep moan, she shuddered against his body.

To her excitement, he wasn't done yet. He was the first man she had ever been with who made her orgasm multiple times. Not that she had several men to compare him to, but still. Lowering her back to her feet, he made sure she could stand without toppling over, and ran his hand through her wet hair, covering her mouth with his leaning in to devour her. Stepping back, she smiled up at him and slipped down to her knees, taking him into her mouth. The sound of his moans heightened her excitement. Pushing him back against the shower wall, she sucked and played until she felt his grip tighten in her wet hair and he swelled in her mouth. Right when she sensed he was going to lose it, she got back on her feet. Turning her heart-shaped ass in his direction, she bent forward, grabbing onto the soap holder to steady herself.

The water sprayed off her small back as he grabbed her round hips and entered her from behind, thrusting faster. The moans coming from behind her heightened her anticipation. Closing her eyes, she focused on the intensity. Feeling her body tightening on the verge of eruption, she pressed back, inviting him to explode inside her in frenzied ecstasy. He pulled her back against his chest, wrapping his arms around her, reveling in the intoxication of her warm body. He would never get used to this amazing woman.

CHAPTER
EIGHT

WITH SOME REGRET, they left the shower. Mac busied herself in front of the mirror applying makeup. She pinned her hair back, wearing a slinky black silk robe, when Hudson walked up behind her. He'd dressed in a dark-gray long-sleeve button-down with dark-black jeans and a nice pair of black-and-gray cowboy boots. She breathed in. "You smell amazing."

"You like that, huh?" he asked.

"Yeah, what is it?"

"A little something special I picked up for the occasion."

"And what occasion is that? You still haven't told me what this big surprise of yours is." She looked up into his eyes, but he gave nothing away. He was so good to her and didn't hesitate after finding out about her family. He hadn't run away. Come to think of it, he was the first person in her life who hadn't turned tail when they found out about her past.

"You'll have to wait and see." He handed her a box wrapped in maroon paper with a pretty white bow.

"Now, what's this? I didn't get you anything."

"Open it."

"Okay." She untied the bow.

"Rip it off. I want to see what you think."

She smiled up at him and ripped the paper and ribbon from the package. The top of the box pulled free to reveal a beautiful red cocktail dress with soft silk fabric. Pulling it out of the box, she held it to her chest. "It's beautiful," she said, pushing up on her tiptoes to give him a kiss.

"I hope it fits," he said, looking a little unsure of himself.

"I've never had anyone buy clothes for me before. Where did you find it?"

"In a little boutique downtown."

She slipped off her robe and pulled the dress on, and to her surprise, it fit every curve. She wasn't sure how he knew to buy her something with stretchy spandex material. It hugged every inch of her in all the right places. She couldn't remember the last time she'd walked into a store and bought something off the rack with her curvy figure. Everything fit too tight in the hips and bust and loose in the waist, but somehow he had found the perfect dress. She turned to show it off.

"Wow," was all he could say in response.

"I like it too. I can't believe you found something that fits."

"Don't give me too much credit. I showed the lady at the shop a picture of you, answered a few questions, and she took it from there. I'll have to go back and thank her."

She went into the closet and pulled out a pair of black strappy heels. She did a final touch-up to her hair and makeup and walked up next to him, lacing her arm through his. In the four-inch heels, she still didn't make it to his shoulder. "Are you ready?"

"Absolutely, my lady." He helped her on with her long black coat and bent over to kiss her, getting a little red lipstick on his lips. Taking her hand, he led her out to his truck and opened the door for her to climb in. He whistled when she hiked up the little dress to climb up. He had thought to warm the truck ahead of time since her legs were bare; in December, the cold was relentless. The long black coat she wore over her little red dress didn't stop the frigid air from climbing up her legs.

He pulled into the Historic Davenport Hotel and handed the valet his keys and walked around to the other side of the truck to help Mac down. They went into the magnificent hotel with floor-to-ceiling, wall-to-wall Victorian-style ornate fixtures and wall-to-wall red carpet. She'd been inside before, but it always took her breath away. It reminded her of pictures of an old Victorian-style castle. After dropping their bags in the stunning suite he'd reserved for them, they headed back out for dinner.

He tucked her in close as they walked around the corner, away from the hotel.

"So, are you going to tell me where we're going?" Mac asked.

"Well, Churchills, of course." He smiled.

"That place costs a mint. Are you sure?"

"Oh, I'm sure."

They walked into the warm dining area. The scent was inviting, with a welcoming mix of sweet and savory. The large dark-wood beams that crawled along the ceiling against the ivory walls gave it an elegant, old-worldly appearance. A waiter passed by with what looked like a chocolate bag filled with fruit and cream and Mac wondered how much she could eat in the tight little dress. She had only heard about this place, but never dared to come on her minimal government salary.

"Do you have a reservation, sir?" a young, dark-haired woman asked Hudson.

"Yes, it should be under Gavin Hudson."

"Of course, sir, right this way." She led them to the back of the restaurant where an elegant, set table with crisp white linens and high-backed, deep-red leather chairs waited. Mac sat down when Hudson pulled her chair out for her. Looking around her surroundings, it was like he'd swept her into a romantic fairytale. The restaurant staff tucked them into a private area, away from the rest of the diners. The hostess laid a black linen napkin across her lap and one across Hudson's. "Your waiter will be right with you," she said and walked away.

Within minutes, a tall man in a crisp white shirt came up with a bottle of white wine. "Sir and madam, welcome to Churchills. My name is Joseph, and I will be your server today. Can I interest you in a glass of our Merlot, or would you like time to look at the menu?"

"No thank you," Mac said. "I'm not much of a wine person, but I would love a mule if possible."

Hudson grinned. "I would like one as well."

The man left, looking disgusted at their request.

———

Mistress Gennavie made herself comfortable at a table for one on the other side of Churchills. For the occasion, she had platinum-blond hair with a wide-rimmed black hat pulled to the side, concealing half her stunning porcelain face. She'd picked a plain black business dress with a simple string of pearls hanging from her neck. The only indulgence she allowed herself was the crimson-red lipstick across her full lips and the deep-red nail polish on her fingers. The last thing she wanted was to draw attention. She had changed her eye color to brown since her natural green made her more memorable. Tonight wasn't the night to be remembered.

Gennavie had been planning for this moment since the day Mac put her husband away. They would release Vincent one day; she would make sure of it. But in the meantime, she would take comfort in destroying Mac. People rallied around Mac and highlighted her in the media as some kind of princess, but that time was over. She couldn't have planned it better, she thought, taking a sip of her wine and waiting for Mac's world to come tumbling down.

"WHAT DO you think we should order?" Mac asked, perusing the menu and cringing at the prices. Prior to meeting Hudson, she had been on her own for so long, she wasn't used to this kind of pampering.

"What would you like? We can have anything, but I suggest the chocolate sack at the end of the meal."

"That sounds amazing, but the portions here are huge, and not much is going to fit in this sexy little dress." She ran her hand down her flat stomach wrapped in tight red fabric. The dress fit like a glove, and she felt sexy with the open straps running down her strong back. The front pushed everything up to reveal full mounds of tanned cleavage. It was revealing, but Hudson liked it much better than her military uniform.

Hudson was staring at her with a strange look on his face. "I was going to wait to do this, but now is as good a time as any." He got up from his seat, walked around to her other side, and looked down, fishing the little box out of his pocket. He knelt on one knee and took her hand.

At first, confusion crossed her face and then she understood what this night was all about. How could she be so stupid? Of course… She smiled at him as he faced her.

"You are the most amazing and sexy woman I have ever met. You make me laugh and sometimes cry, and you kick ass like no one I have ever met." He took a long breath, trying to keep his hands from shaking. "You're my best friend. Would you be willing to spend the rest of your life with me?"

She couldn't stop smiling. The thought of this day was so unreal to her when she was always worried about her family getting in the way. If she said yes prior to her mother going to prison, Hudson would have a mark on his head. It wasn't safe yet since her mother still manipulated and wielded her power from prison, but things were much better than they were.

Realizing she still hadn't answered his question and left him kneeling in anticipation, she put her hand on the side of his face. She covered his mouth with hers, showing him what she thought of his proposal. "Yes," she whispered, and realized most of the restaurant was watching as applause broke out.

Hudson stood up as she slid into his warm embrace. They both couldn't stop smiling. He was about to return to his seat when the man coming through the front door caught his attention.

Officer Joe Romero from the Spokane Police Department was talking to the hostess, who turned and pointed to their table. They knew Joe well, but this was the last place either of them thought he would be. Mac hoped it wasn't a fresh case she was being brought into.

Officer Romero headed toward their table. Hudson and Mac stood next to each other. Mac's gut twisted as if a train was barreling down on top of them. "What do you think's going on?" she said.

"No idea," Hudson responded. "But if Joe is here, it can't be good."

Joe approached, looking at the floor, not making eye contact until he got to the table. "Hey Mac, Hudson, I'm sorry to interrupt your dinner," he said, running his hand through his graying hair. "You look stunning, Mac. I'm so sorry about this."

"What's going on—or should I ask what you're sorry about, Joe?" Mac asked, a shiver crawled up her spine.

"I'm afraid I'm here for Hudson."

"What do you mean, you're here for Hudson? For what?" Mac asked, her voice sounding strange and high-pitched in her own ears.

Hudson and Joe were good friends. Joe assisted them during the Chief Deleon case and helped Hudson find Mac when she went after the chief and killed him in self-defense. During that same case, Mac saved Ali, who was now Romero's girlfriend. Mac looked at Hudson, trying to gauge his reaction, but he stood still, his mouth gaping.

Joe cleared his throat. "The FBI is pushing for the arrest of Hudson for murder. I volunteered to pick you up so nothing would go wrong. Given your size, I didn't want anyone to overreact."

"What do you mean...murder? Hudson didn't murder anyone." Mac's voice was getting louder.

"Please stay calm, Mac," Joe said, placing his hand on her arm. "We're sure this is a misunderstanding, but a lot of pressure is coming from on high. They have evidence that points to Hudson's involvement. You need to let me take him in without incident so we can work this out."

"What evidence do they have against me?" Hudson choked out.

"We can't discuss it here, and you should find an excellent attorney before you talk to me or anyone else," Joe said. "Now, are you going to come with me, or do I need to call for backup?"

"No, I'll go." He turned to Mac and wrapped her in a hug. "It'll be okay. I'm sure this is all a big mistake."

"I know it is. What can I do to help?" she said, her hands shaking at her sides.

"Find me a talented lawyer and notify my leadership. If this hits the press, all hell will break loose."

"Say nothing until I get you an excellent attorney," Mac advised. "Use your right to remain silent until help arrives."

"Yeah, I will," he said, and dropped his hands to his sides, allowing Joe to walk him to the door. He looked back as they were leaving. Mac's heart was being torn from her chest at the look of fear in his eyes.

She stood frozen in place next to their decorated table in her pretty dress, not able to move, her strappy heels rooted to the elegant carpet. The entire restaurant was staring at her. Somewhere in the background, one of the waitstaff dropped a glass, pulling her back to reality, and the world around her went back into motion.

CHAPTER
TEN

MAC PAID the bill and made her way back to the valet at the Davenport Hotel. There, she realized she didn't have the parking ticket or the keys to the room Hudson had rented. They were all in his wallet with him. She walked into the hotel and waited until the tall, thin blond woman at the front desk beckoned her forward. "Are you all right?" she asked.

Mac hadn't realized she was crying. She hated crying in public, or anywhere else, but the tears came. Her mother had always said, letting people see you cry is a sign of weakness and is unacceptable. Even as a little girl, she remembered getting in more trouble for shedding tears than for doing anything else. Taking in a few quick breaths and one long, deep one, she grabbed a tissue out of the box on the polished wood counter and blew her nose. She looked up at the woman, who was waiting for her to answer. "I'll be okay, but I need a key to our room and my boyf…um, my fiancé was, uh, called away. Can you give me a room key so I can go back in to get our stuff?"

"Did you want to keep the room for tonight?" the woman asked with kindness in her voice. The irrational need to lash out swept through Mac, but she knew it wasn't her fault.

"No, right after he proposed, someone took him away," Mac said, not sure how else to convince this woman to give her a key.

"Oh my, what a beautiful ring!" The woman reached over and grabbed hold of Mac's hand. "Congratulations, you are one lucky lady." She took another moment to inspect the ring. "Yup, he did a good job picking it out."

"Thank you." Mac wasn't sure what else to say. "Now, is it possible for me to have a key to the room?"

"Oh, no problem; I saw the two of you here earlier. You've got yourself one handsome guy."

"Thanks," Mac said, waiting for the key, but the blond looked at her with her big doe eyes. *Give me the damn key before I come over the counter and beat your scrawny ass!* Mac thought to herself, all the while plastering a smile on her face. "Um, can I have that key? I need to clean up and make a few phone calls."

"Yeah, sure." She pulled a pencil from behind her ear, made a note on a piece of paper, pushed some keys on her keyboard, and ran a plastic keycard through a little machine. "Here you go." She handed the key across the counter. "You're on the sixth floor. And I'm sorry your special night got messed up by the military. Stay as long as you like. I'll make sure no one bothers you."

"How did you guess we were military?" Mac asked.

"Your fiancé has a military discount on file. Plus, my boyfriend is in, too, and they have that look."

"Yeah. Thanks for the key."

"No problem; let me know if you need anything," the woman said as Mac was walking away.

"Will do."

Mac walked into the elevator, her mind off balance and disoriented. She couldn't believe Joe took Hudson. Standing in the elevator, it took a moment before she figured out she needed to insert her room key to make the elevator move. As soon as she got to their room on the sixth floor, she slipped off her sexy black heels and checked her phone. What kind of evidence could they have? She rolled her neck, the stress creeping into her back and shoulders. It would be a long night.

The large king bed sat in the middle of the luxurious room, taunting her. The staff had turned it and left little chocolates on each pillow. She loved chocolate, but right now her insides were twisting like she might throw up. On her side of the bed lay an elegant present. Hudson must have left it as a surprise when they returned to the room. That was it. She crumpled onto the bed and had herself a good, long cry.

When she ran out of tears, she went into the bathroom and cleaned up her face. Removing the long black streaks of eyeliner and mascara, she started dialing numbers.

CHAPTER
ELEVEN

GENNAVIE STRIPPED off the elegant black hat and put the large binoculars up to her face as Mac came into her room. She pulled her blonde wig off her head and took a seat as excitement crawled through her body. It had all come together so seamlessly. She'd rented the room across from the one Hudson paid for. It was a good thing the man planned. Otherwise, she'd miss the show. She had an open view of the room Mac walked into. Satisfaction coursed through her body when Mac crumpled onto the bed, destroyed. Her open view of the room allowed her to see Mac's face scrunched up, her makeup smeared, and her beautiful long, dark hair unpinned and falling down her back.

Then, it ended.

How dare she recover like that? Shock gripped Gennavie when one minute Mac was sobbing and the next, she was cleaning her face like nothing had happened. Maybe she was deranged or just that tough. Gennavie figured the woman would at least take the night to be distraught, like any other respectable woman would.

Mac slipped out of her little red dress and got down to business. Gennavie liked the dress and thought it was a tasty little piece. She felt a brief pang of jealousy at how well Hudson took care of Mac. He had done well, and Mac looked breathtaking in it. Mac was the first woman

Gennavie had ever met who was her equal in the looks department. "Good thing I'm smarter," she said out loud to the empty room.

It killed her not to share her victory with Vincent. It was almost anticlimactic when she didn't have anyone to gloat with. Maybe it was time to recruit a new partner for now. She didn't intend to give up on Vincent, but he was going to be away for a while. Mac convinced him to sing, and he was dumb enough to tell her everything from his first kill to all the kills they enjoyed together. Now he was waiting for sentencing with the death penalty on the table, thanks to the incompetent defense attorney. Gennavie licked her lips, thinking of all the fun she'd had with Anika.

The defense attorney cried and begged to be spared like they all do, but it was her time to pay for her sins. Gennavie took great satisfaction in showing her who was in charge and making her suffer. Since Vincent lost his freedom to hunt with her, she had been striving to regain that power. But it wasn't the same without a partner, without Vincent.

Gennavie sat on the luxurious bed. She could get used to this as she sank her stocking feet into the lush carpet after abandoning her heels on the way in. Last summer, she had been living in her beautiful house in Seattle, Washington, in her orchestrated dual life with her new husband. A respectable military career by day and a deadly mistress of the night.

Because of her uncle's financing and the money she inherited when her parents died, she had been used to a life of luxury. The military provided a perfect cover. He helped her escape some charges surrounding a time she whipped and beat her boyfriend within an inch of his life. Her uncle called in multiple favors, and before long, she was in an unfamiliar state with a new identity waiting to start basic training. It had been a beautiful plan. When she landed at Joint Base Lewis-McChord in Tacoma, Washington, she settled into her double life. The stunning home she rented was perfect for entertaining her prey with her own custom torture chamber.

Vincent had only enhanced things. They had both been part of the safe confines of the military, with promising careers. On the weekends, they would reveal their true personalities seducing and killing people as often as they wanted. The locals didn't know who was behind the murders until Mac came along. She ruined everything.

They had been so careful. For the first time in her life, she had been happy and in love, or at least as close to love as she was capable of. She enjoyed the power and control that killing in front of Vincent gave her. He had been sadistic in his own right, and they fed off each other. She could almost taste the blood in her mouth as she remembered the addiction they shared that had no cure.

It would be difficult to replace Vincent, knowing she was such a rare unicorn. He was different. She'd met no one who had an insatiable appetite for both sex and murder as she did. Maybe she needed a pawn to distract her until Vincent was back. There was no shortage of killers who would be happy to do her bidding. So many naughty men to choose from. And then there was Vincent; she wasn't sure how she was going to spring him out of prison, but she was the type of woman who put her mind to something and didn't fail.

The thought of them being free to kill again together was tasty, but it wouldn't happen overnight. The first order of business: Mac had to pay. Having Hudson ripped from her arms right after he proposed was oh so tantalizing, but it wouldn't be enough. Hudson needed to be hurt the same way as Vincent. She wondered how many lines Hudson would cross in prison to protect himself. Only time would tell.

She brought the binoculars back up to her eyes to see Mac pacing on the soft carpet in what she had to assume was Hudson's old t-shirt and a pair of sweats. Mac looked in total control as she spoke. "How dare you? Crumble, dammit. This is supposed to destroy you," she said to the window, knowing good and well Mac couldn't hear her. Things would need to get worse, much worse.

CHAPTER
TWELVE

"WHAT THE HELL do you mean, they arrested Hudson?" Captain Stanton said. He had been Mac's boss and the base's defense attorney for the last few years. They worked well together, and Mac trusted him. He had always taken care of her and had her best interests in mind.

"We were out at dinner when Spokane police officer Joe Romero came to the restaurant and arrested him. He said he was being brought in on murder charges."

"I thought you worked with Joe at one point, and you were friends, or at least had a professional relationship."

"Yeah, he said he volunteered to pick up Hudson, so things didn't escalate. I appreciated that part because of the reaction Hudson had received in the past. He's such a big guy and sometimes people think he can be violent because of his stature."

"Makes sense. Who else have you told?" Stanton asked.

"You so far. I'm planning on calling Hudson's commander after this and then, at some point, I'll have to tell his mother." Mac exhaled. "I'm not looking forward to that one. She has already been through so much with the loss of her younger son to drugs."

"Don't worry about all that yet. We first need to find Hudson's representation. Where is he being held?"

"Joe texted; they will hold him for now at the county jail on Mallon. Can you go out there?" Mac asked, desperation laced through her voice.

"Sure, I have a buddy who might help. I think he's not only going to need a JAG attorney, but also a civilian one. I won't be able to represent him because of you, but I can make sure he's well taken care of. If the military had jurisdiction he'd be on base, but since he's downtown, they're keeping it."

"True, thanks for heading down. I'm going to call his command and will meet you in twenty," Mac said, leaving little room for argument.

"At this hour they won't allow visitors, Mac. You're going to have to cool your heels. The only person permitted is going to be his lawyer. Let me take care of him and make sure he isn't talking to anyone for now. Trust me on this Mac, we'll get him squared away."

Mac glanced at the clock on the nightstand. It was after 2000 hours. "Do you think your friend will be available this late?"

"He owes me a favor. Call Hudson's commander and notify him. I'll do my thing and call you when I'm done."

Mac hung up the phone and took a deep breath. This had to be some crazy nightmare. Why in the hell would they think Hudson had anything to do with a murder? A better question was whose murder he was being charged with. She couldn't wait to find out and get this thing resolved. If she figured out a way to post bail, at least he would be out of that nasty place. Many of her clients spent time in the county jail waiting for the charges to be worked through, and it wasn't a place she wanted Hudson to stay.

She would have to worry about where they would find the money later. She dialed the number to Hudson's commander. Normal protocol would have been to go through Hudson's first sergeant, but since Hudson was that person, there was only one other person to call. Under the current circumstances, she didn't want to explain the situation multiple times.

Her history with Lieutenant Colonel Dixon, the Security Forces commander, didn't help. He had been Chief Deleon's commander at the time of his death. He accused Mac of murder but softened when evidence showed it was self-defense. Colonel Dixon wouldn't receive this news well either. His squadron took a lot of heat ever since it came to light that his chief had been a serial killer. Now he was about to learn his first sergeant was up on murder charges.

It took a moment to gather her thoughts. She dialed the number, pacing back and forth in the beautiful hotel room. The elegant furniture with Spanish Renaissance-style decorations was nice. It would have been a lovely place to celebrate their engagement. The small box Hudson left on her side of the bed caught her eye. Walking over, she slipped the bow off the box, ripping into the cream-colored paper. Hooking her finger under the lip of the box, she lifted it up. Inside sat an elegant, sheer black nighty. Her breath caught in her throat, thankful the phone was still ringing and had yet to be picked up. Not that she expected him in his office at this hour, but she figured it was worth a try.

Disconnecting the line, she called the command post. The base agency ran 24/7 and could connect to leadership without giving out their personal numbers. Most leadership carried Blackberries or government cell phones, but she didn't have access to any of Dixon's numbers. "Command post, Senior Airman Forton, how can I help you?" a strong female voice came across the line.

"Hi, this is Master Sergeant Evelyn McGregor. Can you connect me to Lieutenant Colonel Dixon?" The line clicked on and off in her ear. It was part of the secure line. She had been inside their facility a few times when she worked exercises as a unit deployment manager. The sterile environment allowed no cell phones or smart watches once they walked in. She waited while Forton verified her.

"Yes ma'am, of course. Give me a minute."

"Sure, thanks," Mac said, stretching her arms above her head. The muscles along her neck were cramping, and she wondered if it would be wise to take something. All she could do was hope and pray Hudson was doing okay. She was thankful he was such a formidable human. It would go a few different ways for him. The inmates might think he was a threat and leave him alone. They might think he was a challenge and a way to prove themselves or, in the worst case, someone wanted him to be their bitch. She hoped it was the former rather than any of the latter. Everyone had their limits, and she had yet to experience Hudson pushed that far. He had a breaking point like anyone else.

The phone clicked in Mac's ear a few more times and then Forton came back on the line. "I'm connecting you now."

Before Mac said anything, the deep voice of Lieutenant Colonel Dixon came on the line. "Dammit Mac, this better be a fucking emergency."

She stayed silent for a moment, not wanting to come across like she was trying to defend herself. "Sir, I have some bad news you won't like for several reasons."

"Spit it out, dammit." He wasn't a kind man and always came across to Mac as being agitated, even during pleasant encounters when nothing was wrong. Or at least nothing she was aware of.

"Sir, you might want to take a seat."

"Master Sergeant McGregor, tell me what is going on or I am hanging up on you."

"Sir, they arrested Hudson." Silence on the other end. "Sir, are you there?"

"I'm here, Mac." His voice changed, dropping into more of a fatherly tone. "Take me through everything from the beginning and leave nothing out, even if you think it might hurt Hudson."

"Well, sir, I have little information. One minute he was proposing to me at Churchills and the next Spokane police were arresting him for murder."

"Does he have representation?" Dixon asked.

"Yes, Stanton and a civilian attorney are on their way to the jail now."

"That's good. Do you think there is anything to the charges?"

"No sir," Mac answered with conviction in her voice.

CHAPTER
THIRTEEN

MAC STAYED at the hotel overnight, figuring it wouldn't do her any good to go back to his place or hers. She took a quick shower, pulled her wet hair into a ponytail, and headed out the door. After a little research the night before, she figured out a video appointment would be necessary. She hated that she couldn't see him in person, but it was the best she could do. At 1000 hours, she had an appointment scheduled.

She pulled into the Spokane County detention facility with twenty minutes to spare. The last time she had been here to visit a client, things were different. Being part of the legal team, there was little pomp and circumstance, but this time she was a regular visitor. Even then, it took some time to process through security and she didn't want her appointment eaten up by formalities. It took her two tries to get Hudson's big one-ton truck parked between the lines. He'd left the keys in the hotel room.

Similar to her previous visits, they checked her in and asked some questions, and a young guard led her back to a small visiting room with a nineteen-inch screen. Hudson waited for her in yellow prison pants and a top reminding her of scrubs the staff would wear in a hospital.

Cinderblock walls surrounded her, with a chair that looked like it had more bodily fluids on it than she wanted to think about. The place had a faint disinfectant aroma, attempting to cover the scent of urine. The soles of her shoes made a sickly sticking sound, and she didn't want to find out why. She swallowed hard and took a seat, teetering on the edge of the cushion.

"Hi hon, how are you holding up?" she asked, talking into the little screen. He looked exhausted with bags under his eyes, clearly not sleeping a wink. Guilt tickled the back of her brain for staying in the fancy hotel room and sleeping on the luxurious pillow-top mattress. She had been so exhausted after everything was over, she slept well. Sleep was a fickle beast in her world, and most nights she woke several times with nightmares, but not last night.

"I'll be okay. It's not too bad so far. I don't think the other inmates know what to make of me, and I think they might have screwed things up."

"What do you mean, other than they arrested the wrong guy?"

"I'm in general pop and they're supposed to be holding me in pre-trial confinement. My attorney is trying to figure out what's going on, but in the meantime, I'm supposed to keep my head down."

Mac cringed when he referred to himself as an inmate. She never thought she would see this man behind bars. "When is your arraignment?"

"My attorney is trying to have it set within the next forty-eight hours, but he tells me things are pretty backed up. He warned me there's a possibility I won't make bail because I'm a potential flight risk."

"How do they figure?"

"Well, for one, I've been overseas with you, but I'm also in the military and they think I have resources and contacts in multiple locations. They brought up your family's money, or your mother, as ways I may leave the country."

Mac shook her head, knowing the prosecutor was flinging any shit he could find at the wall until something stuck. "Okay, so let's say your attorney is as good as Stanton says he is. Do you have any ideas where we can find the money?"

"No, that's the tough part. I don't have the money needed to post bail for murder charges. Most times they want ten percent, but ten percent of what is the question?"

"I can sell my place. I'm never there these days."

He smiled for the first time. "Nice of you to offer, hon, but by the time the house sells, if we're lucky this nightmare will be over."

"Any idea who they accused you of killing?" she asked, wanting to figure this thing out as soon as possible and release him from this hellhole.

"Not yet, but my gut tells me it has to do with our trip to Holloman. My attorney is still waiting for the evidence to be released to him. All they'll tell me so far is I'm being accused and charged with killing a man, but that's it. They aren't telling me much. All I can do is hope it's a misunderstanding and if not, it was self-defense."

"Do you think they're referring to the bodies at my mother's compound? It was clearly self-defense, and we have an FBI agent who can testify for you. I'm sure we would only have to ask Coleman." He was one agent they worked with in New Mexico and Mexico to take down her mother's cartel. He was a tremendous asset in getting all the prisoners out and to safety. When Mac's mother kidnapped her at gunpoint, the two took down the guards at the compound and went after Mac. Mac killed Alejandro Vedrio's son, Gabriel. Hudson shot and killed Alejandro after he fired on them, hitting Coleman in the leg. They had all killed that day, but only out of necessity. None of them should warrant murder charges. At least Mac didn't think so.

"No idea, but if you can do anything…" he let the statement hang. "Other than asking your mother for help."

"Don't worry, I won't, but I think bringing Lola in to do some digging might be a good idea." She paused for a moment, not sure how she was going to approach the next subject. "I'm going to have to call your mom. If the press gets wind of this, it's not how she should find out."

"Yeah, I hate to cause her pain after everything she's been through. Please tell her I love her, and I didn't do this."

"I'm pretty sure she's already going to know, but I'll tell her. In the meantime, I'll contact Lola and ask her to work her magic." An orange timer popped on her screen, indicating her visit was about to be over.

"Keep your head down. Don't fight unless you have to, and I'll do everything I can to get you out."

The thought of him being in this mess because he went to Holloman to help her was terrifying. She felt guilty for being the reason he was in this place. Not that she put him in here, but she was still responsible. As the screen went blank, she said, "Love you" with a lost sensation, in the small, unsterile room, staring at the spot where Hudson's handsome face was only a moment ago. She turned and waited for the guard to open the door and escort her out. Leaving Hudson in this awful place made her want to scream.

AS MAC CROSSED the parking lot to Hudson's truck, she clicked the remote start on his key fob. The freezing wind bit her cheeks and made her nose run. She slipped into his truck and plucked her phone from her jacket. Looking through the window, she didn't see anyone. The creepy sensation that she was being looked at kept gnawing in the deep part of her brain. Her paranoia was getting worse. She needed to get back in for a session with Chaplain Bastion.

He'd convinced her this was normal for someone who went through the trauma she had experienced. He suggested she might suffer from PTSD, which would explain why she was always so jumpy and hypervigilant, or at least that's what he called it. That was the last diagnosis she wanted. Most people lost their careers once they received that label. Still, it was unnerving when she kept getting the same weird sensation. She'd react to the littlest things, but when she turned around, no one was there. It was fraying her nerves, and the nightmares weren't helping.

She looked down at her phone and closed her eyes. She liked Momma Hudson and hated telling her the news, but waiting wouldn't make it any easier. She was about to hang up when Momma Hudson's voice came on the line. "Hi Mac, honey, how are you doing?"

It surprised Mac when Hudson's mom had her number programmed into her phone. "Hi, sorry to call you."

"You can call me anytime, hon. Now tell me, did my boy put a ring on your finger?"

"Yes ma'am, he did last night, but it isn't why I'm calling."

"Of course, you want to discuss wedding plans. Well, let me tell you, I have some ideas if you want to hear them."

"No, I mean yes, I want your ideas, but I need to tell you something first."

"Well, spit it out, honey."

"They arrested your son on murder charges last night, right after he proposed. He told me to tell you he didn't do it." Mac sat, waiting for his mother to respond, but she said the last thing Mac would have expected.

"Are you sure?"

"Of course I'm sure. I just left the jail where he's being held."

"No honey, are you sure he didn't kill someone?"

Mac stayed silent for a moment, not sure how much to share with his mother. "I mean…he had to defend himself and, well. But it wasn't murder," she said, stumbling over her words, trying to make the right things come out.

"I see," Momma Hudson said into the phone. "I'm getting on an airplane and coming down to help you two figure this thing out."

"Not that we don't want to visit with you, but now isn't a good time. I'll keep you posted as things move forward, but for right now, I need to figure things out. Please stay put and I'll take care of your boy," Mac said, trying to sound reassuring but not believing it either.

"Are you sure, honey? I got nothing goin' on and I'd love to come out and give my two favorite people a hand."

"I may need your help soon, but for right now, I need to find out who they think he killed. Can you wait until I have more information?"

"Okay Mac, but you call me the instant you have information. Don't you let them hurt my baby."

Mac had to smile at this. Her baby stood over six foot seven and was close to two hundred and fifty pounds. If anyone could handle themselves behind bars, it would be Hudson. He was no one's baby. "You have my word. As soon as I have information, I'll call."

"Okay, you take care of yourself, Mac. I need you healthy for when he gets out so you two can start a family. I need me some grandbabies."

"Yes, Momma Hudson. I'll call you soon." She hung up the phone before his mom had the chance to say anything else. The conversation hadn't gone the way she thought it would. Mac assumed Hudson's mother would believe in her son's innocence and wouldn't doubt it for a second... It made her wonder why.

She needed to head back to base and meet with the chaplain for some much-needed counseling. The same sensation that she was being watched wouldn't leave her. She needed to get herself together if she was going to help Hudson out of prison so they could move on with their lives.

Less than thirty minutes later, she walked into Bastion's office. "Well, hello, Mac; how's everything going since we last met?"

"Not well, I'm afraid," she said, flopping down in her usual seat.

Bastion came around the desk and sat in his chair. "Tell me every-thing," he said in a fatherly tone.

"They arrested Hudson last night after he proposed to me, and now I think I'm being followed everywhere I go, but no one is there."

"Wow, okay, well, that is a lot to unpack," he said, folding and unfolding his hands. "Why don't you start with the first part? What charges do they have against Hudson?"

"Murder," she said, sounding dramatic even to her own ears.

"Seriously," was all he said.

"As weird as it sounds to my own ears, I'm serious. He took me out for a nice dinner, got down on one knee, and said some sweet things; I said yes, and then Officer Joe Romero came in and arrested him right in the restaurant."

"I thought Joe and Hudson were friends."

"They are." She explained everything, not leaving any details out. "I left him in prison, and since last night, I think I'm being followed." She took a deep breath in and blew it out. "I had my suspicions before, and it turned out I was right. I was being followed then and I think someone is tailing me now."

"You have a point. I would stay vigilant, but keep in mind it might be the stress playing tricks on you. That doesn't mean you shouldn't be aware of your surroundings. If someone were following you, who do you think it would be?"

"To be honest, I don't know. It might be someone from my mother's world, or Gennavie from a while back, or it could be someone else too. We have tons of clients we've worked with over the years whose military careers ended, or who did a stint in prison because of their military convictions. They might think we didn't defend them well enough, or somehow it was our fault they lost their careers and now can't get jobs with a federal conviction. You never know." As the words tumbled out of her mouth, she knew she was rambling.

"Okay, do you have anyone who can stay with you while this thing with Hudson gets worked out? If you aren't alone, maybe it will settle your nerves."

"There isn't anyone who can drop everything and stay with me. I keep people at arm's length."

"True," he said, "how many people have you talked to about Hudson? Has his leadership been notified?"

"Yes, they're aware, and I told Stanton and Momma Hudson."

"Oh, how did it go with his mother?" he asked, looking intrigued.

"She asked the strangest question. She asked if I was sure he hadn't killed someone. I mean, what kind of question is that?"

He rubbed his fingers over his chin. "A very curious one. Have you ever witnessed Hudson being violent?"

"Um no, well unless it's necessary or in self-defense, but everyone has the right to defend themselves."

"Well, yes, but sometimes there are other circumstances."

GENNAVIE DIALED the number from memory and listened until the familiar sound of her uncle's voice came on the line. "Well, hello, young lady. It's been a while. What have you been up to?"

"Not much, Uncle Frank." She always found herself dropping into a sweet girl's voice every time she talked with him, though they both knew she was far from innocent or sweet. "I need a little living money."

He grumbled into the phone. "The only time you ever call is when you need cash. Why don't you come for a visit so I can lay eyes on you?"

"You are well aware why I can't," she shot back, sounding a little harsher than she meant to. It had been a long time since she'd been home and only thought about her past when she had to. It was when her life changed forever—the first time she experienced that kind of power and dominance. Once it happened, she couldn't turn back no matter how hard she tried, and she stopped trying a long time ago.

Some of her past had been tantalizing and fun, but other parts had been hard. Uncle Frank pulled strings to get her out of a sticky situation when she strangled her boyfriend, Joe, and hurt him much more than she meant to. They dropped him at the hospital and left him at the emergency room door. Her uncle worried she would go to prison for attempted murder.

He'd made some phone calls, and they enlisted her in the United States Air Force. At first, she'd resisted and wanted to stay with him and in her normal, comfortable life. But Uncle Frank was a well-respected defense attorney with years of experience, and he convinced her this was the only way to ensure her freedom. After Uncle Frank tucked her away in the military with her new identity, she liked it. She found it entertaining to find out Joe was still obsessed over her even after she caused permanent damage to his larynx. But by then, she was long gone.

Once she stopped resisting and got on board with the plan, she found she enjoyed the military, and it made for an excellent cover. By the time she landed at Joint Base Lewis-McChord and she met her husband, things became exciting. Until Mac came along, no one ever suspected her or Vincent. She went from being a respected woman and military member during the day and a fierce dominatrix by night to living in hiding without her husband to play with. It would piss any woman off, and she wasn't the average woman.

"We can figure something out if you want to come home. With a new identity and cover story, we can have you set up in no time. Plus, the whole thing with Joe is over. He's not pressing charges, and as crazy as it sounds, I think he's still in love with you."

"I'll keep it in mind, but for now, I have some unfinished business to attend to."

"Tell me you're not going after that woman."

"Not at all. I'm only hanging around to find out what happens with Vincent's trial and to find out if I can help. Don't worry, I'll stay out of trouble. No one has a clue I'm in town."

"I see," he said, his voice heavy with skepticism.

"Don't worry about me. I'm keeping a low profile and staying at a place a friend of mine let me borrow while he was out of town." This was only a little true. The guy who owned the place wasn't aware she was staying, but it was only logistics. He wasn't due home for another three months, and no one seemed to check on his place, so why not?

"Have you been staying away from Vincent? The minute you go near the prison, they'll arrest you."

"Yeah, I'm watching things from afar. Don't get me wrong, Uncle Frank, I appreciated it when you pulled my butt out of trouble. And I have no intention of getting back into it. I'm just a little short on cash since I'm not able to work a job."

"I'll send you whatever you need," he said, staying silent for a moment.

He was waiting for more information, but she didn't have any to give, or at least that she was willing to tell. Her focus was on only one thing: to make Mac's life a living hell in any way she could. Getting Hudson charged with murder was only the beginning. If she could create enough doubt around Vincent's case, they would release him.

Playing without Vincent wasn't as much fun anymore. It was like when she was a little girl and had no friends or siblings to play with because her parents moved around so much. Once she indulged in that particular drug, she couldn't go back. She couldn't find the same level of excitement without him. The need for him to make things tantalizing again was something she couldn't live without.

Her thoughts went back to the times they played together and the power she had. She needed to update him to keep his hopes up, and she needed a little attention. Celibacy wasn't in her DNA. When they made her, they threw away the mold. Dominating was her natural personality, and when she was in the mood, she enjoyed being dominated. She knew who she wanted to play with. "Thanks, Uncle Frank. I'll be in touch." She hung up the phone before he responded. For such a powerful man, he became such a wuss when it came to her. She had that effect on men, but she wished her uncle wasn't one of them.

Her friend would be over soon, and she intended to use him for everything he was worth. Less than an hour later, there was a knock on her door. She answered wearing thigh-high boots and a little black leather skirt with a red corset. The outfit pushed everything into the right places. She allowed her stunning green eyes and deep red hair to show, swept up on her head. "Thank you for coming," she cooed.

"Umm, hi," the man at her door said.

"I thought I told you to come out of uniform." Gennavie pulled him by the tie into the house so no one would identify him. The house sat off the road on more than an acre of land. Someone would have to be looking to witness anything, but she never could be too careful. At least he was on time. She hated to be left waiting.

"Mistress, please accept my apologies. I got stuck at work and didn't want to be late."

She liked them to grovel at her feet. This man wasn't attractive, and he would do anything to touch her. Her five-inch heels set her at eye level with him. His round face and small eyes were too close to his nose, making him look like a lost weasel. He was a little pudgy in the middle, and his uniform belt cut into his sides, making his love handles squish over. But she didn't need to be attracted to him or want to have sex with him. She needed to control him, wield power over him, and make him do what she needed him to.

He had already delivered on part of it; getting Hudson placed into the general population at the prison was a start. She hoped he was being abused and violated the same way Vincent had. If the planets aligned in her direction, maybe someone would stab Hudson and make him bleed. "You have done well, my pet. Now get ready so I can show you what a good boy you've been."

He scampered down the hall with a goofy grin on his face.

MAC WALKED into Captain Stanton's Area Defense Counsel office, hoping to find out something positive. Maybe Hudson would be out of prison by the end of the day. After leaving Hudson there, she hadn't slept a wink. The nightmare was becoming all too real. "Morning, boss, how are things going?" she said because she wasn't sure how else to start the conversation.

"Hi, Mac, take a seat. We have a lot to discuss." She lowered herself into the government-issued client seat with worn red fabric on the other side of his desk. From the look on her boss's face, she wasn't sure she wanted to hear what he had to say. "Okay, Mac, I have good news and bad news. Which do you want first?"

"Give me the good," she said, not sure how much more bad she could handle.

"Fair enough. My friend, Aeddan Bartz, the civilian defense attorney I was telling you about, is on the case. We went to Gonzaga Law School together, and he's the best I've ever seen. I hate to admit it, but the man puts me to shame in the courtroom. If anyone can help Hudson out of this mess, it's him."

"That's great news." She let the words hang in the air, waiting for the rest.

"Now for the bad," he said, taking a deep breath before continuing. "I have no idea how else to tell you this, but the bad news is twofold."

"How bad can it be?" She couldn't keep her voice from shaking.

"Aeddan was able to obtain a copy of the evidence on the case, and it's not circumstantial like we hoped."

"What do you mean? How on earth can they have factual evidence of a murder he didn't commit?" Mac asked, doing her best to remain calm but not succeeding. "Who the hell are they accusing him of murdering?"

"Lieutenant Colonel Daniels, the staff judge advocate from Holloman Air Force Base. Someone murdered him while the two of you were there."

"It doesn't mean Hudson killed the man because we were in the area."

Stanton lowered his voice to keep Mac calm when he delivered the next bit of news. "His prints are on the murder weapon."

Mac sat back in her seat. "It can't be true. Someone had to place his prints. I read an article once about transferring prints and planting evidence."

"We don't know any of that right now. All I can tell you is Aeddan is working on it, but this thing isn't going away anytime soon. He's going to be locked up for a while."

"Are they moving him to New Mexico?"

"Not yet; Aeddan is working on having him held here pending further investigation. Since it's now a federal case and the FBI is involved, Aeddan has an argument, but we'll have to see if he's successful." Mac opened her mouth to speak, but Stanton held up his hand. "There's more. We need to find him a good area defense counsel who can help him with the military repercussions. At a minimum, they have put him in confinement status, which strips him of all pay and allowances. If he stays in that status too long, he'll end up with some serious financial problems. It may be minimal right now, but it's something to be concerned about. He'll find it hard to cope if he gets exonerated but ends up bankrupt because of a prolonged status."

"What do you mean, if?" Mac interrupted. "Do you think they'll convict him of murder?"

"I never prejudge a case, even when I have personal knowledge of the accused. I'm looking at this from a practical and legal standpoint. We have to plan for the worst and hope for the best. You know it as much as I do."

"Yeah, I understand where you're coming from, but there has to be a reasonable explanation for this."

"Let me ask you this. Could he pull this off?"

"What? Murdering a man? What possible motive did he have?"

"I have no idea, but it's not what I asked. Did he have time to pull it off?"

"Well, we weren't together every second of the day, but I don't think he had enough time, and he wouldn't do this. Why would he do this?"

"Is Hudson a jealous man?"

"No, nothing like that. And, in any case, he only met Daniels a few times when we were working out details to take down my mother's cartel."

"Did Daniels flirt with you at all, or give Hudson a reason?"

Mac's face turned red. "You're acting like he did this."

"No, I'm trying to figure out what the prosecution can bring to the table, like any of the other cases we've worked together. Now I need you to take a deep breath and think about this like it's not Hudson. What defense can Aeddan bring to the table? Can you provide any type of alibi for Hudson? Was he with you most of the time? Was there a big enough gap for him to kill someone? Come on Mac, think. Help me so I can help you," he shot at her, running his hand through his hair and making the short blond strands stand on end.

"Okay, okay," she said, taking a deep breath in and letting it out. She sat back in her chair and remained quiet for a moment. "I'm aware it's not our case and I have one hell of a conflict of interest, but it doesn't mean we can't provide his defense team with every advantage we can. If we can obtain a copy of the case file, would you be willing to run the evidence with me to figure this out?"

"I'm happy to help. First, knowing the time of death is going to be very helpful. If you can pinpoint where you were and where Hudson was during that time, it might take care of this mess."

"Can you find out?" Mac asked, hopeful for the first time.

"Yeah, I can ask if Aeddan will share with us, but the prosecution can't catch wind of your involvement. No discussing this case with anyone at all."

"I'm with you on that. The last thing I want to do is complicate things. The only person I'm talking to is Chaplain Bastion. He's helping me deal with all the stress and stuff," Mac said, not wanting to elaborate on how badly her mental health was spiraling.

"Fair enough, he's the only other person on base who has full confidentiality as long as there's no harm to self or others. Keep that off the table and you'll be fine."

"Yeah, not to worry unless I find out who's setting Hudson up. Then I might cause harm to others." She smiled, trying to make light of the subject.

"Hilarious," he said, not laughing. "What can I do to make this easier for you?" he asked with genuine concern in his eyes.

"Not much boss. You've been more than supportive. I'm putting you behind because I haven't been focusing on cases. Maybe I can at least research an ADC to help Hudson and take it off your plate."

"That's a good start. I'd also like you to retrace your steps while you were in New Mexico, once Hudson arrived. Grab a clean notebook out of the supply closet and start with the day he showed up. If we need to go back any further, then we can. For now, focus on the time Hudson was with you. A play-by-play of all your activities while you were both there. It'll help Aeddan narrow down an alibi and splash some reasonable doubt on this thing."

"I'm on it, sir, and thank you."

"I've done nothing yet," he said.

"Your support means the world to me. I appreciate you getting him solid representation and your willingness to help."

"Let's figure this thing out and that will be thanks enough. Now get to work. We need to tackle this thing from all directions since I'm not sure how well a guy like Hudson will do in prison. If he stays in general pop, it may turn worse."

Mac left his office and went to her own. Another paralegal worked the daily cases with Stanton now, leaving her to work on the more complex cases once they changed her job title to a defense investigator. And that's what she intended to do: hunt down the son of a bitch who was setting up Hudson and find enough evidence to lock him away for life.

She dialed Agent Bardot's number again and waited. She'd worked with FBI Agent Bardot during Gennavie and Vincent's case, and then again during her family's case. If anyone could help her with Hudson's situation, it would be her.

A man's voice came back on the line. "I'm sorry, ma'am, she's not available right now. Can I take a message?"

Mac left her third message and wondered if Bardot was avoiding her.

GENNAVIE GOT up and paced the room. She couldn't sit still and was waiting for the time to be right. The thought of thickening the plot and laying out the next step in her plan took over everything. To guarantee Hudson's stay in prison, she needed to keep stacking evidence against him. Obsession and focus engulfed her brain, determined to destroy Mac and Hudson at any cost. This next layer was something that not even the amazing Mac could get rid of.

She slipped on her black oversized pants, boots, jacket, and gloves and stuffed a ski mask in her pocket. Clips pinned her hair back on her head. The brilliance of the suit she was wearing under all of it was the perfect find. When she found it in a costume shop, it was what she was after. When she put it on, it transformed her body, making her look more like an overweight man instead of her tight and toned self. The wonderful thing about Spokane in December was the ability to conceal and hide her identity with no one looking twice. She pulled the cap over her hair, leaving the face portion propped on her forehead so she could drive, and headed out.

A plastic bag under the front seat held the evidence. She'd borrowed an unassuming Toyota Camry that didn't stick out. The tan exterior blended into any environment, and it wasn't like the owner needed it since they'd deployed him. Twenty minutes later, she pulled down Mac's street to find her little SUV in the driveway, where Gennavie hoped it would be. She needed her to stay put for the night. At almost 0200 hours, it was time to put her plan in motion.

She twisted the steering wheel hard and pulled a U-turn at the end of Mac's street and headed back out of her neighborhood. Ten minutes later, she was on Hudson's street. The night's pitch-black sky engulfed the outside as she rolled past; she saw no signs of life. She stopped at the end of the street, pulled down her ski mask, and got out with a plastic bag in her hand.

The light flicked on atop someone's front porch as she crossed their yard. She dove behind a bush, waiting for the owner of the house to come out, but no one did. Her heart was pounding in her chest, but nothing happened. The street remained quiet as she made her way between the houses and back onto Hudson's street. Earlier in the week she'd checked the place during the daytime and found a back door that should allow for easy access.

She slipped next to his house, sliding her fluff-padded body against the vinyl siding, knowing no one would identify her. It gave her the same rush as when she dressed up for a night on the town to play with unsuspecting victims. No one would ever think she was capable of the things she wanted to do to them until it was too late. In this case, no one would ever suspect she was a woman, let alone be able to identify her for who she was if they caught sight of her. As long as they didn't catch her in the house, she was fine. It would be easy to talk her way out of everything else.

She stayed low, not wanting any nosey neighbors to catch a glimpse of her. They would report her as a man breaking and entering. The last thing she needed was some over-enthusiastic neighbor coming out with a shotgun to protect his neighborhood. She inched up to the gate that connected to the fence, lifted the lock, and slipped into Hudson's backyard without a noise. Once she was in she stood and stretched her back, thankful for the yard's ten-foot fence protecting her from view.

The back door was a simple pin tumbler lock found in most homes.

She slid the lock-picking tools she'd bought on Amazon out of her pocket. It always amazed her what she found on the internet. She was in Hudson's home in less than two minutes. She slipped through the kitchen and down the hall to his bedroom. The small house was easy to navigate, making it simple for her to execute her plan.

Pulling a lock of Anika's hair and the tiny pink thong out of the plastic bag, she placed it under his bed. She tucked it into a tear in the box spring toward the back so no one would stumble on it. The reminder of the fear in Anika's eyes as Gennavie pressed harder on her throat flashed in her mind. A smile crept across her crimson lips as she recalled Anika squirming under her strong thighs as she pressed harder. Anika had been a fighter and pulled at the restraints with all her might, but she had no chance. One thing Gennavie was good at was tying people up. Something about the way Anika's eyes bulged, the smooth skin on her neck turning red and purple under Gennavie's bullwhip—the terror in her eyes, knowing she was about to die—the memory made her excited all over again.

Pleased with how things were going, she wiped away her wet footprints as she backed out of the house. Minutes later, she was out the back door, locking it behind her. She froze in place when a dog barked nearby. Listening for a moment, she realized it was the house to the left. Picking up a branch, she cleared her footprints from the snow, exiting the way she came. The last thing she needed was the dog owner to come investigate. In no time, she made it back onto the sidewalk, around the neighbor's house, and back to the car, taking care to remove any trace of her existence as she went.

Sitting in the still-warm car, she fired it up, relishing her success. This was too easy. She dropped it into gear, not wanting to stay long enough for a nosey neighbor to take notice. Or worse yet, take down the license plate, at least not until she finished borrowing things.

A prickle of excitement crawled up her spine as she drove. This was too yummy for words. During the defense attorney's time of death, Hudson was flying out to meet Mac in New Mexico, but his flight got delayed. She chose that time to kill Anika, betting Hudson would wait at home alone with no alibi. No one could verify he hadn't killed her. A window of time big enough for Hudson to drive out to Anika's home, kill her, and board the plane. No one could verify his location, making it enough to meet the preponderance of the evidence. Gennavie needed it to be easy for the prosecution to sink their teeth into the delicious little breadcrumbs she left behind once they discovered everything.

HUDSON ROLLED his enormous frame off the thin mattress in his cell. His back screamed at him when he tried to stand to his full height. For most of his life, he'd struggled with back problems. The doc said most tall men do, and the thin mattress and metal frame underneath his new bed weren't helping. He had to stand for a moment before the little needles stopped exploding in his feet.

The prison uniform they gave him hung on his trim waist and rode halfway up his calves. He tried to stay quiet, not ready to deal with his new cellmate's crap. His bladder was overfull, and he couldn't hold it. He cringed as the man on the top bunk rolled over. As a big man, it was rare for him to be threatened, and most people found him intimidating or assumed he was violent because of his size. But his cellmate was one of the few that made him uneasy.

The other inmates in the prison called Hudson's cellmate Gorilla Juice. Hudson understood the gorilla part but hadn't figured out the juice reference and wasn't sure he wanted that bit of information.

"Good morning, sunshine," Gorilla said from his bunk. Hudson ignored him, turning his back to the man. "Oh, come on honey, you're not still pissed at me about last night, are you?"

Gorilla had challenged Hudson in front of the other prisoners. They wanted Hudson in their little gang, and he wanted nothing to do with it. Gorilla was a skinhead white supremacist type and wanted Hudson to be part of his muscle. At first, this confused the shit out of Hudson, since he wasn't a white man. He was Greek by nationality with olive skin, but then he realized it wasn't about his nationality, beliefs, or culture; it was about his size. As long as Hudson looked like a white boy, then Gorilla could use him to further his cause.

He realized he couldn't keep his head down. All he wanted was for his attorney to get him out of general pop and into pre-trial confinement, but nothing had happened yet. The wheels of justice were moving at a snail's pace and his attorney told him it was going to take some time. He had never been in prison before but knew enough to guess his choices were going to become limited the more time he stayed. The night before he'd made Gorilla back down, but it wouldn't last long. It would be worse before it got better.

Gorilla gave Hudson three options to consider. "You been thinking about my offers, sunshine?" Gorilla said, still stretched out on his bunk. Hudson remained quiet. "Oh, come on, how bad would it be? I want to make you our friend. That's all. Join us, and we'll make sure no one else fucks with you. If you take me up on my other offer, you'll belong to me and no one else."

Hudson shivered. Gorilla's other proposition was for Hudson to become his bitch. The two men were an even match. Gorilla was soft around the middle and had an abundance of hair, enormous arms and legs, and a bulging stomach that made his issued clothes appear too small. He covered his body from head to toe in tattoos, standing a few inches shorter than Hudson. The man had been in prison for a long time and would kill Hudson without giving it a second thought. If Hudson retaliated and Gorilla died, it would only make his situation worse.

Gorilla swung his legs off the top bunk and dropped to the concrete floor as Hudson pulled his pants back into place, pulling the string as tight as possible. Gorilla smacked Hudson on his ass, and Hudson spun around to face the man.

"Don't touch me," Hudson growled through clenched teeth.

Gorilla pushed his smelly body against Hudson, pressing him against the small metal sink secured to the wall. "You don't understand the situation you're in, sunshine. You see, I run this joint. They put me in this cage before you were out of diapers. I take what I want when I want, and there's no one that's gonna protect you from me. I own the guards and everyone else. So, play nice," he said, tapping his meaty palm on Hudson's chiseled cheek.

The last thing Hudson wanted to do was fight this man, but he wouldn't be anyone's bitch. If he took down Gorilla, the other inmates wouldn't touch him. The prison wasn't much different from the military. The ones in charge stayed in charge, and the lower levels fell into place underneath. A big difference in the military was it had nothing to do with size or ability to fight. Position and rank gave power. In prison, it had everything to do with how well a person kicked ass. Hudson was thankful for his skills in that department and hoped what happened next wouldn't land him in more trouble than he was already in.

Gorilla wrapped his arms around Hudson. With his big gut in the way, his fingers strained to clasp. Hudson felt the metal cutting into his skin, but he didn't move until the big man tilted his head up at Hudson. He slammed his forehead down, hitting Gorilla right between the eyes. He had been aiming for his nose, but it stunned the man and got him to release. Hudson swung, catching the man in the ear and making him scream out in pain, stepping back into the small cell.

Hudson hoped that would be the end, but Gorilla was far from finished. He rushed Hudson, who moved to the side, pivoting past the large man and getting behind him. He wrapped his arm around Gorilla's throat and squeezed. Gorilla threw his weight from side to side, trying to make Hudson release, but he held on, locking his other hand to keep his arm around his neck. Gorilla slowed and then stilled for a moment, and Hudson thought he was going to pass out when he slammed one of his enormous fists into Hudson's face, causing Hudson to release. Metallic blood filled his mouth.

Gorilla took advantage, jumping on top of Hudson, pinning him down, and started wailing on him with his enormous fists. Hudson tried to protect his face, but the blows kept on coming until a shout came from outside the cell. Gorilla paused for only a fraction of a second. It was all Hudson needed to shift his weight and throw the man back, pushing him into the wall. Inmates cheered from all sides. Some were shouting for Gorilla to get up, and others were shouting for Hudson to kick his ass. The noise was almost deafening.

The big man scrambled to his feet, regaining his strength, and rushed Hudson. As the man got close, Hudson swung, making contact with his nose, the cartilage crumpling under his knuckles. Gorilla screamed out in pain. Dropping to his knees, he held his face while blood seeped between his fingers.

After too long, a guard opened the cell. Hudson stepped back, not wanting to take a blow from the metal baton, and placed his hands behind his head, waiting for them to place the cuffs on his wrists.

CHAPTER
NINETEEN

IT'D BEEN JUST shy of three days since Hudson went to prison, and Mac feared she might be losing her mind. Back at his house, she slept on his side of the bed, but it made things worse. She couldn't sleep, and she wasn't eating enough. She jumped any time there was a loud noise. The way people were looking at her made her angry, like she was unstable, but she couldn't blame them. She knew what she looked like, and it wasn't good.

If she didn't figure this thing out soon, Hudson wasn't the only one who would be in trouble. She dialed her sister, Lola. It was weird calling on her regular cell phone, but there was no need for either of them to remain in hiding anymore, not with their mother behind bars. Her sister didn't pick up, and Mac tried to calculate the time difference in Italy. Since it was only 1130 hours her time, she figured it was still before 2100 hours in her sister's time.

As she tried to force her to brain make the calculation, her phone rang in her hand. "Hey, sis, how's everything?" Lola said. Mac remained silent. "What's wrong?"

"Everything," Mac breathed out. She sat on Hudson's bed in his home. Nothing was right anymore. One minute her world was great and she was getting married, and the next their world was in shambles. No warning.

"Tell me," Lola said, concern lacing her voice.

"Hudson is in prison, and I think I'm losing my mind."

"What the hell. Why is Hudson in the can?"

"They arrested him for murder right after he proposed."

Silence on the other end of the line. "Congratulations," Lola said.

"Uh, thanks, I guess. But now I need your help." Mac told her everything from the wonderful dinner out and proposal to everything that happened since then. "And I need you to be careful not to leave a trail. I'm not sure who's behind this but I don't want them coming for you too."

"No worries. You know I can be in and out of anywhere without them being wiser. Who do you think is following you?" Lola asked.

"No idea. Every time I turn around, no one is there. I'm starting to think I'm paranoid, but I keep getting that gut reaction."

"Well, trust your instincts. I would rather you be a little on edge and react than think it's nothing and let your guard down. If you think someone is following you, then you should listen to your instincts. Now tell me what I can do to help."

"I need to find out what evidence they have on Hudson, and I could use some help in finding out who's setting him up and tracking me."

"Do you have an alibi for Hudson during the time of the murder?"

"I'm working on a detailed timeline, but my thoughts keep getting jumbled. I need sleep, but every time I shut my eyes I think about Hudson or my other nasty dreams. Or sometimes, I'm trying to fall asleep and start thinking about our mother's trial."

"Oh yeah, any word on what's happening with her crazy ass?"

"No idea. The last I heard, the Feds, the various states, and Mexico are having a pissing contest about who gets to prosecute her first. It may take months, if not years, to make it through all her trials. No matter what I think of her, I can't imagine getting up in front of a court and testifying against her, but I don't want her free."

"Yeah, me either. It's nice not to have to look over my shoulder all the time or wonder if Olive is safe," Lola said.

"I like that part too, but it doesn't mean it's going to be easy and

I'm still looking over my shoulder. Some asshole is fucking with me and I'm tired of it, and the trial looming isn't helping."

"We'll worry about it when it happens. For now, do you or Hudson still have painkillers from your injuries last winter?"

"Yeah, I think some is in the bathroom. Why?" Mac asked, knowing she didn't sound like herself and had to think about things more than she should have to.

"Okay, now listen to me. Go around the house and lock everything up. Windows, doors, the whole nine. Check the house the same way you would clear a crime scene. Once you're done, I want you to go take one painkiller and sleep. Give me some time to do a little digging."

"Do you think that's such a good idea? What if Hudson needs something?"

"There's nothing you can do for Hudson right now. You're no good to anyone in this state. If you don't sleep, you might cause more harm than good. Now go do what I tell you and I'll call you when I have something." Mac stayed silent for a moment. "I'm going to hang up, but I want you to turn off your phone and sleep."

"Yes, ma'am," Mac said. Her sister was right, and she didn't need to be anywhere. The line disconnected. Her sister was always abrupt and didn't end things with pleasantries.

She shot Stanton a quick text telling him she needed a little time and would be in contact later. Then she made her way into the small bathroom and rummaged through the medicine cabinet looking for the medication with her name on it, only to realize hers were back at her place, but Hudson's prescription still sat on the little white shelf.

Taking his medication would go against the Uniform Code of Military Justice and fell under the misuse of a controlled substance, so she shouldn't do it. She plucked it off the counter and looked at the prescription, not sure how much she should take. She decided on only half.

CHAPTER
TWENTY

POUNDING on the door brought Mac out of her deep sleep. It was dark outside. She checked her phone to see it was after 1800 hours and she'd missed several calls from Joe Romero. The knocking continued.

"Just a sec," she hollered, and pulled herself out of the nice warm bed. She was wearing one of Hudson's oversized shirts and a pair of old sweats when she made it to the door.

She looked through the peephole. Joe stood on the other side with four other officers in uniform behind him. Mac opened the door a crack. "Joe, what is this?"

His normally well-kept dark hair stood to one side like he had woken up only moments before. Soft bags hung under his eyes, and her heart sank. It couldn't be good. "I'm sorry Mac, we have a warrant to search the house."

"Did something new surface?" Mac asked, panicked and still half asleep with the medication in her system.

"The FBI believes he might be involved in another murder, and he might be a serial killer. I'm here to convince them they're wrong."

"Joe," Mac said, listening to her own voice shake, "how worried should I be right now?"

"It's going to be fine. Hudson and I go way back. He's a good guy and I'm confident we won't find anything, which is why I told them I wanted to execute the search to make sure it's done right."

"Okay," she said, stepping aside.

"I need you to come out front while they do what they need to," he said, sweeping his arm at the officers. Mac nodded her head, sliding on a pair of boots and Hudson's huge coat hanging by the door.

She followed Joe outside, past the other officers. He nodded at one of them and they walked into the house. "Why don't you sit in my car while they do what they need to? I'm going to make sure things are done properly and I'll be back out as soon as we're finished."

Mac climbed into the passenger side of Joe's police cruiser and waited. She closed her eyes, trying to clear her thoughts, and must have drifted off. When she cracked open her eyes, Joe was climbing into the driver's seat and was shaking her shoulder to bring her back to the living. When she looked at the clock on the dashboard, over two hours passed. "Hi Joe, sorry," she said groggily. "Did you find anything?"

He sat for what was too long for Mac. "I'm not sure where to start. I was so convinced we wouldn't find anything, so I agreed to do the search without pushing back."

"Joe, what in the hell did you guys find?"

"I can't discuss the details of an ongoing investigation," he said, looking out the windshield at nothing. "But I can tell you we found the evidence we were looking for to tie him to this second murder. Do you have any idea how it got there?" he said, making eye contact with her for the first time since he'd climbed behind the wheel.

"No, I have no idea, since you're not telling me what you found or where."

"I'm sorry Mac, but I'm going to have to bring you in for questioning since you were one of the few other people who had full access to the scene."

Mac's head was spinning. How on earth could this get any worse? "Do what you need to." Her voice sounded weak and defeated.

"Do you need to grab anything before we go?" He looked at her with concern in his dark-brown eyes. His attractive features looked drawn and tired.

"Yeah, I'll need my wallet. Is it okay if I change?"

"I'm sorry Mac, it's now an active crime scene. They should clear it in the next twelve hours, but until the forensic specialists from the FBI are done, they won't allow you in."

"Can you go grab my stuff? I'll wait here, promise."

Twenty minutes later, they pulled up to the station. She remembered the first time she'd walked in to find Officer Joe Romero and convinced him to help her in the case involving several missing and dead women. Hudson sent her to Joe. They had been friends for years and Hudson suspected Joe had encountered similar cases that could be connected. This was before Hudson got involved and she fell in love. Only a short year ago, but so much had happened since then. It felt like a lifetime ago. She followed Joe into the precinct, and he led her to interview room one.

Joe left her with the door open and she took comfort in the fact that he wasn't treating her as a suspect. She considered calling Stanton to update him but thought better of it as several officers passed. It would have to wait. Talking to him in private so they could discuss the details was a better idea. Her mind was clearing now that she had a few hours of shuteye on board. The room was small, and she paced it like a caged lioness. She settled into one of the uncomfortable chairs sitting against the metal table secured to the floor.

The noise carried through the thin walls of the government building. She had difficulty making out Joe's voice. It sounded like he was arguing with someone, but she found it impossible to make out what they were saying. Her legs and butt were going numb in the metal chair before Joe came in. "Sorry about that Mac, I had to clear something up."

"What's going on?"

"They want to take me off the case. Conflict of interest because Hudson and I are friends."

"I want you on this case, Joe, but they have a point."

"Yeah, so I agreed to finish the interview with you and then step back."

"Who's taking over?"

"The FBI, if I had to guess. They're getting jurisdiction, since it's a multi-state murder investigation."

She made a mental note to call Agent Bardot again. She still hadn't heard and had to wonder why. After all the help they had provided during the last two cases, maybe Bardot would help them. "Who do they think Hudson killed this time?" Mac said, listening to how ridiculous the words sounded coming from her lips.

"An Air Force attorney, the same one who defended Vincent Wolf, Gennavie's husband."

"You're shitting me. Why on earth would Hudson kill Vincent's defense attorney? He helped me put his ass away."

"The FBI thinks he's involved with Gennavie and is helping her."

Mac remained silent. She didn't know what to say other than she knew in her heart it wasn't true. The man Hudson was couldn't be capable of slaughtering women. As she let the thought sink into her brain, she reminded herself she thought the same thing about her mentor, Chief Master Sergeant Deleon. "What can I do to help?"

"We've already verified you were in New Mexico at the time of the defense attorney's death, so you're not a suspect, but do you have any way to verify where Hudson was right before he flew out to visit you?"

Mac thought about this. She didn't want to give the first answer that popped into her head because it was no. So, she remained silent. This couldn't get any worse.

CHAPTER
TWENTY-ONE

MAC PULLED into the prison parking lot where Hudson was now housed. After being interrogated by Joe and making an official statement about what she had first-hand knowledge of, she went back to her place and got a few more hours of rest. Not sleep, but at least she let her body sink into the cushion mattress on her bed. It was weird to be at her place without the scent of Hudson lingering on the sheets. In the night's quiet, she found herself doubting Hudson and his involvement in the murders. She had to see him. Look him in the eyes and make sure.

They led her into the same room they'd put her in before. She tapped the screen, expecting Hudson to be on the other side, but it was blank, so she waited. After ten minutes, she got up and knocked on the door to get the guard's attention. The man looked up from his station on the other of the bars with a look of disdain at the interruption. He walked over and opened her little room. "Yes."

"I'm supposed to meet with inmate Gavin Hudson but he's not on the video," she said as the knot in her stomach grew. Referring to him as an inmate made her want to cry out.

"Yes, he's being brought down from the infirmary."

"Why in hell is he in the infirmary?"

"An altercation took place."

The blood drained from her face. "Is he okay?"

"Yes, now take a seat and he'll be on video in a few minutes."

The way the man was talking to her like she was insignificant and what happened to Hudson was unimportant pissed her off to no end. "What can you tell me?"

"Nothing," he said, pointing to the chair she had been sitting in. She went back and sat and waited. It took them thirty minutes before Hudson's beaten and broken face appeared on the screen.

She gasped; the handsome face with the chiseled jawline that she loved so much was almost unrecognizable. The right side of his face was black and blue. A long, thin cut ran down his cheek and his left eye was swollen shut. "What happened?"

He tried to smile at her, but the right side of his face was so swollen it came across as a lopsided grin. "It's not as bad as it looks," he said, trying to soften things. "You should look at the other guy."

She stared at him. The words got lost in her throat. Someone had beaten the man she loved, and she was about to deliver more bad news. He looked back at her from the little screen, waiting for her to ask questions, but she didn't. "Oh, come on, hon, we'll make it through this. It's going to be okay. I need you to stay with me and be strong. I can't face this alone."

"No, it's not," she shouted, not meaning to.

"It's not what?" he said, looking confused.

"It's not going to be okay. Nothing is okay. Everything is shit, and it keeps getting worse."

"Okay, babe," he said, leaning back from the screen. "I know this looks bad, but my attorney says he has evidence to help me out of this jam and he's making headway in pulling me out of the general population after the attack."

"You don't understand. This isn't going away," she said, taking a deep breath, pushing back the tears stinging her eyes. She wanted to tell him in person, but she had no idea when she would be with him, hold him, be in his warm, powerful arms. Her heart ached thinking about it.

"What are you talking about? I didn't kill Daniels. We can beat this.

We need to find the evidence." He let his words trail off when he saw the look in her eyes. "You don't think I did this, do you?"

"They found evidence of a second murder victim last night," she said, not answering his question. "Joe and his guys came to your place and conducted a search warrant."

"Nothing should be in my house. It has to be planted. What did they say they found?"

"Joe wouldn't give me the details, but he said it was what they were looking for to connect you to the murder of Vincent Wolf's defense attorney." The look of confusion on his face told her he didn't remember. "Our case last summer, Gennavie's husband."

"Oh yeah, okay," he said, taking a deep breath. "Any idea who's doing this to us?"

"No, but I intend to find out," she said, looking into his eyes. She studied his features. Underneath all the swelling was still the man she loved, and no matter how much evidence they brought forth she still couldn't imagine he had done this, and never to a woman. He could kill in self-defense and so could she. But that they were accusing him of killing a woman told her it was impossible. Hudson was many things, but his personality toward women was of respect and kindness. She couldn't imagine him hurting one, let alone murdering one. He was her gentle giant, and he couldn't be capable of this. She refused to believe it until someone showed her iron-clad evidence he was guilty.

CHAPTER
TWENTY-TWO

LATER IN THE EVENING, Mac was back at Hudson's place. She needed to be near him, and the only place she connected to him was at his house. It wasn't the healthiest thing for her to do, but it was what she was capable of and it was the only place she could think. After cleaning up from when the police executed their search warrant, she pulled out an old piece of cardboard Hudson had tucked into his garage and began making it into a makeshift evidence board.

She put the cardboard on his kitchen table, and with a large black Sharpie she started writing everything she had so far. Lieutenant Colonel Daniels' murder happened prior to when they escaped her mother's compound, but she didn't have the specific details. She remembered Jax telling her he had been dead for days before anyone discovered him, but how many days and what was the time of death?

She reminded herself to ask Stanton if he'd received any additional information. If she couldn't nail down where Hudson was, she couldn't provide a solid alibi. Hudson had arrived in New Mexico on the twenty-seventh of October. She picked him up from the airport and they stayed in El Paso for the night, but then she remembered the weekend he'd flown in to see her at Holloman. It was right after he found out about her crazy family. The fear he was going to run away was still fresh.

But he didn't. He surprised her by taking her in his arms and convincing her in more ways than one that he was here to stay. She smiled, remembering the mind-blowing sex they had once he convinced her he was committed to her. Electricity ran down her spine at the thought of him touching her. The things he could do with his fingers and his mouth were indescribable. She missed him and wasn't sure how long she could do this without him.

It was crazy to think how only last year she had been independent and faced the world alone. Hudson came along and now her world was empty without him in it. She never thought she would find someone like him and now that she had, she had no intentions of letting him go. He'd stayed in her corner and didn't give up on her when she was facing off with her mother. Now it was her turn to rescue him.

Thinking about him being beaten and broken in the jail cell made it hard to concentrate. She jotted down everything she could think of about the time he was with her at Holloman Air Force Base, putting El Paso for the times they weren't in the location of the murder. The time he came down for the weekend and surprised her and the time he came back to help her face off with her family kept intertwining in her mind. She couldn't recall a big enough gap in time for him to kill Daniels, but it was far from ironclad. If she had more information, like the exact date and time of death, she might narrow it down to something useful.

After staring at her list for over an hour, she got up and stretched. Her eyes were getting heavy, and she needed more sleep. She crawled into Hudson's bed and grabbed one of his old t-shirts, pulling it up to her chest so she would sleep engulfed in his scent. She closed her eyes, thinking about his warm body pressed up against hers. How his strong hands slid down her back. The jolt of electricity that shot through her body when he kissed her neck. She would roll over to meet him and he would kiss her, making her lose all thought. Her dreams were filled with his mouth, sucking on her nipples and his fingers between her legs, making her wet and wanting.

She would roll back over and press her body against his and he would reach around cupping her breast, entering her from behind, pulling her in until they were moving as one. She coiled around his large shaft, anticipating the euphoric explosion that was coming. Her head was spinning with anticipation when something crept in. "Just ignore it," she whispered in her dreams. She tried to force the noise out. To stay in the wonderful dream she was having, but the incessant noise kept coming.

She cracked one of her eyes open, finding herself in the dark room in Hudson's bed with his t-shirt pressed against her face. It took her another minute to figure out what had pulled her from her sleep and the wonderful sensation of Hudson against her. Her phone was ringing. "Somebody better be dead," she said out loud, but regretted it. The last thing they needed were more dead bodies.

She picked up her phone and hit the button, but no call was coming in. It took a moment for her to remember Hudson was one of the few people on Earth who still had a landline. He said it came with the house and he never got it disconnected. She slid out of bed and into the kitchen to answer. As she picked up the receiver, she heard a dial tone. The clock on the wall told her it was already after 2300 hours, and she wondered how long it would take her to go back to sleep. She placed the receiver back in its cradle when it started ringing again. She snatched it back up. "Who is this?" she said, irritation laced through her voice.

"Hello, this is a collect call from the Texas State Prison for Evelyn McGregor. Say yes if you would like to accept."

"Yes," Mac said in a whisper.

"Evelyn darling, hi. How is my girl doing?" came her mother's voice over the phone like she was calling to catch up.

"What do you want, Mother?"

"Oh, come on darling, is that any way to treat your own mother?"

Mac had no idea what her mother was after or how the hell she'd gotten Hudson's home number, but Mac wanted nothing to do with it. "It's late and I need to sleep. Say what you want to say or I'm hanging up," she growled.

"Very well," Reina said, dropping her voice from friendly to all business. "I understand Hudson is in a bit of a bind, and I'm calling to offer my help."

"You're in prison, Mother, and I don't want the type of help you have to give."

"I have many friends, darling. I can protect Hudson until he gets out of this awful situation."

"How do you know what's going on? Are you having me followed?"

"Oh, don't be so paranoid. I have people and they talk to me. I understand your poor boy toy got his ass beat by a man named Gorilla." Reina chuckled in Mac's ear. "I couldn't imagine how awful that must be for you."

"You mean you have spies."

"Oh darling, they don't like to be called that. They like the title 'information gatherers.'"

Mac remained silent for a moment. "What do you want in return?"

"I want you to come for a visit. If you agree, Hudson will be safe."

It was never simple, and she had no intention of getting help from her mother. If she was sure of anything, nothing was free. She would owe Reina for the rest of her life. "No thank you, Mother. Hudson and I can handle this."

"Okay, if you think so. Call me if you change your mind," Reina said and hung up the phone. Mac wasn't sure if it was because her time was up or if that was all she had to say. Either way, Mac wasn't biting. The last thing she needed was to be in debt to her mother.

CHAPTER
TWENTY-THREE

"HI JOE," Mac said into the phone, trying to keep her voice casual. She sat back in her office the next morning fidgeting with a pen. Stanton hadn't been able to obtain any additional evidence from Hudson's defense attorney, which meant they were in a waiting pattern and Mac had little patience.

"Mac, how are you holding up?" She smiled at the genuine concern in his voice. For a cop, Joe was a nice guy who cared about people. Most of the people she met in law enforcement had walls up and wouldn't let people get too close, but not Joe. He was one of the nicest people Mac had ever met.

"I'm okay. How are you?" She hated the small talk, but she needed him to open up. "How's Ali?" she asked, hoping if she got him talking about his girlfriend, then maybe he would continue talking.

"She's amazing and has been asking to have you over for dinner. I can't discuss the case with you, but if you're open for dinner tonight, she'd be thrilled."

Ali had lost her sister during one of Mac's first cases. Her sister had been the victim of the first man she hunted down. Ali had almost become a victim herself, but Mac came to her rescue. That's when Ali and Joe met, and now they were living together. It would give her some leverage for information.

"Sounds amazing. I'd love to catch up with her. It's been too long. Can I bring anything?"

"Nope, just you. How about six tonight?"

"I look forward to it."

The timer on Hudson's stove dinged. Her day flew by and now she was running behind. Joe said to show up, but she couldn't come empty-handed, so she cooked a pan of brownies. Hudson's oven differed from hers, and it took more time than expected. She left the house with the piping-hot pan right out of the oven and laid it on a towel in the passenger side of her vehicle.

It was ten past six when she arrived. Ali opened the door, looking radiant with her dark hair pulled up in a bun. She engulfed Mac in a hug as soon as Mac dropped the brownies on a hot pad in the kitchen on the tiled countertop. "It's so good to see you. How have you been?" Ali asked.

"Hate to say, I've been better, but tell me about you first," she said, looking at Ali. She'd moved into Joe's home, which was a simple one-story, two-bedroom place. There was nothing fancy about it except for the woman who lived inside. Something was different about Ali, but Mac couldn't put her finger on it. Joe was nowhere to be seen, and she hoped it didn't mean he wasn't coming. Ali watched as she scanned the room.

"Don't worry; he'll be here soon. He got held up at work. We should wait to tell you, but I can't. I'm so excited," she said, bouncing on the balls of her feet like a little girl with a secret.

"Tell me what?" Mac said, smiling, remembering the first time she met Ali. She was working as an exotic dancer and was the target of a killer who ended up abducting her from the club she worked at. Ali worked at a strip club but wasn't a stripper. The word was too ugly and plain for what she did on that stage. She remembered the night she and Hudson went to see Ali. She was the most magnificent woman in the place, with her exotic almond-shaped eyes, long, dark hair, and toned body. When she took the stage, everyone in the place fell silent. Mac smiled, thinking of the look on Hudson's face. He was trying not to stare but couldn't help it. Neither could Mac. Once they sat down with Ali, Mac liked her. She was fearless and wouldn't allow anyone to run her from her life.

"I'm pregnant, and we're getting married," Ali blurted out.

"Holy shit, that's amazing. When?"

"Well, we're getting married in a small ceremony next month. Come," she said, grabbing Mac's hand and leading her into the family room where they sat down on a worn brown leather sectional. "You're going to be my maid of honor, and Hudson is Joe's best man." She said it like it was a foregone conclusion. Mac looked at her like she'd lost her mind, and then it hit her. Joe hadn't told her. Why wouldn't he tell her? "What's wrong? Don't tell me you aren't going to be here. You can't go on a trip again. I can't imagine walking down the aisle without you. If it wasn't for you, I would be dead and would have never met my Joe. Please tell me you can come."

Joe walked in. "What are you two ladies talking about?" he asked, taking off his heavy coat. He assessed the room and smiled. "You told her, didn't you?"

Ali looked sheepish. "I couldn't help myself," she said, getting up from the couch and hugging Joe, planting a soft kiss on his lips. Seeing them together made Mac miss Hudson more. She was happy for them, but it pulled at her heartstrings, knowing she couldn't have the same thing with Hudson. In her world, things didn't work out like they did for Joe and Ali.

"Congratulations, Joe. I'm excited for both of you," Mac said, pausing and letting the joyful news settle over the room.

Ali cocked her head to one side as fierceness crossed her dark eyes. "I was telling Mac how we would like to have them at the wedding, but there's something I don't know. What is it?"

Joe ran his hands through his hair. "Let me change, and I'll catch you up on everything." If Mac had to guess, he planned to come home early enough to tell her but got held up.

CHAPTER
TWENTY-FOUR

HE CAME BACK into the room in a pair of slacks and a button-down for dinner. Mac was in her nicer jeans and one of the few tops she owned that wasn't a t-shirt, but with Ali in a beautiful, colorful dress she felt a bit out of place.

Ali crossed her slender arms over her chest and looked from Joe to Mac. "Okay, spill it."

So, Mac did. She told her everything she had, including Joe's involvement. Ali's eyes got wide at first and she glared at Joe. "You arrested Hudson right after he proposed?"

"Hon, I had no idea he was going to pop the question," Joe said, his shoulders drooping as he tried to explain.

"How could you arrest your best friend?" Ali said with accusation in her eyes.

Mac reached over and placed her hand over Ali's. "Don't give Joe too hard a time. His heart was in the right place. He was protecting Hudson by making the arrest. Most people find Hudson intimidating, and they may have overreacted if they didn't know him."

"I guess it makes sense," Ali said. "Now how do we get him out of prison before our wedding so the two of you get hitched as well?" Mac smiled, appreciating her enthusiasm and her belief that they could resolve the situation. Mac wasn't so sure. The oven timer dinged. "Dinner's ready. Now sit your asses down so we can eat and figure this thing out." Ali was one woman Mac didn't want to mess with, and she had to smile at Ali's optimism. She needed to remember to think that way herself.

Joe pulled a ham out of the oven, carved several pieces of the sweet meat off, and placed them on three plates. It filled the house with an amazing aroma, and Mac's stomach growled. She tried to remember the last time she ate, and her brain pulled a blank. Ali put out a bowl full of little sweet potatoes with Hawaiian purple bread. They took their seats, with Ali sitting between them. She grabbed both their hands in hers. "Dear Lord, keep Hudson in our prayers and give us the strength to get him out of prison. A-men."

Mac appreciated the thought. After all she had been through, she wasn't sure God existed, and if he did, he had one hell of a sick sense of humor. "So, Joe," Mac said, "what can you tell me?"

"I can't discuss an active investigation. Not even with you, Mac. I want Hudson to be exonerated as much as you do, but they're taking me off the case, and my hands are tied."

"What about the murdered defense attorney? How did she die?" Mac asked, hoping he would shed some light.

"All I can tell you is the tip came in as an anonymous caller. They found the woman mutilated in some gruesome ways. I can't imagine Hudson doing that to another person, not a woman. He's the gentlest giant I've ever met," Joe said. "But we found evidence in his house, tucked away in a nice hiding place. The DNA results matched the attorney. Again, Mac, I can't give you the details of what we found, but it points back to Hudson. Other than you, has anyone else been in the house?"

"No, just me." Mac thought about it for a moment. "Did the evidence you found have Hudson's DNA on it?"

"Not that we found, but the FBI said he wore gloves," Joe said.

Mac looked over at Ali and saw her mind working.

"Does Hudson's place have a security system?" Ali asked.

"No, Hudson figured no one would break in if they found out who lived there," Mac said.

"Sounds like Hudson. Any sign of a break-in?" Ali asked.

"Nothing that they reported back to me," Joe said.

"I've been to Hudson's place. It would take me less than three minutes to break in, plant the evidence, and be back out on the street. Why the hell isn't it being considered?" Ali said, crossing her arms.

"How do you know how long it would take to break into a house?" Joe looked at her, not hiding the surprise in his eyes.

"I wasn't always a good girl, Joe. Don't look at me like that. When my sister and I were young, we had to fend for ourselves and make a little money every now and again. That sometimes involved breaking into houses. Enough about me. How likely is it that someone broke into the house and planted evidence?" Ali pushed.

"I guess it's possible, but no evidence suggests it. I can go back and canvass the neighborhood in case anyone got a look at someone prowling around the night we received the tip. At least, it would bring reasonable doubt into Hudson's case."

"You do that," Ali shot back with a scowl on her face.

"Ali, brilliant suggestion," Mac said. "I can help if you don't think it'll muddy things too much, Joe."

"Joe will do anything he needs to do to get Hudson back home to you," Ali answered for him.

"Trust me, no one wants Hudson out of prison more than I do, but getting angry with each other won't solve anything," Mac said.

"Yeah, it's just these damn hormones, and this must be awful for you, Mac. I couldn't imagine what I would do if some monster was setting up Joe."

TWENTY-FIVE

MAC SNUGGLED BACK into Hudson's bed with nothing new to work with except for more theories. She drifted off into a restless sleep to find Hudson waiting for her. He was behind iron bars with plexiglass in between, and she couldn't get to him. She tried to talk, but nothing came out. He looked like he was staring at her, but then she realized he was looking right through her. He couldn't see her or hear her, no matter how loud she screamed. She tried a different tactic, pounding on the glass separating them, but he didn't flinch.

His large body stood slack. His broad shoulders, normally pressed back with perfect posture, hung forward with his massive arms dangling down at his sides. The prison uniform hung on his frame from recent weight loss. He ate six or seven times a day and hit the gym on almost every day of the year, but the man who stood in front of her was a shell of himself. She was having a hard time connecting him with the once-powerful man who'd stood next to her. His face cracked and broke like a shattered mirror. The black and blue surrounding his hazel eyes brought tears to her brown ones. It was almost too much to look at. She needed to save him before he broke the rest of the way, turning him into something she didn't recognize. It hurt to her core to see the man she loved look this way.

She reached out and pressed her hand to the plexiglass separating them, sliding it between the bars. This time, he saw her and placed his large hand, dwarfing her small one. She looked deep into his eyes, where pain swam. The thought of him spending one more day in this hellhole was more than she could bear. He had been so good to her in the short year they had been together.

The door opened behind Hudson. A large man stepped into the tiny cell. Mac tried to warn Hudson to turn around, but he kept looking at her and ignoring the man behind him. She couldn't make out the man's face, but he was huge. Bigger than Hudson, bigger than any man she had ever seen. He almost didn't look human, but more like a gorilla. Mac screamed, pounding on the plexiglass, trying to make Hudson turn around, but his sad eyes never left hers.

A huge hairy arm wrapped around Hudson's head, and Hudson closed his eyes. His face looked peaceful for the first time. The enormous man behind him pulled hard with one swift, massive thrust, snapping Hudson's neck. Hudson's eyes shot open, locking with Mac's, and then went vacant. The light she loved in those eyes went dim and then out as he dropped to the cold cement floor. The man behind Hudson laughed as Mac screamed out.

Mac woke the next morning covered in sweat. The scream still lingered in the air. Hudson's sheets stuck to her body. She pushed her wet hair out of her face and took several deep breaths, thankful when she realized it was only a dream. She had an uncontrollable desire to lay eyes on him. Make sure he was okay.

She pulled her tired body out of bed, dragging the wet sheets with her, dropping them in the laundry room and heading for the kitchen to start the coffee. Hudson's t-shirt she'd worn to bed clung to her body, which still glistened with sweat. She glanced in the mirror to see her eyes looked sunken into her head, her limbs sluggish as she prepared the old drip coffee maker in Hudson's kitchen. She heard a noise outside but figured it was only kids passing the house on the way to school.

By the time she got out of the shower with her coffee in hand, she felt more like herself. Every day she remained free and enjoying the luxury of taking hot showers and drinking hot coffee while Hudson sat locked away, having to endure God knew what. It nagged at her. She felt she should suffer right along with him. The coffee was wonderful this morning, and she had to wonder what they were feeding Hudson. Was he getting coffee? She couldn't imagine being stuck in a cage, not knowing what the next day would bring, always on high alert. Never sure if some guy was going to come in the middle of the night.

She passed by the front window thinking about Hudson's situation and almost dropped her cup of hot coffee on the hardwoods. Outside, the front lawn was covered in reporters, cameramen, and equipment. She recognized a few of them from her early press conference and cringed.

One of them caught sight of her at the window and the entire crowd erupted, pressing forward to grab a better look. She looked down in horror, remembering she only had a t-shirt and socks on. It barely covered her front and back side from view. She stepped back into the kitchen and out of view as the cameras erupted, engulfing the window in blinding flashes. She prayed no one could snag a good shot of her in little to nothing. "Shit, shit, shit," she said as she slipped behind the front door and checked the deadbolt to make sure she'd locked it the night before. With everything going on, she was too absentminded to be sure.

She slipped back into the kitchen, avoiding the windows, looking for her phone. It wasn't in the kitchen, so she headed to the bedroom to find her uniform pants so she wasn't so exposed. She hoped they hadn't caught sight of her when she came out of the shower. She found the press invasive and violating, not thinking twice about respecting someone's privacy. This wasn't her home, but her temper still flared at the violation. They were stomping all over Hudson's lawn, making a mess of things. Lord knew what the neighbors were thinking at this point. It was bad enough someone was setting Hudson up for murder, but it was a different issue to mess with a man's home.

She remembered the call she'd received only a few short nights ago. Would her own mother do this to her? She always thought the worst of Reina, no matter the situation. Her mother was capable of many things and sending the press to cause issues for Mac was not beneath her and the most likely option. She remembered a time when one of her mother's suppliers had double-crossed her and tried to take Reina for millions by selling her inferior product. Her mother launched not only a vindictive assault against the man in charge, but had also smeared his reputation to where he and his operation shut down. As far as Mac was aware, the man never recovered. Her mother was capable of almost anything if she thought it enhanced her position. Even in prison, Reina wouldn't take her betrayal lying down. She would either use Mac to her advantage or get revenge.

She tried to think like her mother, but a mental block prevented it. What would she have to gain from destroying her reputation and taking Hudson from her? And was she capable of doing it from prison? Mac wasn't sure of any of it, but this had her mother written all over it. Her mother had her location. The collect phone call proved that much. "How does she know where I'm staying?" Mac wondered out loud. Did she know about Hudson's situation because she somehow had something to do with it? So many questions and so few answers. The one she was struggling with the most was Daniels. He died before Mac launched her assault on her mother. Could she have planned that far ahead? Did she have Daniels murdered and then plant evidence somehow? What about the defense attorney?

CHAPTER
TWENTY-SIX

"CAPTAIN BOOM, this is Master Sergeant McGregor. I need help."

"I'm in the middle of something, Mac. This better be important." Boom sounded like she was screaming into the phone.

"Ma'am, I'm at Hudson's house, and outside the front door are thirty to forty reporters. What the hell am I supposed to do?"

"Shit, what the hell do they want? Have you gone outside?"

"No, ma'am, I haven't gone out yet. I've been staying away from the windows and keeping my head down. I didn't realize they were out there until after my shower."

"Dammit Mac, have you told anyone about Hudson's case? Have you been talking to anyone?" she asked, not hiding the accusation in her voice.

"No, ma'am, I've talked to Joe Romero, the officer investigating the case, but that's it. Oh, and my mother called from prison the other night to offer to help get Hudson out of the can."

"You told your fucking mother about Hudson? The same woman who has more connections than God. Have you lost your mind?" Boom's voice felt like it was coming through the phone and knocking Mac around.

"Of course not. She already knew. I don't know how, but it sounded like she had more information than I do. It makes me wonder if she isn't involved somehow."

"In what? The circus outside his house or getting him put up on murder charges? Your mom has one hell of a reputation, but do you think she's capable of all that?"

"Never underestimate her. I have nothing to back up my theory, but it's pretty damn convenient she would call right after he goes to prison."

"Okay, let me make some phone calls to find out who she's had contact with. You do realize Texas is over two thousand miles away. Do you think she can the media riled up while sitting in a Texas federal penitentiary?"

"I don't know what she's capable of, but you have to admit it's weird, and I don't believe in coincidences," Mac said.

"Okay, do nothing, and don't think about opening the front door. Let me find out what we're dealing with, and I'll be right over. Text me the address."

"Thanks, Captain Boom. I owe you one."

"Don't thank me yet. This may be a bigger shit show than we're expecting," Boom said, and hung up the phone.

Mac let her boss and Hudson's boss know what a shitstorm was likely coming their way. Bad press about the military wasn't positive for anyone. Any time a military member was in the media spotlight, it was rarely good. There were always staunch supporters of the military and other people who either didn't understand what the military did or had a twisted view. She remembered going to a civilian job interview once when she was thinking of getting out, and the person interviewing her commented on how feminine she looked for a military member, like all women in the service were supposed to look a certain way.

The military had some unique criteria, but for the most part, people went to work like everyone else and then went home to their families. Aside from the deployments, combat training, and exercises they had to deal with for the most part, they were like everyone else. Not trained killers like some people thought, and the media sometimes twisted the military into being. The misconception that everyone who served was a walking time bomb with severe PTSD was a popular one that got tossed around the media. On the contrary, she'd met some of the most down-to-earth, regular people in her military career.

Giving the media even a little of herself would be dangerous. They would twist facts into something to sell regardless of whether they were true. She was well aware she wasn't supposed to talk to the media without prior authorization from her chain of command and Public Affairs. As it stood, they were keeping her prisoner in Hudson's house. She took a quick peek out the window and found the group in front of the house had almost doubled. Neighbors and the media lined the street, and the press seemed to multiply like rabbits.

This was getting out of hand. She looked at her phone again, wishing it would ring with someone who would give her an answer. She was confident the media wouldn't try to break down her door. At least not with the other news channels out front. If left to their own devices, then maybe, but not with the entire neighborhood bearing witness. Her distrust of people mounted. She had always kept her private life private because she didn't want to be linked back to her mother's drug cartel, but also because she liked her privacy.

Her phone rang in her hand as she was pacing the living room for the hundredth time. "What did you find out?" she said as a way of greeting.

Captain Boom remained quiet for a moment before she spoke. "Well, Mac, it turns out you're correct."

"About what?" she said, hearing the impatience laced through her voice. "Sorry, it's getting a little crazy here."

"I can see a satellite view of Hudson's place and it's swarming with people. Are you still inside?"

"Yup, I'm not leaving this house. Those people will eat me alive," Mac said, her voice sounding strained to her own ears.

"I'm on my way, and I need you dressed and ready to go by the time I arrive. Your ABUs are fine for this unless you have your blues with you."

"My blues are at my place."

"Okay, put yourself together, wear minimal makeup, put your hair up, and look professional," Boom said.

"What's your plan?" Mac asked, trying to keep the phone in her hand from shaking as she paced.

"It looks like your mother leaked parts of the information. I was able to find out she did an interview with a reporter in Texas who was following her story. The reporter tipped off a friend of his at *The Washington Post* and that's why we're here. The article in the *Houston Chronicle* did an overview of Hudson's arrest and how Reina thinks he's a bad influence on you and she wants to protect you and keep you away from Hudson. Respect is due to the reporter for the *Houston Chronicle*—he did his research and highlighted all of Hudson's accomplishments, painting him in a favorable light. He clarified Hudson has not faced trial or received a conviction for the crime and is merely under suspicion for murder. That's the angle we're running with here."

"That doesn't sound too bad," Mac said, not at all surprised Reina was stirring the pot. "Any information about what my mother hopes to gain from this?"

"Her attorney wouldn't talk to us. Claimed attorney-client privilege, but if you ask me, she's trying to discredit you as a witness against her," Boom said. "I just got here. Be right in."

The petite woman barged through the crowd of reporters without so much as flinching. When she made it to the front steps and was standing higher than everyone else, she turned and addressed everyone. "Good morning, I am Captain Boom from Fairchild Air Force Base. I ask that you hold your questions for the moment until I can confer with the woman you're holding captive."

The seasoned reporters kept quiet for the moment, knowing how Boom operated, but a young guy from the back shouted, "No one's stopping her from leaving. We just want to ask a few quest..." He stopped talking when he saw the look on Boom's face. And one of the nearby reporters slapped him on the shoulder and told him to shut up.

Mac didn't understand the strange encounter taking place and didn't know what to make of it, but she was glad Boom was on her side.

CHAPTER
TWENTY-SEVEN

MAC FLIPPED the deadbolt to unlock it, letting Boom in and relocking the door. "Thanks for coming. What's the plan?"

"I'm going to start off by highlighting Hudson's distinguished military career. Making it very clear he's a suspect, but they have no definitive proof of his involvement. I'll highlight how the Spokane County Jail messed up and put him in the general population as a military member and his attorneys are working to have him released or moved to pre-trial confinement until they've concluded the investigation. If we're lucky, the public attention will move things along. You'll stand by my side and say nothing unless I tell you to. You're to look like the supportive girlfriend."

"Fiancée," Mac corrected.

Boom raised an eyebrow. "Congratulations, when did that happen?"

"The night of his arrest."

"Oh, well, in that case we'll keep it at you being supportive. Don't answer questions unless we confer beforehand. As you saw in your last encounter with the press, they'll do anything to get a rise out of you."

"Got it."

The two walked out onto the small front porch and waited for the crowd to go quiet. A hush fell over the enormous mass of neighbors and reporters as they waited. Boom covered what they'd discussed, outlining Hudson's military career, and how he served his country for over sixteen years with not so much as a blemish.

"So, why is he in prison?" a young blond woman in the front row hollered out.

"He's a suspect in a murder investigation, but they haven't charged him with anything. He's innocent until proven guilty," Boom made a point of highlighting.

"Then why is he in general pop?"

"A fantastic question for the warden at the Spokane County Jail." Boom was going to have to apologize for it one day soon. She liked Warden Juliana. As a tremendous supporter of the military, he took good care of the troops who got in trouble, making sure the proper authorities knew and the press did not. Here, she thought, throwing the focus in a different direction was worth it. As soon as she was done here, she would give him a heads-up. She went through and high-lighted everything she and Mac talked about.

Mac stood in silence with her hands clasped behind her back. Several reporters threw questions her way, but Boom answered for her. "Master Sergeant McGregor will not be answering questions today. She's here to support Hudson and is unwilling to discuss his case or her mother's case."

Mac stepped forward. "I believe Master Sergeant Gavin Hudson is innocent of all wrongdoing and is being set up. I support him and will continue to support him throughout this ordeal."

"What if he's convicted?" a large man with three chins in the middle of the crowd asked.

"If he's wrongfully convicted, I will always stand by his side," Mac said with conviction in her voice.

Another barrage of questions started. Boom shut them down and, with one swift movement, pushed Mac back inside the house and toward the back door. "Wait here, I'll be right back."

Mac listened to the front door open and close. She heard Boom say, "That's all for today folks, we'll hold another press conference as soon as we have new information."

Moments later, Boom was back inside.

"Do you think that'll get them to leave?" Mac asked, ruffling her brow.

"Not on your life. They'll stay camped out here until you leave. They figure it's only a matter of time before you have to go somewhere."

"Great, so I'm stuck."

"I didn't say that. I said it's what they would expect. Come with me." Boom led her to the back door. "The brown house to the left. I need you to jump the back fence, pass through the neighbor's lawn, and come out the gate. A black SUV is waiting for you."

"What about the neighbors?" Mac asked.

"They aren't home and have no pets outside, so you should be able to pass through with no issue. I'm going to go back out front and distract them while you make a clean break."

"This is fucking ridiculous," Mac growled. "But thank you for rescuing me. Where will the SUV take me?"

"Back to base. I'll meet you in my office."

Mac waited while Boom made her way back outside and headed for her car, listening to the eruption of questions being pelted at Boom. She grabbed her bag and headed out the back, placing her military hat over her head to stay in uniform but also to conceal her. The backyard wasn't large and it only took Mac a moment to reach the six-foot vinyl fence. Stepping back, she placed an outdoor chair against the edge, pushing herself up. Her arms shook as she tried to hoist herself up the rest of the way. As she threw her leg over the fence and was getting ready to drop to the other side, she heard, "Hey, she's running," from behind her.

She glanced back, and a chubby red-headed man busted through the gate on the side of the house. "Son of a bitch." She dropped over and took off running through the neighbor's yard. Vehicles came to life behind her. At full speed, she came around the front of the neighbor's house where the promised black SUV was sitting. Coming down the street toward them was a parade of news vehicles of all kinds. It looked like a sea of reporters coming to attack. Mac grabbed the door and yanked it open, climbing into the passenger seat. She recognized the man behind the wheel as Master Sergeant Right. Boom's right-hand guy in Public Affairs.

"Thanks for the ride," Mac said. "How's your driving?"

"I drove in the indie circuit before coming into the military. I think I can handle these clowns."

Mac smiled and leaned back in the seat, trying her best to relax, but there was no chance of that.

He dropped the vehicle into gear, squealing the tires as the wall of reporters inched closer. He flipped a U-turn, heading in the opposite direction, only to find a wall of cars blocking both sides of the street. One van had parked diagonally in the middle of the street with the center door of their panel van open and the cameraman shooting footage. Right slammed on the brakes only inches from the guy blocking the street. Mac had to smile at the look on the guy's face.

Right backed up and drove up one of the nearby lawns, clearing the van by centimeters and took off hitting the gas going far faster than they should have down residential streets. Mac looked back. The cameraman in the van scrambled to pull his equipment back in to join the chase. He was helping by blocking the rest of the media vehicles. "Nice moves," Mac said, smiling.

"Thanks. Do I want to know what you did to deserve all this attention?"

"Nah, long story. I'm sure Boom will give you the lowdown, but for now, can you bring me back on base so we can figure out the next move?"

"You got it."

CHAPTER
TWENTY-EIGHT

LATER IN THE EVENING, Mac walked into her home exhausted and beat up. After being chased and getting to base, she had to sit through what felt like a full interrogation. After much debate, they released her. At first, the base leadership wanted to confine her to the base until this thing blew over. They said it was for her own safety. She convinced them her home was secure, and no one had reason to know her location.

Because of her past with her mother and her desire to stay off anyone's radar, she bought her house through a company her dad helped her set up. She and her sister Lola had all their assets hidden under company names and were untraceable by their mother. The current setup helped her out here as well. At a minimum, it would take the press a while to figure out her location. She promised to be careful. As soon as she arrived home, she took her Ruger out, cleaned it, and loaded it. Not that she had any intentions of shooting at the press, but she didn't know who else was out there looking for her.

She smiled as she cleaned the small handgun. Hudson had bought it for her last birthday. Her ability to handle a weapon as well as he could didn't intimidate him, which made her smile. He liked it when she fought and protected herself. The last time she tried to get into a serious relationship before Hudson, the guy couldn't handle it. He found it emasculating when she didn't need his protection. He would ask her, "If you don't need my protection, then do you need me at all?"

There were many times she tried to explain to him she never wanted to need a man. She wanted to be his equal. They would balance each other out without needing any protection. When she had protected herself and didn't need him, he couldn't handle it. She had to give him credit; he lasted almost six full months.

Hudson was different. He loved her ability to kick ass, and she found it hilarious and empowering that it turned him on when she fired a gun, or he saw her in hand-to-hand combat.

He was the first man she ever met who not only wasn't threatened by her but understood her, and she was determined not to lose him. She thought about going to the prison, but the visiting hours were over. After everything that had happened, she wanted nothing more than to snuggle up against his warm body and sleep for hours, but she knew it wasn't possible.

She settled into her worn tan couch with a hot cup of tea and began looking through the case surrounding the dead defense attorney. Lola forwarded the files to her after hacking into the police department's system. Mac didn't enjoy breaking the law or encouraging her sister to, but she also didn't think the wheels of justice were going to work in their favor.

Mac picked up her computer and clicked on the link her sister sent her. A picture of a stunning woman with short, dark hair and large brown eyes stared back at her from the screen. She had an angular facial structure and Mac wondered what nationality she was. The next page contained the basic information about the victim. Anika Wilson, Area Defense Counsel at Joint Base Lewis McChord in Tacoma, Washington. It listed her address on the outskirts of Seattle.

She flipped to the next page and stared at the time and date of death. The time and date of death coincided with when Hudson should have been on a plane to New Mexico, but his plane got delayed. That was how they connected him with the murder. The evidence would have been easy enough to plant. She clicked on the next file and the first autopsy photo came up. The same beautiful woman lay on the bed. She almost looked asleep, aside from the gruesome ligature marks along her otherwise perfect skin and what looked like the mutilation of her genitals.

Mac stared at the picture, knowing Hudson couldn't do something like that, but someone wanted to make sure it looked like he did. The mutilation spoke to a sexual sadist who got off on torture and was the only way he could obtain sexual gratification, but why make it look like Hudson, and what did this guy have to gain by framing him?

She flipped to the next page in case they found any DNA evidence. The coroner's report read, *The body was void of seaman, fingerprints, or fibers on or near the victim. It appears they have wiped all evidence clean. We found a faint film of a bleach solution on the skin and under the fingernails. The skin appears scrubbed postmortem.*

The next page had some notes from the forensic team, who processed the scene. Mac read, *A disinfectant found on and around the deceased body. The wood floor appears swept and mopped. All surfaces wiped off any prints. Unsub may have worn gloves. No skin cells or hair follicles in the bathroom and bedroom, including the victims.*

One of the officer's reports stated, *There were no nearby neighbors. The victims' home sat off the main road and pressed back into the woods. We have questioned all surrounding property owners with negative results. Evidence of a four-wheel-drive vehicle parked off to the far left side of the property showed tire indentations from the weight of a heavy vehicle with large tires. Disturbed soil and branches suggesting the covering of said vehicle.*

It wasn't much to go on, but at least Mac could check if there was any possibility Hudson had access to a four-wheel-drive vehicle. The ligature marks on the body also gave her pause. It would have been helpful if the perp strangled Anika with his bare hands, but he'd used a rope. It would be much easier to eliminate Hudson since he had huge distinguishable hands, and they could lift prints from the body. No other information was helpful in eliminating Hudson as the killer.

She rubbed her eyes, trying to stay focused, but after such a long day her brain was swimming. She made a mental note to ask Lola to investigate the cases the attorney was working on at the time of her death. There may be a link there. And then she thought about Hudson. Maybe this was about him and him alone. Who in his past would want to destroy him? Her mother might use this as a convenient situation to discredit Mac, as Boom suggested.

A headache was creeping through the back of her eyes. She wasn't getting anywhere and needed rest. After a hot bath and some melatonin to help ward away the insomnia kicks and nightmares. She snuggled deep in her bed, missing Hudson's scent as she drifted off to sleep. She fell into a deep slumber, not remembering when her head hit the pillow.

Woken from a sound sleep, she cracked her eyes open. Living off the beaten path meant that sometimes there would be animals around her property making noises. Not unlike the defense attorney, she realized.

She grabbed her gun from the nightstand as she caught a glimpse of a man dressed from head to toe in black. Mac lay still as the figure passed outside her window. Her assailant was short and appeared overweight, but with no skin showing. The intruder wore black clothing that covered every inch of his body, including his hands. She hoped to get a look in his eyes, so she at least had some way of identifying him. She slipped out of bed with her gun in hand. Crouching on the floor, she fluffed her pillows, lining them up in the shape of a body, and slipped under her bed.

Seconds after her body slid under the mattress, her entire room erupted in bullets. It sounded like a high-powered automatic rifle to Mac's trained ears. One pierced through the mattress and into the floor only inches from her head. She scooted her body further against the wall her old headboard rested on. Stuffing from the mattress and wood pieces from the box spring rained down around her as she covered her face, trying to protect her head from any stray debris or bullets, knowing full well if she caught a bullet her hands wouldn't do a damn bit of good.

A black pair of combat boots became visible. They were the same style most military members used to wear a couple of uniform styles ago. They'd since changed them to a tan color that didn't require polishing. From her vantage point, she could see that her assailant had tucked the boots and the bottom part of the baggy black pants into the top. The boots looked large and out of place compared to the rest of the man as he stepped closer to the side of the bed.

The assailant grabbed the edge of her bedding and pulled it away, revealing the pillow-person Mac had left behind. Mac took a deep breath and shot at the feet, but the person moved at the wrong time and Mac missed by centimeters. Mac inched forward, watching the person flee. She inched closer to the edge to get a better shot, aimed, and fired at the retreating form. Her bullet pierce his side. The strange popping sound that followed made Mac pause. By the time she was out from under the bed and in pursuit, there was no sign of him.

TWENTY-NINE

MAC PULLED herself to her feet and went into the bathroom to check on herself. A wild-haired woman with bags under her eyes stared back from the mirror. She patted herself down, looking for wounds, but only found a few minor scratches that stung until she reached down, and her fingers came back covered in slick red blood. It took her a moment to find some gauze and bandages to wrap around it. The bullet hadn't gone in but took a nice chunk out of her leg.

She went back into her bedroom, which had more holes in it than Swiss cheese, to find something to put on before she called the authorities. It was unnerving that he came for her in her own home. It confirmed someone had been following her, but at least it wasn't only about Hudson. They were both being targeted.

She pulled out three pairs of sweatpants before she found one that hadn't suffered a bullet wound. After getting a bra in place and kind of putting herself together, she dialed Joe's number. It was 0200 hours on a Sunday night, and she was sure he wasn't going to be happy to receive her call. She thought about his fiancée, Ali, lying next to him, expecting their first child, but she couldn't trust anyone else.

It rang several times before Joe's voice came on the line, laced with grogginess. "Hello," he grumbled into the phone.

"Joe, I'm so sorry to wake you, but someone shot up my place and I didn't know who else to call."

The sound of him shuffling around and sitting up in bed came through the phone. Ali's voice was in the background, asking him what was happening. "Mac, are you hurt?"

"No, I'm fine, but whoever it was had every intention of killing me. You'll see what I mean when you arrive."

"I'm on my way."

Less than thirty minutes later, four cop cars with their lights blazing pulled into her drive. She went around the house, turning on all the lights to make sure no one came in and shot her. She placed the gun back in her safe, just in case. She didn't view the police as trigger-happy, but there was no reason to make things more intense than they needed to be.

Joe was the first one through the door. "Have you cleared the house?" was the first thing out of his mouth.

She nodded her head. Despite the situation, she had to smile at his dark hair standing out on one side. "I went from room to room and did a perimeter check. The only thing left behind were some tire tracks."

He came over to her and wrapped her in a brotherly hug. She saw Ali come through the door seconds later, still in her nightgown and a robe. Mac was grateful for friends who didn't stop to so much as put on day clothes when she needed them. They'd jumped out of bed to come to save her, not stopping long enough even to brush their teeth. "Are you okay?" he said, pulling away from the hug.

"No, I'm fucking pissed. Some asshole tried to kill me." Her body vibrated with anger; she sucked in several slow breaths to try to calm her nerves. "Thank you, guys, for coming," she said as Ali wrapped her in a warm embrace.

"Holy shit, Mac," was all Ali had to say as she pulled back and plucked a chip of wood out of Mac's hair.

Joe was stalking around her house, transitioning from concerned friend to cop mode with his notepad out. "Okay Mac, walk me through everything."

Mac walked back through the kitchen and into her room. Both Joe and Ali stood speechless for a moment. The small room looked like it had been through a woodchipper. Bullet holes splintered through every wall. Joe walked over, pulling a latex glove from his sweatpants and putting it on. He pulled out his pocketknife and dug at the white drywall until he could pry the bullet out. "I'll have my guys run ballistics to see if there's a match in the system," he said, more talking to himself than the two women in the room.

Uniformed officers walked around her house looking for evidence, and Mac felt useless. She shouldn't touch or do anything in order to protect the chain of evidence, but it didn't help her fidgeting. The light-blue comforter she was sleeping under looked like an explosion had gone off in it. She watched as Joe pushed the thin metal frame of her bed aside to reveal multiple bullet holes, wood splinters, and parts of the mattress pad embedded in the wood flooring.

Joe whistled and shook his head. "How in the hell did this guy miss you? There must be fifty or sixty bullet holes. Where were you?"

"I pressed up against the back wall. It sounded like an automatic assault rifle. The AR-15 can empty about sixty rounds a minute. I'm not saying that's what it was because I didn't get a good look at it, but that's what it sounded like. It sounded like he changed out the clip once, but my ears were ringing so I can't be sure," Mac said.

"Okay." Joe's eyes scanned the room. "Anything else you can tell me?"

"Yeah, his boots looked like the wrong size compared to the rest of his body. I'd swear when he passed by my window, he wasn't much taller than me. I was waking up when I heard the noise, but if I'm right, this is one short dude."

"Did you look at his face?"

"Nope, head to toe in black. I couldn't even tell you what color his skin was." Mac closed her eyes and sat on the edge of the mutilated bed. Joe waited. "There's one other thing. It sounds weird, but when I shot him, it didn't sound right."

"What do you mean?"

"It sounded like air being let out of a bag or something. I mean, he looked overweight, but…" She ran her hand through her hair. "Maybe I was only hearing things, but it was weird."

"Okay, good to know. Anything else?"

"Not that I can think of." Mac turned to look at her shredded bed. "Joe, look at this."

She stepped further back to make sure she was seeing it right. Joe came up next to her as she pointed. "Is it just me, or did all the bullets miss the mass of pillows in the middle? No way he would have missed like that unless it was on purpose."

GENNAVIE CLIMBED into her borrowed car and settled in for her trip to Seattle. She was groggy after last night. She'd taken a bullet in her fat suit and would need to buy a new one. Dammit, Mac got close. She had no intentions of killing her mortal enemy. Death would be an easy way out. Mac needed to suffer the same way Gennavie herself was suffering.

A wicked smile slipped across her face as she thought about Mac. How freaked out she must be right now. Gennavie had taken away her man, driven her out of Hudson's home and his bed, and had now driven her out of her own home. The military wouldn't allow Mac to stay in her place after what happened. She would be relocated someplace else. If she had to guess, it would be back on base. She laughed out loud. The military thought she would be safe on Fairchild, but Gennavie knew differently. She had her own military ID now and had been on base fucking with Mac on several occasions.

It was easy to access the base and blend in when she looked like she belonged. Her time in the Air Force gave her more than contacts. It gave her the ability to blend into the military world with no one taking a second look. Being one of them made things so much easier. She missed her career and wished to have it back, but at least she would take Mac's career as a consolation prize. Mac wasn't supposed to die yet, just suffer. She still had a use for her.

Maybe while she was in the Seattle area, she would pick up another fat suit. So far, it has worked. If she hadn't had it on last night, she might have been nursing a bullet wound instead of replacing her disguise. She didn't think she would need it for a while, but she had to be fluid. Her plan was going so well.

Her drive to Seattle was boring, but she wanted to visit with the guard who was taking care of Vincent for her. It was quite convenient. The two brothers were twins, so she had to be careful not to mix up their names, but they sure were fun to play with. She wondered if the brother in Seattle knew she was sleeping with the brother in Spokane. They had both gone into corrections for the state of Washington and came in handy.

Joseph, the brother in Seattle, would feed Vincent information for her and keep her updated on how he was doing. She needed Vincent to survive until she pulled him out. She hadn't figured out how to get him off death row, but she was in contact with someone who said she would make it happen as long as Gennavie delivered.

The other brother, Johnathan, was busy doing her bidding in the Spokane County Jail. He'd agreed to put Hudson in with the meanest and biggest inmate they had in the general population. She hoped to hear about that little arrangement soon. Hudson ending up in the infirmary pleased her. Maybe if all went well, they'd gang rape Hudson soon.

She pulled into the driveway of Joseph's small house. It wasn't much to look at, but it served her purposes. Today she wore a short black wig with her long muscular legs wrapped in thigh-high spiked boots and a long winter coat with nothing else underneath. He pulled the door open as she was about to knock. "Hey you," she said, giving him a seductive smile.

"I thought you were going to be here an hour ago. I have to go to work."

"Oh, come on, sugar, you can be a little late for me, can't you?"

He looked unsure of himself. Like his brother, he wasn't much to look at—average. His round face and small eyes looked back at her. He was thinner and in better shape than his brother, but still held a bit of a pudge around his middle, but much like his brother, he was easy to control and wanted nothing more than to touch her. "I shouldn't be late." His voice cracked, and his eyes shot to the floor.

"As you wish," she said, opening her coat so he saw she wasn't wearing anything underneath. "I understand if you must go, my pet." He didn't move and only stared. He reached out, but before he touched the coat she slapped his hand hard, and he pulled back. He wasn't going anywhere. "Now, tell your mistress what you've been up to."

He still hadn't taken his eyes off the opening in her coat. "I did everything you asked. I've been giving your hubby extra food and supplies every day. He's getting extra-special treatment, and the guards are making sure no one messes with him." He stepped back. "But after…"

"But after what?"

"After he killed one of the head gangbangers last night, no one's going to fuck with him. He did some nasty things to the guy."

"Which guy was it?" Gennavie's eyes lit up with interest.

"The same one who raped him when he first got dropped in the can."

Gennavie's smile got bigger. "Nice. What did he do to the guy?"

"A beautiful lady like you doesn't want to know the gruesome details, right? Let's have some fun instead." He reached out for her coat again to peer inside, and she slapped his hand away with a light growl.

"You can touch when I tell you to," she said, smiling at the bulge growing in his pants. "Now, tell me the details of what Vincent did and I will let you have a little."

"He didn't only shank the guy like a normal prisoner would. He found an old rusty pipe and shoved it…" The color drained from Joseph's face, and Gennavie knew it had to be good.

"Tell me what happened, my love," she said, inching closer and running her blood-red fingernail down the side of his cheek.

"Your husband beat the man to within an inch of his life and then lodged a one-inch-thick rusty pipe up the guy's ass. Vincent propped him up on display right inside his cell for everyone to see. We're not sure how the guy got in, but it was some fucked-up shit. His legs were dangling over the pipe with a vacant look in his eyes. The doctor said Vincent got the pipe so far inside it pierced through his stomach lining. It took a while for him to die, but the doc said it would have been excruciating."

"I would have liked to see it," she said.

"You would have?" Joseph took several steps back but Gennavie advanced on him, dropping her coat as she went. The shift in his eyes told her he'd forgotten all about the dead guy last night. She pushed him onto the couch and straddled him.

"Now, if I take care of you, will you make sure to give Vincent a message for me?"

"Lady, if you do the thing you did last time, I'll tell Vincent anything you want me to."

"Good boy," she said, slapping him on the cheek. She needed Joseph to help her keep Vincent's spirits up and let him know she was working on his prison break. Joseph was going to be an important part of that plan. She worked on Joseph while she thought about Vincent. It would be such a pleasure to kill with him again. They should relocate once she got him out. Maybe Mexico or some place in Europe. She lowered herself on top of Joseph, bringing her slender frame up and down. At least Joseph was well-hung. She needed the release.

It would do for now, she thought as she pressed her hands down on his neck, getting more excited as his face turned red. She wouldn't hurt him, or would she? He still needed to perform for her soon. She had a few more things to line up.

CHAPTER
THIRTY-ONE

MAC GATHERED the last of her belongings. She wasn't sure how long she would have to be gone, but she hoped this would be over soon so she could feel safe again. It was one thing when she was chasing a bad guy, but another thing when she was being hunted. "Are you almost ready?" her boss asked, coming in from the kitchen.

"Yeah, I think so," she said, looking around her house again. The police had been there all night, and she had yet to sleep or eat. Joe and Ali tried to convince her to come and stay with them in their guest bedroom, but she didn't want to put them in danger. If someone was hunting her, they wouldn't stop just because Joe was a cop. And, with Ali pregnant, she wasn't willing to take any chances. Her pride wanted to fight back and not let this asshole run her out of her own home, but she was losing steam. She would pay anything to have her normal life back with Hudson in her arms.

"Any idea who might be behind this?" Stanton asked.

"I have no idea," she said, hanging her head.

"I'm sure the police will figure things out. In the meantime, let's get you settled on base where you'll be safe. Our boss wants you to stay on Fairchild. He's not yet ready to order you there, but he doesn't want you wandering around in the community without protection."

"I understand," she said, never remembering being this tired or worn down in the past. Maybe after some sleep, she would fight, but not now. She remained silent as her boss drove her to base. He walked her into the small temporary housing at the back of the base.

"Are you sure you're going to be okay?" he asked again.

"I'll be fine. I just need a little sleep."

He left her there to get settled, promising to come by and check on her later in the day. She lay down on the uncomfortable bed, not bothering to take off her shoes or clothes, and closed her eyes. The first thing she saw was Hudson and the gigantic man looming behind him from her dream. Her eyes shot open again right before the part where he plunged the knife deep into his neck.

She picked up her phone and dialed the prison. If she heard his voice, then maybe she would rest. It took talking to four different people before they transferred her to Warden Juliana.

"Yes, may I help you?"

"Sir, thank you for taking my call. I'm Master Sergeant McGregor from Fairchild," she said in her most official voice. "Would it be possible to speak with inmate Gavin Hudson?"

"Inmates aren't supposed to receive personal calls, Ms. McGregor."

"I understand, sir, but there has been an emergency that I need to speak with him about. He's not supposed to be an inmate. They haven't convicted him of anything. Can you tell me why he's locked up with criminals?"

"Ms. McGregor, I know who you are," he said, never raising his voice. "And your boyfriend's status is being reviewed. What is the nature of the emergency?"

"Someone tried to kill me last night," she said.

"I see. Are you able to come during visiting hours?"

"No sir, I'm being told to remain on base until the authorities can figure out who's trying to harm me."

"Very well, please hold."

Mac let out a deep breath. While she waited, she thought about how much to tell Hudson. There was nothing he could do behind bars.

After sitting on hold for over ten minutes, she heard his deep baritone come over the line. "Hey beautiful, what happened?"

She let go of the breath she was holding. Relief swept through every inch of her body. "I'm not sure where to start. How are you doing? Are your injuries healing?"

"I'll be okay, only a few bumps and bruises. Don't worry about me, I can take care of myself. The good thing is no one will mess with me right now. The guy I fought with backed off and all the other inmates are avoiding me."

"Well, at least that's good news…" She let the words hang.

"Spit it out, Mac. What happened?"

She told him everything from the beginning of the evening, reviewing the case about the defense attorney and then the guy who broke in and shot her place to hell. He remained silent for more time than she would have liked. "Say something."

"We have to get me out of here, Mac. I won't be able to handle it if something happens to you."

"I'm glad you weren't there with me. Even though it was scary as hell. I don't think he meant to kill me."

"What do you mean? He made your bed into a war zone."

"Yeah, but he shouldn't have missed. A rifle like that should have hit me, no problem."

"But you weren't in the bed."

"Yeah, but he didn't know that."

"True, so you're saying it was to scare the shit out of you?"

"That's my theory. Someone is trying to destroy us, but I don't think they want us dead. You're in prison and they've taken me off all my cases. Everything's on hold and someone is messing with me."

"What do you mean, messing with you?"

"Everywhere I go, I can sense someone watching. Someone has messed with my shit and there are things missing. Little things either out of place or altogether gone."

"Like what?"

"My hairbrush. Things moved on my desk or not the way they were when I left. I had my car broken into the other day. Nothing taken, but things weren't where I left them. Last night, I was reviewing the case file on the murder of the defense attorney and now it's gone."

"Are you sure you didn't move stuff and forget where you put it?"

"No dammit, I'm telling you. Someone is screwing with us and after last night I'm positive I'm not imagining things."

"Who do you think would be behind something like this?"

"That's the problem. I have no idea. The guy in my house last night didn't look familiar."

"Can you identify him?" Hudson asked.

"No, but the height and weight didn't click with anyone we've put behind bars except for maybe Vincent Wulf, but he's in prison himself. Plus, Vincent is a skinny guy. This guy had some fluff around the middle."

"So, what do you think our next move should be?"

"I'm not sure, but we have to do something and soon. If we don't, whoever's doing this might decide they're done playing with us."

"Do me a favor and stay on base and work it from there. My attorney tells me there's a good possibility that I'll be in pre-trial soon. Some screw-up with paperwork, but he thinks they'll have it fixed. I'm advocating to be released into military custody. At least then, I can be out of this shit hole and with you."

Mac let a tear slip down her cheek. The thought of him being safe and back in her arms was more than she could hope for.

CHAPTER
THIRTY-TWO

HUDSON LAY awake on the hard slab they called an inmate bed. The paper-thin mattress did little to help his sore back. His hands wrapped behind his head on top of the nonexistent pillow. He listened to his new roommate snoring above him. After his scuffle with Gorilla Juice, they'd moved him in with yet another roommate. This guy was half Hudson's size and scared shitless. He looked more like a schoolboy than a convict. The guard told Hudson he was in on some financial scheme, shaving money off the top at the company he'd worked for.

They brought him in the night before and he'd already taken a beating once. Hudson assumed he wouldn't fare well and wondered if that was why they put them in the same cell, hoping Hudson would provide protection. He couldn't imagine what it would be like to find himself in this world and not have the ability to defend. He had a different perspective on the world because of his size and abilities. He felt protective of the small man but didn't want to be involved. The last thing he needed was more trouble if it meant he would be stuck here.

The man above him snorted in his sleep and then went back to a rhythmic purr. He needed to figure out how to get out of this place, not because he worried for his own safety, but because the woman he loved was being hurt. He couldn't imagine what he would do if one of those bullets found its mark. She could take care of herself, and he loved that about her. Such an attack would reduce a lesser person to shreds. It had only pissed Mac off. He wondered if the person who was coming for her knew that. She was the bravest and fiercest woman he'd met, and he couldn't live without her.

The lights flicked on in the west wing and crept through the prison. During the processing, the officials had taken everything he owned, and he lost track of time when they sedated him in the infirmary. He stood and waited for his cell to open and for them to file through the long line of people waiting to eat what the prison referred to as breakfast.

His new roommate dropped to the concrete floor next to him. "Morning," he said, looking half-asleep.

Hudson didn't want to know this man. He wanted out of here. "Morning," he muttered.

"I'm William, but most people call me Billy. How long have you been here?"

"Too long," Hudson muttered back.

Billy looked up at his new roommate. "Can I stick with you for a while?"

"It's a free country," Hudson said.

"Thanks. Have you ever been on the inside before?"

"You ask a lot of questions," Hudson said, thinking about the last time they arrested him and he sat in a prison cell. He liked it less this time around. At least before he understood why he was there.

"What do you think we'll have for breakfast?" Billy asked.

"Nothing good."

The two men filed out into the line of men dressed in baggy yellow prison uniforms. Billy slipped in close behind Hudson as they walked. A little too close, but he tried to understand. The last time he was in prison, he'd learned to keep a low profile and hoped he could do the same thing this time around. There were prisoners behind him shuffling around more than normal. He was about to turn when Billy got thrown into Hudson's back. The man let out a scream that sounded more like a little girl.

Hudson pivoted to the side. "What the fuck?" was all he could get out. He was face to face with Gorilla, but this time, he had friends. Two large men had flanked him on the left, and two more stood to his right. Hudson weighed his options, not sure if he could take all five men or if he wanted to try.

"This isn't about you, sweet cheeks," Gorilla said, baring his teeth like a wild beast. His sagging skin creased around his eyes. He held the back of Billy's neck, lifting him off the ground, and shook him back and forth. "This little shit has some things to answer for."

"What could this guy do to you?" Hudson asked.

Billy looked up at Hudson and mouthed, "Help me."

Hudson looked down at the row of inmates in both directions to find that the guards had vanished. They were nowhere to be seen. Typical, he thought. He took a deep breath in and blew it out. This wouldn't end well. "This guy is less than half your size. It's one thing to take me on, but Billy here doesn't have a chance."

"That's not my problem, sunshine. I'm on orders to teach Billy here a lesson. He stole from my boss and now my boss wants him to pay."

Hudson figured if he kept him talking, maybe the guards would show up and do their job. "Who's your boss?"

"I don't have to tell you shit, sweet cheeks."

"Aw come one Gorilla, tell me why a big badass like you is going to break this little man," Hudson said, the knot growing in his stomach. He shouldn't be involved, but he couldn't stand by and witness this man take a beating that would end his life. No matter what he'd done.

"This little shit stole one and a half mil from Reina," Gorilla said as an enormous grin spread across his face.

Hudson's face turned pale as he looked down at Billy, still dangling from Gorilla's grip. "How the hell did you do that?" he asked Billy.

"I've been her finance guy for the last three years. Not that hard once she trusted me," Billy explained.

"You didn't think she'd find out?" Hudson asked.

"Nah, her boy Carlos was planning on taking her down. Said she was a fool and didn't know the first thing about the drug trade. He was helping me siphon the money, and we were going to split it, but then he got himself killed and now I'm in here."

"That reminds me, pretty boy," Gorilla snarled. "Reina said if you give her what she wants, this will all go away."

"I have nothing to give that woman," Hudson said.

"Oh, I think you do. She wants her daughter in exchange for protection and to make your little situation here go away."

Hudson stared at Gorilla like he'd lost his mind. He couldn't believe Reina had this much pull in Spokane. He knew she had a lot of reach but didn't think she'd be able to plant people in Spokane to go after him in prison. But then, why not? She was capable of kidnapping her granddaughter to get what she wanted. He was being used as a tool. He would never help Reina, no matter what it cost him, but he needed time. "Tell her I'm off limits and so is Billy here until I've made my decision."

"That's not my call, sunshine," Gorilla said. "And I'm outta time." They looked down at the long line of inmates to see a group of guards coming their way.

"That's my deal. Take it or leave it. Do you think Reina will be happy with you if she thinks there's a chance of getting her daughter back and you went and fucked it up?"

Gorilla dropped Billy into a pile on the floor. Billy gasped and spit as the guards rushed in.

"Suit yourself, but you've bought yourself a puppy and twenty-four hours. If you don't have an answer and a plan by then, Billy here is dead. And I might throw you in for fun." Gorilla turned and faced the bars, putting his hands in plain view as soon as the guards reached them. Hudson followed suit along with the rest of Gorilla's men.

Hudson braced himself for a guard to hit or restrain him. Dammit, all he wanted to do was get through this until his attorney got him out of it. They weren't having a bail hearing because charges were still being drafted. One guard was as big as he was, and the last thing he wanted was more trouble.

The big man came up behind Hudson and pressed the cold metal baton into his back. Hudson told himself not to react, not to resist. "What the hell's going on here?" the senior guard asked.

"Nothing," Hudson said. "Just a conversation."

"What about this?" The guard pointed down at Billy, who was

getting to his feet. A deep red mark in the outline of Gorilla's hand had formed on the back of Billy's neck.

"We were just having a conversation," Billy repeated. "No harm in that, right, um, sir?"

He took one look at Gorilla and his men. "Yeah right. Take your crew and head to the back of the line and leave him alone. We don't need any trouble out of you, Gorilla."

The large men walked away, and Hudson saw Billy relax. "What in hell were you thinking stealing from one of the most powerful drug queens in history?" Hudson whispered under his breath.

"Carlos made it sound so easy. He was going to take down his mother, and I was going to help him. The deal was that he would protect me, but then he had to get himself killed and now I'm here." He repeated the same story from before.

"You need to figure out a way to make a deal," Hudson said. "Is there anything you can offer Reina that she wants more than you dead?"

"Yeah, I can restore all her accounts if she allows me access to a computer. Carlos had me hack into her entire portfolio and start moving money. He didn't know where it all went, but I do," Billy said, looking proud of himself.

"Well, if you want to make it out alive, then make a deal. I'll be out of here soon, and you'll be on your own with Gorilla and his goons."

"But all that money," Billy whined.

"You can't spend it if you're dead."

MAC STALKED BACK and forth in the tiny temporary house they'd put her in on base. She hadn't slept, and she was losing weight. The weight loss thing would have been welcome, but this wasn't the way to drop pounds. The one thing she'd learned while growing up in her mother's bat-shit-crazy world was to always stay in control. It was time for her to take the wheel. This son of a bitch had to stop, and being on the defense was getting old.

She picked up her cell and dialed Lola's number. "Hey sis," she said when the line picked up.

"Auntie Mac," Olive's tiny voice sang.

"Hi hon, how're you doing?"

"I'm wearing my pink boots," she said in a singsong voice.

"Oh, I bet you look cute."

"Yup, Mommy said so."

"Speaking of your mommy, honey, is she around?"

"Yup."

"Can I speak with her?" Olive had turned three years old, and it thrilled Mac that she was back home safe with her mom and dad. After their mother Reina kidnapped her and held her as leverage, it had made Lola uneasy. They both thought their mother was capable of reaching out and hurting Olive again, even from prison.

"Mommy, Auntie Mac's on the phone," she said in her loudest voice.

A few seconds later, Lola's smooth voice came on the line. "Hey, you. How are you holding up?" Mac gave her a quick update. "Holy shit. What are you going to do?" Lola said in a whisper, not wanting Olive to repeat the cuss word. Mac laughed out loud despite the situation when Olive's little voice sang, "Shit, shit, sit, shit." Lola growled into the phone. "Of course that's the word she picks up. What's your plan?"

"I need all the information on Hudson regarding the murder of Lieutenant Colonel Daniels and Anika, the defense attorney."

"I'm already way ahead of you on it. So, from what I can gather, the only actual evidence they have for the Daniels case is the prints on the murder weapon. Everything else is circumstantial. They suspect he killed Daniels while you were working the case," Lola said, blowing out a long breath.

"Okay, where did they find the murder weapon? Or is there anything else surrounding the case that might help?"

"Nothing concrete, or at least nothing that made it into the reports. In the defense attorney's case it was an anonymous tip about her murder, and the evidence found under Hudson's bed. Nothing else stands out. You looked at her case file, and the torture Anika suffered, but the exact cause of her death remains unclear," Lola said. "Do you have an alibi for Hudson at the time of Anika's death?"

"You're going to love this one." Mac paused.

"Somehow I don't think I will," Lola said.

"You remember on his second trip out to see me how his flight got delayed?"

"Yeah."

"That's when someone killed her. It gave him the exact time he would need to drive to her house, murder her, and still make it to the airport. Someone is fucking with the two of us hardcore, and they've been planning it for a while."

"What about the blood?" Lola asked.

"What blood?"

"Wouldn't Hudson have blood all over him? Shouldn't there be some evidence left behind, like fibers or prints showing he was present? Nothing is in the police report I hacked into in New Mexico."

"According to the report you gave me, the scene was clean. The investigating officer commented how impressed he was with the thorough job," Mac said.

"There has to be a way to poke holes in the evidence. It looks bad right now but..." Lola trailed off.

"Agreed. I've had enough of this shit. I'm stuck on base at the moment, but I think it's time I take a brief trip to New Mexico and start working this boots-on-the-ground style. I'm not getting anything done sitting around here with my thumb up my ass."

Lola remained silent. "Mac, if someone is hunting you, I'm not sure if that's such a good idea. What if they get to you while you're traveling?"

"No idea, but what I know is I can't sit here and let some asshole destroy us."

THE WORLD WAS SPINNING out of control and Mac was sitting in the middle of the vortex. There had to be additional information. She finished her timeline only to find there were a few windows of opportunity the prosecution would point to where Hudson could have killed Lieutenant Colonel Daniels. She dialed Jax's number, hoping she could help.

Jax picked up on the first ring. "Hey Mac, it's great to hear from you. How is everything going?"

"Hi Jaxs. Not great." Mac gave her a rundown of her current situation and waited while Jax processed it.

"What the fuck, Mac? Is there anything to the evidence?" Jax asked.

"No, just the prints on the murder weapon and that he was in the vicinity. Can you find out the exact day and time of death so I can tighten things up on my end? If I can provide him with an alibi, it would be a step in the right direction." Mac had an extensive relationship with Jax. Not only were they friends, but they used to be stationed together at Holloman Air Force Base in New Mexico, and they worked the last case together involving missing airmen and her mother's drug cartel. Mac found and rescued Jax's best friend and brought her back from what would have been a death sentence. If Mac's brother Dominic had his way with Sergeant Mia Hannick, she would have ended up dismembered and left in some undisclosed location. Mac had landed on Dominic's table and endured his torture. She wouldn't wish that experience on anyone. Every time she thought about waking up strapped to his table, she shivered. She hadn't intended for both her brothers to die, but the world was a better place without them. Their mother had done a number on both men.

"Yeah, but it won't hold up in court. You're his girlfriend and have a vested interest in getting him exonerated. Spouses, most times, cannot be compelled to testify for or against their spouses for the same reason. The prosecution will tear you to pieces in cross-examination. There has to be more than your words."

"Yeah, they arrested him right after he proposed. This fucker is hitting below the belt, and I need to figure out a way to get ahead of it. Any ideas?"

"Um, congratulations. Do you have a way to get the case file on Daniels?" Jax asked.

"My contact is working on it, but she hasn't been able to infiltrate. Alamogordo doesn't have everything in digital records. As backwoods as the little town is, it wouldn't surprise me if they kept their case files in bank boxes." With over thirty-one thousand people, the only reason the little town was thriving was because of the military installation and White Sands Missile Range. The police station housed fifty-five officers, but several were still in training and their technology left a lot to be desired, according to Lola.

Jax stayed silent for a moment. "Okay Mac, let me do some digging. You made a lot of friends on this base after the last case and a few enemies. Let me reach out to a couple of folks in the legal office and people who were close to him to see what I can find. Maybe it will point us in the right direction."

"Thanks, Jax. I owe you one."

"Think nothing of it, Mac. Keep your head down and let me do my thing. I'll call soon."

Mac set her phone down and continued to pace like a wild beast. Her system was jittery like she had meth in her, or some other drug that would mess with her. One of her clients, Jimmy, had a serious meth problem and popped hot on his urinalysis four times. He was about to go in for another one. He was paranoid and thought the world was out to get him. When they sat down with his addiction counselor, the doctor explained he was experiencing meth psychosis. It caused their client to experience not only paranoia, but a distorted version of reality. Mac's mind was spiraling on the edge, and she needed to get herself under control or she would lose. She wondered if it was how Jimmy felt all the time.

Bending down, she laced her boots up and grabbed her keys. She needed a change of scenery and couldn't stay locked up here anymore. Heading out to the tiny carport attached to her temporary housing, she climbed into her SUV and headed to the park on base. A little bench that few people knew about sat in the far corner. It would give her the opportunity to do some searching without interruption. It was one of the few winter days in Spokane when the sun was shining and it wasn't bitterly cold. Pulling into the tiny parking lot attached to Miller Park, she climbed out. As she'd hoped, no one was around on the beautiful afternoon.

The large pavilion provided plenty of shade and a place to plug in her laptop if she needed it. She settled in place and fired it up, sifting through the news articles surrounding Daniels' murder. She came across one that read:

On Saturday, October 15, 2022, at 0245 hours, officers from the Alamogordo Police Department received an anonymous call reporting a murder at the residence of Lieutenant Colonel Daniels, United States Air Force. Daniels was the Staff Judge Advocate from Holloman Air Force Base. They found his body in his bedroom, naked and covered in several stab wounds. All details are not yet available.

Soon after, officers located the murder weapon behind some bushes on the side of the house. Preliminary evidence indicates a break-in gone wrong, and the officials are waiting for the evidence to be processed in this case. Eyewitness reports revealed a dark-haired female was with the victim prior to his death. The New Mexico State Police have assumed the criminal investigation and are being assisted by the Alamogordo Police Department.

Lt. Col. Daniel's cases are being reviewed to flush out possible suspects who might have a motive to kill Daniels after his office prosecuted them. The Alamogordo Police Department, in conjunction with the New Mexico State

Police, has set up a tip line and is offering a reward for any information in connection with the murder of the decorated and honorable military officer.

Mac stretched her hands over her head and took a deep breath. The woman with Daniels was interesting, and she wondered if it might be her first solid lead in the case. Maybe Lola could find some camera footage on the mystery woman in question. It always amazed Mac and kind of creeped her out how many cameras watched society every day.

A shiver ran up her spine, and she looked around. At first, she thought it was nothing, but then she caught movement to the left of the restrooms. She gathered up her laptop and shoved it in her backpack while heading back to her SUV exposed out in the open. The second she clicked the little button on her key fob, the entire world exploded, and her body flew into the pavilion, slamming her back into one of the picnic tables. As she flew, she thought she saw a man running in the opposite direction, but she couldn't make anything out. It all happened too fast. It looked like the same short, heavy-set man that took shots at her, but she couldn't be sure.

There was no sound, just a high-pitched ringing in her ears. The world came back into focus. A pair of tennis shoes ran in her direction. A man put his hands on her head and was speaking into his phone, but Mac couldn't make out what he was saying when the darkness crept across her eyes.

CHAPTER
THIRTY-FIVE

MAC'S BODY shifted from side to side, but she couldn't move. The ringing in her ears subsided, and she made out several figures looming over her. Thinking she was being attacked, she fought until one of the larger men restrained her and stuck a needle into her arm.

When her mind cleared again, she was in an ambulance strapped to a gurney, traveling at a high speed toward the hospital. She cracked open her right eye and then her left, trying to make them focus, but the bright lights were too painful. Her throat was raw like she'd swallowed glass, and the scent of burnt hair surrounded her. With her eyes closed again, she reached over to the medic and touched his arm. "What happened?" she breathed out.

"Your vehicle exploded, ma'am. Lie back and close your eyes. We'll be at the hospital in a few minutes."

"Shit," was all she could muster before she passed out again.

A faint noise in the background kept tickling at her subconscious. When she peeled her eyes open, Captain Stanton sat in the hospital room in what looked like an uncomfortable chair. She wondered how long her boss had been waiting.

"Mac, you're awake. Let me call the nurse." He reached to push the button attached to her bed.

"Wait," she said, touching his hand. "First, tell me what happened.

Am I okay?"

"I'm happy to report you're doing pretty good, all things considered. According to the Explosive Ordinance Division on base, there was enough C-4 strapped to the bottom of your car to take out half the city block. Miller Park took some damage but somehow the way you landed on the side of the pavilion blocked most of the debris that should have hit you. You have a minor concussion and a hell of a bruise on your back. Your ears might ring for a bit, and you'll have to submit to some hearing evaluations for a while, but all things considered, you're going to be just fine." He smiled down at her. "You scared the shit out of me."

She reached up and touched her hair and winced when it crunched under her hand. Then she touched her eyebrows and breathed a sigh of relief when she found them right where she'd left them. "Did you tell Hudson?"

"Not yet. I gave his attorney a heads-up. He said he would brief him on the situation when they met this afternoon."

"Thanks," Mac said, as she moved to sit up and dropped back down when her head swam. "My insurance company is going to drop me for sure after this."

"That's the least of your worries. When you're up to it, we need to put our heads together and figure out who's behind these attacks before they do actual damage, or worse yet…" He let the words dangle in the air.

"I think it was the same guy running from the scene just before the explosion. He slipped behind a brick wall right before."

"The Office of Special Investigations will be in to take your statement soon. They're taking joint jurisdiction of your case with the local authorities now that there's been an attack on the base. OSI thinks you're being targeted because of your mother. What do you think?" Stanton asked.

"I mean, it's possible, but what would she have to gain by killing me?"

"If this guy wanted you dead, he had plenty of opportunity. The fact that you're still in one piece tells me there's something else at play here."

CHAPTER
THIRTY-SIX

IT TOOK days of waiting and exams for them to release Mac. By the time they were done poking and prodding, she'd had enough. It didn't help when they took turns interrogating her. Some of the OSI agents came at her hard and tried to accuse her of somehow being behind the attacks. It crossed her mind more than once that they held a grudge against her after what happened to their fellow agent in New Mexico. Agent Tarran had taken it upon himself to run an illegal investigation against Reina, Mac's mother, and was using a young airman as bait to do it. At first Mac had suspected he was overzealous, but later found out Tarran was in love with the wife of one of the major players. Tarran made things personal because he was running on emotion rather than his training in the field. As far as Mac was aware, he was still being investigated for his part in the murder of one of the young airmen. She'd have to ask Jax how it all turned out.

Mac sat on the edge of her hospital bed, waiting for Stanton to arrive. He'd volunteered to pick her up and take her back to her temporary lodging. They posted a guard outside the house twenty-four hours a day. The thought made Mac's skin crawl. She hated being watched and hated even more having her privacy and freedom taken away. The thought of being a prisoner inside the little house would be intolerable. She needed to put a stop to this.

Stanton walked in with a half-cocked grin on his face.

"What are you so happy about?" Mac asked. He said nothing at first. "Come on, give it up. I could use something to smile about right now. Did you and your wife find some time alone?"

"I wish. That's never going to happen with the kids always running around. But I have some excellent news for you."

"Spill it."

"Hudson's defense attorney was able to work a deal with the judge overseeing Hudson's case. Turns out the judge is pro-military and has a son in the Army. At the bail hearing, Hudson's commander swore under oath the military would hold him on base and ensure his presence in court. He's going to have to be remanded to base housing until his trial, but at least the two of you will be able to see each other."

Mac let the first grin in a while slide across her face. "That's the best news I've heard all week. How much is the bail?" she asked, bracing herself for the news.

"They set bail at ten thousand dollars, but if we can find a good bail bond company, they can secure bail for ten percent. It should only cost you guys about one thousand for his release. Do you have that kind of cash on hand?"

"I can scrape together five hundred and maybe Hudson can come up with the rest. We never sat down and did a deep dive into finances. Something for another day, but all I can do is hope he has it. Can I see him?"

"Not a chance. Sorry Mac, I have two armed Security Forces members outside the door waiting to escort us back to base. You will be on lockdown until we figure this thing out. The base wing commander thinks the only way he can keep you safe is by limiting your movements. These attacks are getting out of hand."

He was right, but it didn't make her any more comfortable with the situation. "What are the rules for this lockdown situation? Am I able to buy groceries? What about things I need from my house?"

"I've volunteered to pick up anything you need as long as we leave you behind closed doors. It sounds harsh and you might go a little stir crazy, but at least you'll be alive."

Mac dropped her sore body back onto the bed, her legs wobbling beneath her. She couldn't wait to get her hands on the slimy son of a bitch ruining her life. Taking a deep breath in and letting it out, she had to remind herself not to take her anger out on Stanton. He was doing everything he could to support and help. "Thank you for volunteering."

"Don't thank me yet. Not until we get you and Hudson clear and safe."

"Do we have any new information about Hudson's cases?"

"No, his defense attorney is hoping the two of you can sit down and tighten up the timeline so he can start poking additional holes in the case. Right now, he convinced the judge that a real possibility exists someone planted evidence against Hudson. He used the attacks against you as leverage to show someone has a vendetta against the two of you. Have you found anything else?"

She told him about the mention of a dark-haired woman being seen with Daniels before his death, but nothing more. When they walked out of the room, two large armed men flanked her at either side. "Ma'am," one of them said, "I need you to put this on until we have you secured on the installation. Once you're in the house, you can remove the vest, but you are to wear it any time you step foot out of TLF. Do you understand?"

"Yes, sir," she murmured, defeat and exhaustion crawling through her body.

Mac and Stanton rode back to base in a reinforced Humvee with bulletproof plating. Every time a vehicle came close, Mac would jump. The flack vest was suffocating her. It was not dissimilar to driving into a combat zone instead of heading back to base to a temporary house. Her lack of control was pissing her off.

They cleared the front gate without incident. Once they pulled into temporary housing, the Humvee stopped.

"Ma'am, I need you to wait while we clear the house before you go in." He was out of the vehicle and in the house before Mac responded. Within minutes, the two men came back. "All clear. Sergeant Edson is going to post himself outside your door. If you need anything, please tell me," Sergeant Preston said, indicating he was the one in charge. He pulled a card from his breast pocket and handed it to her. "If you need anything at all, Sergeant McGregor, don't hesitate to ask. We take it personally when someone goes after one of our own."

Mac walked into the house sandwiched by the two men, who were swinging their heads from side to side, watching every movement on the street. Once she was in the house, Sergeant Preston locked all the doors and secured the windows.

"Can I grab a ride back to my vehicle?" Stanton asked.

"Yes, sir."

"Mac, I'm going to take care of this. If all goes well, I'll be back with Hudson soon. Have your money ready to transfer as soon as I have things set up."

"No problem. Thank you for getting him out of that shithole."

"It wasn't me, but I'll take partial credit for hooking him up with Aeddan Bartz. I told you he was the best." Stanton smiled and walked out the door with the two armed men, leaving Mac to wander around the empty house.

Sergeant Edson took up his post outside the front of the house under the carport. Mac wondered how long he would have to sit out in the cold.

She poked her head out. "Can I get you anything?"

"Don't worry about me." The young sergeant smiled. "My relief is coming in about an hour and they're bringing a vehicle for us to stay in."

Having him posted outside was necessary, but she wouldn't relax until Hudson was back.

CHAPTER
THIRTY-SEVEN

"WHAT DO YOU MEAN, he's being released this afternoon?" Gennavie screamed at her boy toy.

Johnathan shrank back from her and flinched when she threw up her hands. "Mistress, it's not my fault. I tried, but I don't have the power to keep him in if the judge was releasing him. There's nothing I can do." He reached out to touch her, but she whipped around and slapped him across the face so hard he fell back onto the floor.

"So, you're telling me I don't have a use for you anymore," she seethed.

"Yes, mistress. I mean no."

"Well, which is it?" she screamed at him, thankful that her borrowed house was far enough away from other people so they wouldn't hear her. She needed to make someone experience her pain, and poor Johnathan was the closest target.

"What if we stack more charges? If the judge thinks he's continuing to break the law or violating the conditions of his bail, then he'll be right back in the can, and this time he won't get released until his trial," Johnathan said. "He'll never make bail a second time. See, I can still help you. I promise."

She looked over at him. Pitiful, she thought. Just like she liked them. Easy to control and willing to do anything for her, no matter what it cost.

Gennavie sank into a white overstuffed chair and thought about her slave's proposal. "Come, rub my tired feet while I consider," she said, slipping her feet out of her five-inch heels.

He didn't hesitate to drop onto the floor and catch her foot in his hand before it hit the carpet.

The idea had merit, but what kind of crime could she set him up for? She had murdered no one in a while. Not since Anika. Another kill would be a welcome addition to her week, she thought, but maybe she needed to do more. Stack the deck a little.

Jonathan slid his hand up her leg and began massaging her calf. She allowed it for now.

Every time she thought about Hudson getting out of jail, her anger spiked to a whole new level. Worse yet, Mac would reap the benefits of having Hudson back. The man at her feet might serve a purpose, after all. Someone had to pay for this indiscretion.

"What are you willing to do for me, my pet?" She glared.

"I'll do anything you want me to. Just say the word. But why do you want this guy behind bars?"

"Because Mac has to suffer. She put Vincent away, and now I…"

He looked up at her with hurt in his eyes. "Am I not enough for you? Would it be so bad if Vincent stayed in prison, and you were with me?"

She wondered how long it would be before he and his brother began talking about things. But for now, he would suffice as her plaything. Neither one of them was anywhere near Vincent's equal. He was the only person on Earth who knew her and how to push her buttons. He made her feel powerful and in control instead of insignificant, like she'd felt as a child when her parents died. She needed to wield that control now.

"Will you do anything for me?"

"Yes," he whispered, bowing his head in submission.

"As you wish. Take off your clothes and lay face-down on the bed," she commanded.

"Yes, mistress." He stood and walked toward the bedroom, stripping off his clothes as he went.

Following behind him, she grabbed her bull whip. The stress relief would do her good. He tensed as he lay on the bed, waiting for her to punish him. She cracked the whip and the tip sliced through the tender skin on his left butt cheek. A trickle of blood ran down the side. Another mark appeared seconds later and then another as her whip worked its magic.

She circled him, knowing she wouldn't be able to do what she needed to. The little whimpering man still had a purpose, and for that she would let him live for now.

Smiling, she told him to flip over on his back. When she tortured his front side, she was careful not to leave any visible marks. She needed him in uniform and looking professional.

HUDSON COULDN'T STOP SMILING. He was waiting in his cell to be out-processed, but his cellmate Billy was sulking. "They're gonna kill me," he muttered.

"I'm not your assigned protector. I told you how to fix it. The rest is up to you."

"Yeah, I sent the word up the chain to see if Reina would bite. Hope she takes it."

"If she does, don't do something stupid like that again. No matter how much cash is involved."

"What about you? What are you going to do when you get out?" Billy asked, pushing his glasses up on his nose.

"I'm going to find out who's doing this to us."

"Who's us?"

"The less you know, the better. Keep your head down and fix what you did."

A guard showed up at the cell door.

"Today's your lucky day, Mr. Hudson," he said, looking down at his clipboard. "You're being remanded into the custody of the Air Force."

Hudson took a step back from the door as was protocol and waited for the guard to open and escort him out. Many of the guards had been rough with him, but this man was professional and treated Hudson with respect.

Hudson walked away with a slight pang of guilt for leaving Billy to face his consequences alone. He wondered if the small man would make it through the night when he passed Gorilla sitting at a table. Gorilla gave him a sickly smile and nodded. It would be way too soon if Hudson ever had to see him again. He couldn't wait to be back in Mac's arms. Even if they were under siege, they would conquer this assault on their lives as long as they were together. After hearing what happened to her at Miller Park, he was prepared to do anything to stay with her and be able to protect her.

They led him into a small changing room where the guard removed his handcuffs and left him to change back into his civilian clothes. The last time Mac came to see him flooded his thoughts. She'd looked amazing and had agreed to be his wife. He couldn't believe how lucky he was to be with her and only hoped this bullshit hadn't changed that. He couldn't imagine life without her. His future made little sense without her in it. The room was small, and he had a hard time getting his dress clothes back on, but he emerged in the same dark jeans and button-down he wore on their special night.

When he came out, Stanton and his defense attorney, Bartz, were waiting for him. Stanton was holding an extra-large flack vest in his hand. Both men had their own on under their shirts. "What is that for?" Hudson pointed to the vest.

"Bartz was going to come to brief you on the situation, but they approved you for release, so we thought you'd want to go back to her as soon as possible rather than delaying things."

"You've got that right, but why in hell do I need a flack vest?"

Stanton handed it to him. "Put it on and we'll explain on the way to the base."

Hudson put the vest on and strapped it into place, following both men out to an armor-plated Humvee. "Is she okay?"

"She's fine," Stanton said, opening the door for Hudson to climb in.

Inside, his commanding officer, Lieutenant Colonel Dixon, waited for them.

"Hi, sir. Thank you for helping me out," Hudson said, shaking his hand.

"You better not make me regret it, Hudson. I put my neck on the line and it's personal," Dixon said.

"What part of this case is personal for you, sir? Other than your first sergeant getting arrested and some bad press."

"Amelia Churer was my goddaughter," Dixon said, lowering his voice.

Hudson looked at his commander, confused. "I'm sorry, sir, I don't follow. Who's Amelia Churer?"

"She died over a year ago. It was right before you came to Fairchild and our squadron. I'm sure you heard about it. She froze to death after a night of drinking. They were prosecuting the young man with her. The defense attorney working the case is the same one you're being accused of murdering. So, like I said, don't prove me wrong."

"I'm sorry for your loss, sir."

"None of that. Her parents are the ones I'm worried about. They're close friends of my family, and they aren't doing well. Now that the defense attorney is out of the picture, it delays the entire case. No one should have to bury their daughter. They thought they might almost have closure and begin the healing process. Instead, there's another delay until they find a replacement defense counsel. With the trial still looming, it stirs all those emotions back up."

Hudson looked down at his hands, not knowing what to say. "If there's anything I can do to help…" He let the words hang in the air.

"You can help by proving me right and clearing your name so you can go back to work."

"I'll do everything I can. Can someone tell me what's happening?"

By the time they pulled up to Mac's TLF, Hudson's heart was pounding in his chest. Someone had put a mark on their heads, and he was thankful to be back by Mac's side. "Before you get out, I need to know you understand you may not leave and there will be an armed Security Forces member parked outside this house," Bartz said.

"Yes sir, I understand. I don't plan on leaving her side. I'm not going anywhere."

Hudson got out and tilted his head at the guard in the adjacent

Humvee. The two men knew each other since Hudson was in the man's chain of command.

He looked up to the best view in the world: Mac, standing at the window, staring back at him.

HUDSON WALKED INTO THE HOUSE, stripping off the vest as he wrapped Mac in his arms. She was warm and comfortable in his embrace, and he didn't want to let go. He missed everything about her. The scent of her shampoo, the look in her soft brown eyes, her little cockeyed grin when she was being mischievous. He breathed her in, kissing the side of her neck until she shivered under his embrace.

"We can't," she whispered. "They're right outside."

He covered her mouth with a deep kiss that seemed to devour her and unleash her every emotion. "I missed you," was all he said in return as he scooped her up in his arms and headed toward the bedroom. He laid her on the bed. She propped herself up on her elbows as he closed the blinds on the window and pulled the bedroom door shut. The old shades didn't quite close all the way, but they led to the back of the house and their guard was around in front. "You look too sexy in my t-shirt."

Mac smiled up at him. She'd gone back to wearing his clothes.

Hudson stared down at her, not wanting to be apart from her for another second. He slipped over her body on the bed and pressed his mouth against her. His heart was racing, burning with hunger. An insatiable need coursed through his body. The intensity of being denied the ability to hold her, to touch her, made him want her more.

He reached down, pushing the shirt up over her head. He ran his hand down her soft olive skin, letting his fingers tantalize every inch of her body. Pushing her hands above her head, he took his other hand, releasing the hook sitting between her large breasts. The lacy black bra sprang open as he caught her nipple in his mouth. Her moan told him she wanted him to take all of her. Take he would.

He wanted to savor the moment as long as possible as he kissed her bare flesh and listened to her moan. He pulled away, stripping off his shirt as he went. She sat up and unbuttoned his pants, watching them slide down his long legs and hit the floor. He was already rock-hard when she placed her hands around him and stroked. He pulled her up into his arms and pushed her pants down as he went. His breath caught when her little black thong came into view. "Good lord, woman," was all he could say when he bent down to remove the little fabric between him and what he wanted. She stood as he kissed the sweet mound between her legs and let out a soft gasp when his tongue found her sweet spot.

She lowered herself back to the bed, allowing him full access to whatever he wanted. And he wanted every inch of her. His mind was only in one place while he allowed his mouth to work its magic. Her excitement was mounting and bringing him close to the edge. Every time she let out a loud moan, she'd put her hand over her mouth to stay quiet. He loved that she was noisy in the bedroom. It turned him on more than she could imagine. There was no more powerful, erotic sensation than to cause those sounds to come from such a stunning woman. She arched her back, pulling his hair while her body shuddered.

As soon as her butt settled back onto the mattress, he reached up, grabbing both her ankles and placing them on his muscular shoulders. "Now," she whispered.

He would never think of denying this beautiful creature. Lowering himself into her, he pressed the full length of his shaft deep inside. Her nails sank into his back as she moaned "more." He lost all sense of control, moving fast, stroking harder. She pushed up, meeting him, pressing him deeper until her body coiled around him. Her body went still for a moment as she let out a soft, muffled cry when she buried her face in his shoulder. Then her climax reached its peak. He had no choice but to respond in the heat of her body until his world exploded into mindless ecstasy. He collapsed in her arms, unable to speak. They slept after days of restless nights and turmoil. The world was at peace.

———

Gennavie drove by the tiny house they kept Mac and Hudson in. There was a singular Humvee with only one guard. They weren't taking the situation as seriously as they should. The man wasn't looking when she drove past. At 1800 hours, it would only be a matter of time before night fell and she would have her opportunity.

She parked at the base clinic and walked around to the back of the house they were staying in. She couldn't believe it. Not only was Hudson out of prison, but he was making love to Mac. Gennavie dug her nails into the palm of her hands. Anger didn't begin to describe what was coursing through her body. This had to stop. There was nothing more she wanted in the world than to wipe that satisfied grin off Mac's face.

"WELL, GOOD MORNING, BEAUTIFUL," Hudson said when he wandered out of the bedroom and found Mac sitting at the small wooden kitchen table. She smiled up at him, but there was worry in her eyes. "Don't worry, hon, we'll figure this out. It's a matter of putting our heads together."

"I know, I'm trying. I started making a list of possible alibis for the Daniels' murder and Captain Anika Wilson."

"That's a good start. Let's tighten it up a bit."

"Holes exist. Times when we weren't together where the prosecution can say you did these things. What about when your plane got delayed? Walk me through what happened," Mac said.

"That's the problem. Nothing happened. I don't know how someone found out, but I was getting ready to leave for the airport and received a message on my Delta app that said my plane wasn't leaving for another two hours. The last thing I wanted to do was go to the airport four and a half hours before my flight was going to leave," he explained, as he grabbed a cup of coffee and sat next to her at the table.

"Okay, let's work that angle. How long would it take you to drive from your house to Moses Lake?"

He pulled up Google Maps on his phone and punched in the information. "It should have taken me one hour and thirty-three minutes. With my driving, it would have been a solid three-hour round trip, giving me about an hour and a half to clean up and catch my flight."

"Not helpful."

"After reviewing the case file," he said, "how long do you think it would take someone to commit that kind of murder?"

"There was evidence of a hidden vehicle. It would have taken about five minutes to break into the house." She paused, thinking about it for a moment. "With no sign of forced entry, her attacker would need a key, or maybe Anika left her door unlocked."

"That's possible. Didn't you say her place was out in the sticks?"

"Yeah, pretty far down a back road. It would have given the guy tons of privacy to do what he wanted to."

"What about the act itself?" Hudson asked. "Would it have covered him in blood? Was it messy?"

"Nope, the place was clean. Anika had severe ligature marks, a contusion on her head caused by a lamp, and her larynx crushed, but the perp didn't so much as leave a fiber behind. It's almost like the person responsible was in a bubble or a latex suit."

"Okay, so how long would it have taken?"

Mac looked down at her hands. She wasn't sure how to answer without hurting him, but they had to figure this thing out. "For a man of your size, you could have been in, hit her over the head, strangled her, and been out in about fifteen minutes tops."

"Didn't you say they found her tied to the bed? That takes time."

"You've got a point. The pictures of the scene reminded me of someone we both know. The ligature marks, the tied-up bodies, even the slight mutilation to her genital area."

"Gennavie," he said without hesitation.

"And there's more. I found a news article reporting a dark-haired woman seen with Daniels before his death. It's a theory, but my gut tells me she's involved."

"Your gut has been right before," he said, standing up and heading to the sink to put away his coffee cup. "We can bat this thing around more tonight when I return. Take notes if you think of anything."

"You're leaving," she said, sounding pitiful to her own ears.

He smiled and walked back over, planting a deep kiss on her supple lips. "I have to reappear in front of the judge to finalize everything and sign some paperwork guaranteeing I'll appear in court. The bail bondsman is still working through the system, so the only reason I'm out is because Dixon signed for me. This shouldn't take long. I'll be back before you know it."

Seconds later, he was outside the door and back in the Humvee with his vest on.

The house was so empty without him. She hated needing him so much, but with the attacks on their safety she didn't want to be alone. After wearing a path on the carpet, she checked if Jax or Lola had any updates for her. She tried Lola first but only got her voicemail. But when she tried Jax, she picked up on the first ring.

"Hey lady, how are you holding up?" Jax asked.

"All things considered, pretty well. The fucker blew up my new ride, but other than that."

"Holy shit, are you okay?"

"I'm fine, only a couple of bumps and bruises." She gave her a full update on Hudson's status and the article she'd found.

"Perfect. Well, I've been doing some digging too. One of the female attorneys at the legal office said Daniels was seeing a woman. One of her clients. He asked her to take the woman on as a client so he wouldn't have a conflict of interest with her. She was pretty sure they were dating, but Daniels was pretty closed off about those things. After his divorce and his wife left with the kids, he became a workaholic until this woman started coming around. At first, she was happy for him. He had been pretty down for a while, but there was something off about the woman."

"Do we have a name?" Mac asked, a tingle running up her spine from the first genuine lead.

"Attorney-client privilege prevents me from getting it. But at least we know for sure another person is at play here. I'm not sure why the police didn't look into her, but most people don't look at women during a murder investigation. They think we're nurturers, and for most of us that's true, but you and I have seen a few who are more callous and calculated than any man."

"You're not kidding about that," Mac responded. "Thanks for digging. Let me know if you find anything else."

GENNAVIE WATCHED as Mac put down her phone. She'd crouched behind the air conditioning unit outside the house while making her way to the gate, so she got a good look at the guard. He was sitting in the Humvee, looking down at his phone. The young man couldn't be older than his mid-twenties. The right age for him to be an easy target. Most men had a hard time resisting her, and why would this one? They were watching for a short, fat man, not a goddess. The woman of his dreams was the last person he would think of as a threat.

The only problem she ever had with this approach was a time when she tried to seduce a gay man. He looked at her without so much as a grin and said, "Honey, no offense, you're not my type." She'd never been told that before, so she had to ask. "So, what is your type?" He pointed at Vincent. It was fun seeing Vincent seduce someone. He was pretty good at it.

No way she would allow Mac to have sex with Hudson and enjoy him when she couldn't have Vincent. At first, it kinda turned her on watching Hudson do all those tantalizing things to Mac. He was an impressive member of the male species, and she was stunning in her own right. But after the initial enjoyment wore off, she obsessed with how her life had turned to shit while they were still going strong.

Gennavie went around to the opposite side of the house, where the guard wouldn't see her coming. She approached from the passenger side of the Humvee and knocked on the window. He jumped when she did, and she smiled. At first his eyes went wide, and he placed his hand on the butt of his gun. When the stunning woman smiled at him, he removed his hand and smiled back. *Good boy,* she thought as he rolled the window down to talk to her.

"Hi, ma'am. What can I do for you?"

She didn't take offense to the ma'am business. A lot of women thought it meant the person was calling you old, but not in the military. Most of the population referred to each other as ma'am or sir.

"Hiya, sugar. I was wondering if I could slip in with you for a minute to warm up. My car broke down and I have to hoof it to the Auto Hobby Shop to get a little help with it. What do you say?"

He reached over, clicking the locks, and let her in. "I suppose there's no harm in that," he said, looking her up and down like a hungry beast. "I wish I could drive you, but I have to stay at my post."

"What're you watching?" she asked, smiling as she climbed into the vehicle, tipping forward and allowing him to look down her shirt. She'd tucked the new fat suit behind the house in case she needed it. Underneath, she wore skintight leggings and a tight shirt with a nice lacy push-up bra to get this young man's attention. Men would do almost anything for a beautiful woman, and she loved to exploit it.

"I'm guarding the neighborhood," he said. He was being vague, but that was okay. He wasn't useful for information. She only needed him to take a little nap so she could take care of some business. No one was on the street and most of the houses appeared empty. It would only take a few hours. Leaning into him, she ran her long nails along his jawline.

"Um," he said, as she ran her hand down his chest and started massaging him. Within seconds, he was at her mercy. "I'm, um, working. Can I meet up with you later?"

She could see the pleading in his eyes. He was weighing whether she was worth losing his military career, or at the very least getting an Article 15 and losing pay. The look in his eyes told her he was losing the battle between doing what was right and giving in to what was wrong.

As a young man fueled with hormones, he couldn't resist as she undid his pants and pulled him into her hand. She climbed on top of him, not giving him the chance to reconsider. The belt she'd bought was identical to the one Hudson wore the night he proposed to Mac. She pulled it from around her slender waist. The young guard tilted his head back as she continued to massage him. The thumping of his pulse along the exposed skin on his neck was mesmerizing. Lifting off the seat, she wrapped the belt around his neck and pulled, cinching it tight. Flinging her body over the seat, she pulled hard. Kicking and pulling at the noose around his neck, the young man spit, struggling against his restraints until he stopped moving.

At first she thought she might have killed him. It didn't matter. It was important they thought it was Hudson in a rage. The man still had a pulse, but it was thin. She came back over to the front seat, slipping his penis back into his pants and buttoning him up, leaving the belt wrapped around his throat. Careful not to leave additional marks, she spread his fingers wide and injected GHB into his system. It would keep him out for a while and had the beautiful after-effect of memory loss. She didn't need him retelling the story. Not that anyone would believe him, but a girl could never be too careful.

CHAPTER
FORTY-TWO

AFTER HUDSON LEFT, Mac couldn't help but hum to herself as she mulled over their next move. The situation wasn't as bad with him here. Having him back in her arms made the world more at peace. It was only a matter of time before they cracked this thing wide open. She peered out the window. The young man guarding her place was sleeping. Typical, she thought. She and Hudson had had a discussion about the lack of discipline among this latest generation of airmen. Of course, if she had to guess, the leaders ahead of her would say the same thing when she was coming up through the ranks. She'd give him a little time to rest his eyes, then bring him a cup of coffee.

In the meantime, she needed the solitude to think. It was unnerving to have someone always watching. Last night when they had made love, she'd felt eyes on her. Someone was watching the entire time, but afterward she'd checked and found the guard sitting where they'd left him and not peeking through the windows. As she paced around the house, rolling the case over in her mind, her phone rang. "Hi Lola, I've been trying to reach you."

"Hey sis. Sorry, been busy working this recent case. To my surprise, the government wants me to do some work in order to receive pay." Lola had gone back to working with the three-letter agencies as an independent contractor after her latest boss had double-crossed her.

He was giving their mother Reina information about her and her daughter's location, which led to both her soon-to-be husband and their daughter being kidnapped.

"Yeah, they're silly like that sometimes. Me, I'm on lockdown with my thumb up my ass."

"Now that's an interesting visual," Lola said, laughing into the phone. Mac pictured her little sister. She always reminded her of a badass pixie fairy with her red hair and freckles. That woman was a force to be reckoned with, and Mac was always thankful she was on her side. Lola could hack into anything, including all the government agency databases. She made it look like child's play. She got arrested a few times when she was younger until she got good at it. Once that happened, the government decided it was better to have her as an ally instead of an enemy.

"So, were you able to dig anything up for me?"

"Of course. Now it's nothing definitive, but he was seeing someone, and she was a hottie. I visited AFFIRST, the Air Force legal office database. The log on the days she was in the building under the alias she used leads nowhere. The social security number they had for her belongs to a woman who died three years ago in a car accident. I could view her coming and going, but each time she wore this obnoxious wide-rimmed black hat covering most of her face."

"Then how do you know she's a hottie? She might cover her face because she's a troll."

"Not a chance. From what I glimpsed, her face is nothing short of perfect, and her body belongs on the cover of *Playboy*. I tell you, any man would pay good money to touch that woman. If what your friend Jax told you is correct, and he was seeing her, then she had access to him and anything else she might want."

"Great work, thanks. Can you send me the pictures you could retrieve? Did you find anything at or around his residence?"

"A porch camera on a neighbor's house, but it only caught her back as she was going in. I can't even be sure if it's the same woman."

"Okay, thanks for looking. How are you guys doing?"

They chatted for a while and hung up with promises to catch up soon.

In the kitchen, she started chopping vegetables and smiled. Having an awesome boss like Stanton was a gift. He went out and bought her a ton of groceries and went to her house to retrieve clothes and supplies. She sang to herself, swaying her hips back and forth. Her long hair tickled her back as she went. Only the ends had been singed during the explosion, but most of it was still there.

As she turned, crushing pain smashed through the back of her head as darkness clouded her eyes. When she tried to open them again, her vision was cloudy like a strange film covered them, and she felt shooting pain. Goose pimples climbed up her skin and panic crept into her brain when she realized she couldn't move, and she was stark naked. "Who's there?" she tried to say, but nothing came out. Pulling her arms only made the ropes tighten around her wrists. "What the fuck is going on?" she got out. It sounded like a little girl instead of her own voice.

A shift in the room caught her attention, and something scraped across her scalp. "Did you miss me?" came a voice. She strained to turn her head but could only make out a shadow looming behind her. It was dark out and she couldn't make out the features, but it was a woman without question. She thought she recognized the voice but couldn't quite place it. The woman ran her long nails through Mac's hair again, and Mac shrank away. "Oh, come now, that's no way to greet an old friend."

"Gennavie?" Mac asked.

"Yes, my dear." Gennavie breathed out her words as she ran her hand down Mac's body to the gunshot in her leg. She ran her finger around the entry point.

"What do you want?" Mac asked.

"I want you to suffer after what you did to Vincent."

"Vincent landed himself in prison. I didn't put him there, and you should be with him instead of running free," Mac said, trying to figure a way out.

"Free? Free—you think I'm free. You pompous little bitch. I've had to go into hiding from the rest of the world. Because of you, I've had to live in the shadows instead of showing the world my beautiful self. No, this is your fault, and you're going to help me get Vincent out."

Gennavie ripped the bandage off Mac's leg and pressed her long fingernail into the wound the bullet had left behind, causing Mac to scream out in pain. The blood drained from her face as she fought to stay focused. Right before Mac was about to pass out, Gennavie removed her finger that had sunk into her soft flesh and waited while Mac recovered.

"Why on earth do you want Vincent back? He's nothing special. I'm sure thousands of men would do your bidding," Mac said. She needed to keep Gennavie talking until the guard out front came to check or Hudson made it back. If she played to Gennavie's narcissistic side, then maybe she could keep her talking.

"You have no idea what you're talking about. Would you replace Hudson?" she said, letting out a wicked cackle. "As a matter of fact, my dear Mac, you might want to start looking for a replacement. You're not going to want what's left of him once I'm done."

"This is between you and me. Leave Hudson out of it," Mac said, trying to force the pleading out of her voice.

"Not a chance. You're going to suffer like I have. There's no way you're going to enjoy his beautiful body and lie in his arms while I wither away," Gennavie complained.

Mac thought she was pouting. "Tell me, how can I help you get Vincent out of prison? They're looking at the death penalty for him. There's nothing I can do for him. Not even the best defense team in the world can help him now. His testimony is part of the record. A mistrial would be almost impossible," Mac tried to reason, but anger flashed in Gennavie's eyes right before the side of her face exploded in pain when Gennavie's open hand cracked across Mac's cheek.

"Don't spew that bullshit. There has to be a way. All you need to do is cooperate and all this will go away."

"Cooperate how? What do you want me to do?" Mac asked. "Leave Hudson out of this," she tried again.

"Not a chance. You haven't suffered enough."

Gennavie smashed the butt of her gun into Mac's temple. A flash of white passed in front of her eyes, and then nothing.

FORTY-THREE

IT TOOK five hours to work through the court system and get his bail posted. Hudson was exhausted and couldn't wait to return to Mac. At least he wasn't stuck in a jail cell defending himself from assholes like Gorilla. His attorney dropped him off at temporary housing. He was under strict instructions to stay at the house with Mac. Hudson couldn't think of another place he'd rather be.

Something was off as he came around the side of the Humvee to check in with the guard. It was dark out, and at first the man appeared to be sleeping on the job, but the closer he got the more he was positive something was very wrong. The young airman's head lolled to the side in an unnatural position. Something was pulled tight around his throat. When Hudson twisted the knob and pulled, it didn't budge. He tried the back and then went over to the passenger side. It was open, so he climbed in, pressing his fingers against the man's neck. The guy had a pulse, but it was weak. He touched the belt wrapped around the man's throat. His instincts told him he shouldn't touch anything, but he couldn't leave the man like that. It was cutting off his airway. He loosened the belt as much as possible to give him more room to breathe. The man's chest moved up and down without restriction, but he remained unconscious.

Hudson backed out of the Humvee and sprinted to the door,

yanking it open. He shouldn't have left her alone. Guilt and panic flew through his body as he started through the house. He didn't know if the intruder was still there. He didn't have a weapon since he was out on bail. Slipping into the small kitchen, he grabbed a steak knife out of the utensil drawer and continued checking each room as he went.

It was too quiet. Not a sound except for his heavy footsteps as he made his way to the back of the house. Strapped to the bed was the love of his life, unconscious, with a trickle of blood running down the side of her face. He rushed in and dropped to his knees. "Mac, are you okay?" He wrapped his large hands around her face. "Talk to me." But her head lay limp in his hands.

He stood to find the light switch when a sharp needle pierced his skin. He spun around as the room spun with him. The world around him went out of focus. He blinked his eyes several times, trying to push the darkness away, but it was no use. Crashing to the ground, his head bounced off the unforgiving floor.

Gennavie paced around the big man at her feet. "You came back a little too early. Your little lady and I were about to have fun. But this will work too," she said, kneeling down next to him and picking up the steak knife still in his hand. Running the blade along Mac's stomach with her gloved hand, she pressed it into her soft flesh. Not hard enough to kill or plunge too deep and hit anything important, enough to leave a nice ugly scar for Hudson to answer to. "I hope I didn't give you too much. It's hard to gauge these things for a guy your size," she told Hudson's unconscious body. "We'll have to see. Mac was easy. There was such wonderful information on the internet about how much to give a woman her size to make her pass out and not remember much. It kinda makes me worry about our society," she said, placing the knife back into Hudson's large hand and pressing it closed around the knife.

Gennavie had to move before someone started paying attention. She was betting no one would check until the next shift change. According to her intel, it wouldn't happen until morning. She slipped back into her fat suit and was at the back door, disappearing into the night.

"SECURITY FORCES, Sergeant Angel. How may I help you?"

"Hi, is this the police?"

"Yes ma'am, you've reached the Fairchild Air Force police. Are you on base?"

"Uh yeah, and I need to report a crime. Or, well, I think there's something wrong. I mean, I'm not sure."

"Okay ma'am, are you safe?" Sergeant Angel asked.

"Yeah, we returned from overseas, and my sleep is all screwed up. I was sitting outside in temporary housing, and I thought I saw a dark figure slinking out of the back of the house, but I'm not sure. I caught a glimpse of his shadow. There's a Humvee in the driveway with a guy inside, but he's not moving."

"Ma'am, what's your name, and do you have the address of the house in question?"

"Not sure about the house number, but it's off South Graham Road and First Street. It's the second house on the right. I'm in the third. Oh, and I'm Lara Tarang."

"Okay Lara, I'm sending someone over. Please stay in your house until our officers arrive," Sergeant Angel said as he pulled up the house in his database and saw it was the one Sergeant McGregor was staying in. Instead of following the normal protocol of sending a patrol car to see what was happening, he walked down the hall to his commander's office.

"Sir, sorry to barge in. I received a call from a lady who reported seeing an assailant leaving the house we tucked McGregor and Hudson into. How would you like me to respond?"

"Who's on post?" Dixon asked.

"Landry, sir, and he's not responding. The lady who called in said he's not moving."

"Shit," Dixon said, grabbing his keys. "Get a team together and meet me there. No one enters without my go, understood?"

"Yes, sir."

Seven minutes later, First Street was covered with police cars like an infestation. Lieutenant Colonel Dixon pulled up and got out of his car. "Report," he bellowed toward Sergeant Angel.

"Sir, no movement in the house. Permission to approach Landry's Humvee?"

"Keep your head on a swivel," Dixon ordered. Angel and three other Security Forces members crouched low in a single-file line coming around the passenger side of Landry's vehicle. Angel put his phone up to the window and pressed the button, taking a picture of the inside, then twisting his wrist and doing the same for the back before exposing any of his men. He brought it down, seeing only Landry's unconscious form in the driver's seat. There was no way of telling if someone was crouched in the back.

"Sir," Angel said into his radio. "He appears to be alone and uncon-scious. Permission to proceed."

"Go ahead, but stay vigilant." Angel pulled latex gloves over his hands prior to climbing into the passenger side of the vehicle.

"He's alive but needs medical attention. Permission to enter the premises, sir."

"Hold, Sergeant. I'm coming with you. Leave one of your men with Landry." Within seconds, Dixon stood next to his team with his flack vest strapped to his chest. Angel entered first, with the commander right behind him. They fanned out, clearing each room as they made their way to the back of the house where the bedroom was.

"Clear," each member hollered as they cleared the space. Once they congregated at the end of the hall outside the bedroom, Dixon held up his hand for his team to hold. They lined themselves down the wall in case there was an armed assailant still inside. Angel swung around his commander and kicked the door, lunging forward with his gun pushed out in front of them. Strapped to the bed lay Mac, struggling against her restraints. When the men burst into the room, it was too late. Her naked body strapped to the bed was on display for all to see. All four men stared at her for what seemed like a solid five minutes but was only a few seconds.

Dixon cleared his throat and grabbed a sheet lying on the floor to cover her up, as one of his men whispered, "Damn."

"Help me untie her and get medical in here. She's wounded."

The entire team had been so distracted by the sight of Mac on display they hadn't paid attention to Hudson curled up on the floor in a fetal position.

"Sir," Angel said. "Hudson has a pulse, but…" His voice dropped away as he pointed at the knife in Hudson's hand. Blood covered the tip. The entire team looked back at Mac. A thin line of red had already formed on her stomach through the white sheet.

"Don't jump to conclusions yet," Dixon said. "Bag the knife and cuff Hudson."

Angel nodded his head. As he clasped the cuffs on Hudson, he shifted. Angel put them in place and stepped back.

Hudson's head lolled to the side as he forced his eyes open. "What the fuck?" he said, trying to make his words come out. His tongue was thick in his mouth. "Why am I cuffed?"

Dixon walked up and grabbed his shoulder, helping him into a sitting position. "We found you on the floor with a bloody knife in your hand. You have the right to have your attorney present. You also may remain silent."

This made little sense. Someone had attacked him. "No, you don't understand. Is Mac okay?"

"She has a nasty cut and a bump on the head, but otherwise she looks okay," Dixon said.

Mac spoke up from behind him. "Hon, are you okay?" Her voice sounded distant and slurred.

"I don't think so. They said I had a knife in my hand, and they think I hurt you. Are you hurt?" Hudson asked again, worry laced through his voice.

"Yeah." She shook her head and looked down at the red marks on her wrist, and the blood seeping through the sheet on her stomach. "My vision is hazy, and so is my memory. I have little bits of what might have happened, but I think I have something in my system." Mac looked at the medic. "Can you run a tox screen on me and Hudson? It's possible the assailant injected us with something."

"Mac," Dixon said, "is it possible Hudson did this to you? He could have lost his temper and tried to hurt you. It would have been nothing for him to overpower you and strap you to the bed."

"That's not what happened," Mac said with venom in her voice.

"Then what happened?" Dixon shot back.

"I don't know, but I know that didn't. I remember singing to myself in the kitchen, and then the back of my head exploded like…" She thought about it for a moment. "Like something hard hit me. Frying pan, baseball bat, something."

"And then what?" Dixon asked.

"Then I think I remember waking tied to the bed at some point. Someone was here, but everything is hazy, like there's a weird film over it."

"Can you tell me who was here?" Dixon asked, making a point not to look at Hudson.

"It wasn't Hudson. He wasn't even here. He'd gone to court, couldn't have been him."

Dixon turned to face Hudson. "I'm sorry, but until we can process the evidence, we're going to have to retain you. I'm not convinced you're guilty, but evidence needs to be reviewed before we can make a determination. Do you understand?"

"Yes, sir. Please call my lawyer and let him know what happened." He shook his head, trying to clear the cobwebs as the room tilted around him, and he wanted to tilt with it. "Can you keep me on base?" Hudson asked.

"For the moment, yes. For now, we have jurisdiction over this incident. I'll keep you in our facility for now, but you understand you will need to be confined while we sort this out," Dixon said.

"Yes, sir." He did his best to help as Sergeant Angel struggled to help him to his feet. As he got up, Angel patted him down per protocol. He found a small bulge in Hudson's front pocket. When he pulled it out, he showed it to his commander.

"That's not mine," Hudson blurted out, knowing it was what every suspect said when caught with an illegal substance. He only assumed they'd planted it to nail his coffin closed.

"Sir, let the record show a small bag of white powder was found on Master Sergeant Hudson during his arrest for the assault of Master Sergeant McGregor and Staff Sergeant Landry."

An officer in the room stepped forward and photographed the small bag in the palm of Angel's hand.

Hudson hung his head as they walked him toward the door. Mac stared after him, unable to speak until she choked out, "Love you."

FORTY-FIVE

MAC LAY BACK on the bed and closed her eyes while the medic treated the long gash on her stomach. It wasn't deep enough to need stitches, but it would leave a nasty scar. "I need you to lie still," he told her as he placed little butterfly bandages to hold the wound together. "We're going to transport you to the hospital so a doctor can inspect. It looks like you're suffering from a mild concussion, and they're going to want to conduct a forensic medical examination," he explained in a soothing voice. He moved to her head and ran his fingers along her skull, and she flinched, pulling away. "You have a pretty nasty contusion back here."

"Tox screen," Mac whispered.

"What? Sorry."

"Can you pull a vial of my blood? We need to find out what's in my system." She turned her head to Dixon. "Sir, can you order a tox screen for Hudson and the sergeant outside?"

"What makes you so sure you have something in your system?"

"It reminds me of a case I had." She paused, trying to clear her brain. "Client charged with vehicular manslaughter. Witnesses saw her run from a bar, her top ripped, and she was screaming. The guy chasing her ran in front of her car. She hit the gas and slammed her car and the guy into the side of the bar. He died on impact. At the hospital..." Mac took in a long breath. "At the hospital, she woke cuffed to the bed. Couldn't remember anything, said her tongue was thick and everything was hazy. I'm experiencing the same thing now. Run a fucking tox screen."

"What did she have in her system?" Dixon asked.

"It dissolved by the time they thought to test her," Mac said.

The medic helped her sit up. "Sir, can we clear the room while McGregor gets dressed?"

"Of course," Dixon said, heading for the door.

Mac waited while the rest of the men, including the medic, cleared the room. The rape kit at the hospital would be unpleasant. She held the hand of a good friend as she endured the procedure. Her friend cried the entire time. Mac walked out into the hall where she found Dixon waiting for her. "Mac, you're both going to the hospital. Sergeant Angel will ride with you so you don't discuss any of the details. Are we clear?"

"Yes, sir. Thank you for allowing us to go together."

"Hudson is in a lot of trouble. Are you sure you don't want to distance yourself from him?" Dixon asked.

"Sir, he didn't do any of this. I swear to you, he'd rather cut off his own arm than hurt me. Someone else is behind this, and I intend to find out who."

"Get to the hospital and we'll take care of the investigation. Put your trust in law enforcement. No one wants Hudson to go down if he's not guilty."

"Yes, sir." After watching many of her clients get railroaded over the years and only half-assed investigations being done, she had little faith in the investigative skills on or off base. No one cared about this more than her.

She allowed herself to be led out and into the waiting ambulance. Hudson had one hand handcuffed to a metal bar in the back of the ambulance and an ice pack on the side of his head.

"How are you holding up?" she asked, not able to look him in the eyes.

"I would never hurt you," he said in a soft voice.

"I never thought you would. I have no idea how to stop this. Who's behind it? It's lingering in the back of my brain but won't come forward. The entire night is like a distant dream that I can't make out. If I could bring those memories back, then I could stop this," Mac said, cradling her head as she sat on the cot.

"I don't want you doing anything. Let them help you and maybe we can work through it together if they allow you to visit me once I'm back in a cell."

A tear slipped down Mac's cheek. "This is all so horrible. Why would someone want to do this to us? What would they have to gain?"

"I have no idea, but what I do know," he said, reaching out to touch her knee. "What I'm sure of is you need to go into hiding. Get away from me and Fairchild until this is over. I can't make it through this if you're in danger, or worse if…" He couldn't finish the sentence.

"I'm not going anywhere, and I'm not about to leave you," she said, squeezing his hand.

Once they arrived at the hospital, they handcuffed Hudson to a hospital bed and wheeled him in for his examination. She watched them take him down the hall. He didn't resist and did everything the orderly asked him to.

"Hi, you must be Evelyn. I'll be your nurse today. You can call me Susan," a young blond woman said as she stepped up into the ambulance. "I need you to come with me so we can look at you."

"Why the wheelchair?" Mac asked, looking at the chair parked right outside.

"Protocol," Susan said, moving her shoulders up and down.

Mac climbed out of the ambulance, holding onto the side door so she wouldn't fall as her brain shifted. There was something wrong. "Susan, did they tell you I may have some kind of drug in my system?"

"Yes, first we'll draw your blood and then we'll take a close look at the rest of you."

"Um, I don't think the assailant raped me," Mac said, sounding unconvincing to her own ears.

"That may be, but we have to check. Evidence has to be collected."

Mac understood, but she still didn't want to go through the examination. Susan took her into the room and gave her a gown to change into. When she was done, Susan bagged her clothes. The doctor walked in while Susan was taking Mac's vitals and drawing her blood, her silvery-white hair pulled back and away from her face. "Hello young lady, I'm Doctor Irving. How are you?"

Mac gave her a quizzical look. "I've been better," she said, trying to crack a smile, but it was lopsided.

"I bet," Irving said, smiling at her. "Now, I'm going to take a look at you. We'll start with a head-to-toe exam, including a scrape under your nails. Then we'll move to the vaginal exam. Do you have any questions before we start?"

"No," Mac whispered.

"Okay, tell me if you need a break."

Irving ran her hands along every inch of Mac's body, taking care to check the contusion on her head. Susan ran swabs under her nails and cleaned and redressed the wound along her stomach. Mac closed her eyes as the doctor finished and began the second part of the exam. When she did, little images flashed in front of her eyes. Strapped to the bed, a woman standing over her, she was talking, but Mac couldn't make out what she was saying. The woman was touching her, running her hands over her body, but they weren't normal hands, they were like rubber. The woman's face was a blur, but it was a female. Her memory jumped and a short, fat man was staring down at her with a knife in his hands and a mask over his face. He cut her.

CHAPTER
FORTY-SIX

GENNAVIE WAS HUMMING to herself in the kitchen of her borrowed home when her phone rang. Joseph, her Seattle plaything, popped up on her caller ID.

"Yes, my pet," she said as a way of greeting.

"Mistress, can you come visit me?"

"I told you it might be a while." She liked to make them wait. It intensified their want and gave her even more leverage.

"But I have information for you, but not over the phone. It's about Vincent."

She suspected he wouldn't discuss it over the phone because he wanted to be with her, but she was okay with it. Now that Hudson was back in prison with more charges against him than he could deal with, she could move forward with her plans. There was no way she was going to allow Mac the pleasure of keeping Hudson with her.

It wouldn't be long now. Everything was coming together so perfectly. The bonus of being able to fuck with Mac was too enjoyable. Touching her soft skin and watching her respond in her drugged state had done things to Gennavie she hadn't experienced in a long time. What was it about Mac that turned her on so much but also made her want to destroy the woman? Destruction was the only option, but it had been tantalizing to touch and play. Mac's body was taut and muscular in a soft, feminine way responding when she ran her hands down her soft, round hips and between her legs. Gennavie shuddered, thinking about the experience.

Visiting Joseph would do her good. She needed the release. Packing up her things, she went out, dropping them in the passenger seat of her car. Four and a half hours later, she pulled up to Joseph's house, anticipating the torture she was planning to deliver. Walking to the door, she wore a long coat and a sheer dress underneath, hugging every curve. He opened the door before she could knock. "Well, hello my pet. Are you happy to see me?"

"Um, yes mistress." He stepped back so she would come in. His beady little rodent eyes wouldn't meet hers.

Stepping into the house, she slammed the door shut behind her. "Joseph, what are you not telling me?"

He stepped back from her. "I failed you, my mistress. You told me to protect Vincent, but they retaliated against him last night for the awful thing he did with the pipe. I wasn't on shift, but they hurt him bad. He's going to live, but he's in the infirmary with several stab wounds, and they…"

"What did they do to him, my pet?" she asked, moving closer, placing her hands on his face and forcing him to look at her.

"They gang-raped him. It was brutal. According to one of the nurses, they ripped him down there." He looked down at himself and pointed. "And attached a wire to his junk. It didn't cut all the way through, but it will be a long time before he is, um, normal again, if he ever is." The fire flashed across Gennavie's green eyes, and he took a step back from her. "I'm sorry," he whimpered as her hand cracked across his bare chest, leaving a welt with long scratches from her fingernails.

She took several deep breaths, knowing it would do her little good to destroy this man. He still had his purpose, and she needed him to deliver a message to Vincent to tell him her plan was coming together. The last thing she needed was for Vincent to give up on her. She needed a little more time and some release. "You did your best."

"You mean," he said, with a surprised look on his face, "you'll forgive me?"

"Yes, my pet. I need you to give Vincent a precise message for me. Do you think you can do it without fucking it up?"

"Yes, mistress, anything for you."

She told him what needed to be said and made him repeat it several times. When she first told him, his eyes grew wide, but then he relaxed the more she made him repeat it. Once he was done and had it verbatim, she smiled. "Okay, now you may get ready."

He scampered off down the hall, and she tried to keep the thought of a mutilated Vincent out of her mind. It would sure be a pity if Vincent wasn't able to perform for her. Her mind went back to the mind-blowing sex they had after their first murder together. The wetness between her legs as her body responded. Time for stress relief, she thought as she followed Joseph to the back room. He was there, naked on the bed, waiting for her.

Everything started out fine. Strapping his hands to the bed, she whipped him like she had before, hitting the same scars she'd left on his buttocks the last time they played. Baring her teeth, she started whipping harder as he cried out. The excitement engulfed her senses. Her primal, animalistic need to cause harm, do damage, to make him hurt the same way she did after hearing what happened to Vincent left her feeling unhinged.

"Please stop," he screamed, but she wouldn't stop. Large gashes formed on his back. She moved to the other side and whipped him again, leaving large marks in the opposite direction. He twisted around to shield his backside from her blows. His hands twisted in a strange pretzel when she pounced on top of him. "Please no," he begged. But he was hard, and he wanted her. Her mind went blank. She pressed forward, pushing her whip into his neck as he thrashed from side to side, trying to buck her off him. It was no use; she was a wild animal and couldn't stop even if she wanted to.

Over an hour later, Joseph was close to death, lying in a bloody pile of human waste. This wasn't supposed to happen. Now she would have to find a new informant. Someone who would deliver the message to Vincent. She stormed from the house, livid with herself for losing control. Dammit, it was all Mac's fault. If it wasn't for that little bitch, everything would be fine.

CHAPTER
FORTY-SEVEN

MAC RETURNED from the hospital to find her temporary housing swarming with Security Forces and investigators from the Office of Special Investigations.

Dixon stood out in the yard waiting for her when one of his troops dropped her off. "Hi, Mac. What did the doc say?"

"I'll live. We should get the tox screen back in the next few hours. She put a rush on it. Other than that, I feel like a train wreck. How close are they to being done?"

"I'm sorry Mac, but you can't stay here. When they're done, I'll take you someplace safe. Stanton and I will be the only ones who have your location."

"How is Hudson?" Mac asked.

"He cleared medical and is being booked into confinement. I've talked with the FBI. After a lot of negotiations, they've agreed to leave him on base for now, in case there is something to this conspiracy theory thing."

"What do you mean, in case?" Mac said, her shoulders tense.

"I deal in facts, not in a phantom person who's planting evidence. That's not how this works. I am an open-minded man, and I'm willing to concede someone is after you. Hudson was in prison when someone shot at you, and we may prove he was still working through the process at the jail during Landry's attack."

"How is Sergeant Landry?"

"Minor damage to his larynx, but the doc assured me he would make a full recovery," Dixon said.

"Was he able to remember anything?"

"No, but I'll engage again once his mind clears. He wasn't making much sense when I tried to question him earlier."

"Will you allow me to visit Hudson before you take me wherever it is I'm going?" Mac asked, melting into the seat.

"I think we can arrange it," Dixon said as one of his men walked out of the house.

"Sir, I think you should come look."

"What do you have for me, Sergeant Angel?" Dixon asked, looking back at Mac, who followed him into the house.

"Sir, this guy is good. We didn't find a print, fiber, or anything else except for…" He paused long enough to lift the sheet on the side of the bed. The commander and Mac both knelt. "It appears the assailant might have been waiting under the bed until Hudson left. No telling how long he was under there, but it appears he might have been waiting for a while."

"How do you know it wasn't Hudson playing some kind of sick prank?" Dixon asked.

"Size, sir," Angel said. "Look at the outline in the dust. Someone was lying in this spot and then slid out from under the bed. If it had been Hudson, the dust would have been disturbed for the entire length of the bed, but here it was only…" He grabbed a measuring tape from his bag and took the length. "This person couldn't have been taller than five foot four to five five. Hudson is at least a foot taller, if not more. I'm not sure he would fit under."

Dixon stood at his full height. "Good work, Angel. Document the scene and make sure you take excellent photographs before anyone disturbs anything."

"Already done, sir."

"Very well. Is there anything else? Did you find anything in the kitchen used to hit Mac over the head?"

"No sir, but I think a pan might be missing from the kitchen. No telling, with this being temporary housing, but most sets have a medium-sized frying pan. Under the cabinet, we found a small skillet and a large one, but nothing in the middle."

"Very well, document everything and put your report on my desk by COB," Dixon said, turning to Mac and pointing toward the front door.

She had remained quiet the entire time, taking everything in. At least some evidence showed Hudson wasn't responsible, but she didn't know if some dust bunnies under the bed would be enough. Then she thought about her and Hudson's activities earlier and shivered, wondering if the guy was under the bed while they made love. The sensation that they weren't alone the entire time crept through her mind again. Anger coursed through every inch of her body at the violation of privacy.

Mac followed Dixon out to the front lawn. "Sir, I would like to talk to Hudson prior to going anywhere. There's something I need to discuss with him."

"I can't have the two of you getting your stories straight," he said, crossing his arms. "As you well know, this is an open investigation and allowing the two of you to collaborate will not be possible."

"Sir, I assure you we aren't collaborating about anything except maybe to find out who's doing this to us. I only need five minutes alone with him. If you'd like, you can send Stanton in with me so he can monitor the conversation. No talking about the case against Hudson. You have my word, sir."

He stayed silent for a moment, mulling over her proposition. "McGregor, I'm not questioning your integrity, but you have a skewed view of the situation. I suppose it wouldn't hinder the investigation as long as a third party is present. I'll send Stanton with you so long as you promise to allow him to take you to a safe place as soon as you're done."

"Agreed, sir. Thank you for protecting Hudson on base and not dropping him back in with the wolves."

"Go, Mac, before your time is up. If someone is after you, it may not be safe even in the Security Forces building."

Stanton pulled up and smiled at Dixon.

"Thanks, sir," she said, walking to Stanton's car. When she climbed into the passenger seat, the realization hit her for the first time: she might put him in danger. His beautiful wife and kids slipped through her mind. She only needed a few minutes with Hudson. It would be time for her to distance herself and go to work. This shit needed to end. It was one thing to go after her, but something else to go after the people she cared about.

STANTON AND MAC walked into the Security Forces building. It was not the first time they had been there together, but these circumstances had never crossed Mac's mind until today. In the past, it had been to visit clients. The first time she met Hudson seemed like yesterday. They were at Security Forces to meet with their client, a young airman accused of killing his wife in base housing. They found him covered in her blood and most people thought he was guilty, except for Hudson. The man she now loved with every fiber of her being didn't have to help, but he did. He helped her track down the man who murdered multiple women on and off base and saved one of his troops from sitting in confinement for the rest of his life.

Now Hudson was sitting in a tiny cell of his own with no one to protect him. At least he wasn't back downtown. She'd hit her limits and wasn't going to wait for this asshole to start the next round. This was going to stop. They led Stanton and Mac into the same interrogation room where they met with the young Airman Johnson after they found his wife murdered in base housing last year. Ten minutes later, they led Hudson in with his hands cuffed behind him. The confinement NCO acknowledged them, attached Hudson's cuffs to the table, and left.

"Hi hon, what did the doctor say?" Hudson asked, trying to plaster a smile on his face.

"I'm fine. I don't have a ton of time. I'm going away for a little while, but I need you to be safe and trust me." Hudson remained silent. An entire conversation passed between the two of them without saying a word. "Stanton, can you work with Hudson's attorney to make sure he stays here and doesn't end up back downtown?"

"I'll do everything I can, but they'll fight us on it," Stanton said.

"Will I be able to reach you?" Hudson asked.

"Not for a while, but I'll figure out a way to send word. I have Bartz's information, but no news is good news. If you don't hear from me, it means I'm making progress."

Stanton furrowed his brow. "What are you talking about here, Mac? Where do you intend on going?"

"I'll explain everything later. We aren't sure who we can trust. I'm positive our conversation is being recorded." She nodded her head to the small black dome in the room's corner.

Hudson cleared his throat. "Stay away from her. You know it's not worth the price."

"I will," she said, touching his hand knowing he was referring to Reina. Stanton looked at both, confused, as they got up to leave. "Take care, love, I'll be in touch soon," she said and walked out the door. The only way to make this stop was to exonerate Hudson. If she found evidence that cast enough reasonable doubt to trigger his release, then they would hunt whoever was doing this to them together.

One thing at a time. First Daniel's case and then the defense attorney. She would have to leave the drug charges and assault charges from this afternoon to Bartz. Once she and Stanton were outside the building, she stopped him. They could plant listening devices in his car. She may be paranoid, but she'd rather that than fail. "I'm going to disappear for a while. Don't tell anyone where I've gone for my safety and yours. Tell Daniels you have me tucked away in a safe house somewhere."

"Where are you going, Mac?" he asked with concern in his eyes.

"I'm going to solve these cases one at a time. If I'm sitting in a house somewhere hiding, things will get worse until I figure out what he wants. If he wanted me dead, I'd already be. He wants something else, and I intend to find out what it is."

"Anything I can do?" Stanton asked.

"Keep my secret and I'll be in touch." She was about to climb into the passenger seat when she paused. "If he thinks you're hiding me, he may come for you. Please take precautions for you and your family."

"You have nothing to worry about."

Mac stayed on base that night, gathering her things and making reservations for the next morning. She used an alias from when she was a kid. Her dad set it up for her to keep her and her sister under the radar. They traveled like that until they became adults. Once grown, they tucked Mac into the military under her father's name and her sister and dad started working for the three-letter agencies and stayed under the radar. Lola worked with the FBI, but her dad went into a black hole called the CIA. They didn't know where he was for the longest time. When their mother crossed the line and kidnapped Lola's daughter, he came out of hiding. Mac hoped her dad and maybe her uncle, the police chief in El Paso, Texas, would help her out. The last person she wanted to ask for help from was her mother.

The price for asking Reina for help was too high. If she did, it would cost her more than she was willing to give. Anything would be worth saving Hudson, even if she couldn't be with him.

CHAPTER
FORTY-NINE

Holloman Air Force Base, New Mexico

MAC LANDED IN EL PASO, Texas, and picked up a car, paying cash for everything. She knew it was impossible not to leave a trail in this digital world where there were cameras on every corner. Every time she interacted with someone or made a transaction, even in cash, it could put her in danger. She needed to find her answers and return to Fairchild before her stalker could figure out where she was. Then maybe she'd be a step ahead of him instead of reacting. He seemed to always be in the driver's seat, and she was tired of it.

Two hours later, she checked into a local hotel sitting off the main road. Alamogordo, New Mexico, wasn't big, with a population of over thirty-one thousand people, and it was important to only notify a few people she was in town. The place she was staying in wasn't anything glamorous, but it served her purpose. A semi-uncomfortable bed with furnishings dating back to the early seventies, with an old box television sitting on a rickety stand threatening to tumble at any moment. It provided her with a place where she could have a clear view if someone came down the road and no one could find her. It was the precise reason she chose the place. The long-deserted road left no place for anyone to hide.

She hoped the man coming for her didn't have access to the Security Forces database and could look up her profile showing her entering Holloman Air Force Base. It was something she couldn't avoid, but still sat in the back of her mind as she walked into the Area Defense Counsel's office to visit Jax.

"Hi, why the hell didn't you tell me you were coming?" Jax said, throwing open the door after Mac knocked. Mac explained her reasoning as she followed Jax into the office. "So, what you're telling me is you have a psycho trying to kill you?"

"I don't think so," Mac said, rolling her neck from side to side and trying to make her body release the tension from the day of traveling. "I think if he wanted me dead, I would be dead. He wants something else, and I need to figure out what. The only place I have to start is Daniels' murder case. Can I look at the case file?"

Jax walked back to her office. "The base didn't maintain jurisdiction of the case because the murder occurred in town. All I have are the preliminary reports you've already seen. They didn't bother to investigate the woman seen with Daniels prior to his murder. She kept a low profile and never looked at any of the cameras, but one paralegal in the office had a conversation with her when he was checking her in for legal help. He said she was hot and flirtatious. If Hudson was our client, I would sit Sergeant Thota down with a sketch artist and throw a firestorm of reasonable doubt all over the case. Of course, this woman is not a concern for the locals who solely focused on Hudson. Their theory is a woman couldn't do such a thing. In their chauvinistic minds, a guy is the only one who can be this violent."

"Maybe I can get them to listen. Where can I find Thota?"

"Be careful. He was fond of Daniels. We all were, but Thota was worried about getting involved. He has orders out of here. Orders he's been waiting on for almost two years. They stationed his wife and daughter at Hickam Air Force Base in Hawaii. The Air Force separated them the entire time, and from what I understand, they are having some real financial issues with the travel back and forth and having to pay for two separate households. Keeping one place going is hard enough, let alone two," Jax explained, handing over Thota's address and phone number.

"I appreciate it. I'll be kind and won't involve him unless I have to."

"How long are you staying?" Jax asked, handing Mac a cup of coffee.

"Not sure. Long enough to figure this thing out and exonerate Hudson. Please don't let people know I'm here."

"Well, that's obvious," Jax said, running her hand through her short blond hair. "What can I do to help?"

"Only eyes and ears. If anyone comes looking for me or starts asking questions, I need to know."

"Can do. Where are you staying?"

"The less intel you have, the better. You can reach me at my usual number if you need to get ahold of me," Mac said.

"Isn't that dangerous? A half-assed hacker can track a cell phone."

"I have it forwarded to a burner bouncing off multiple cell towers. My sister set me up with the tech. I'm not sure how it works, but she assures me no one will track me."

"Cool, how's Lola?" Jax asked.

"She's good and working to find a video of the mystery woman for me. If anyone can, it's her. I gotta go, but I'll be in touch. Tell me if anyone comes hunting."

Jax leaned in to give her a hug at the door. "Keep your head down, Mac. If there's anything I can do, don't hesitate."

"Thanks," Mac said, and was back outside. She jumped in her rental car, switched locations toward the back of the base, and called Lola.

"Hey sis, have you checked your SAT phone yet?" Lola said by way of greeting.

"No, what do you have?"

"So far, I have inconclusive video footage of the same dark-haired woman," Lola said. "It might be usable to cast reasonable doubt if you provide footage of this woman leaving Daniels' house on the day of his murder. I can only catch glimpses of her, but she matches the general description. I'm also putting together a video chronology of Hudson's movements on the day in question."

"You're amazing. Thank you. Anything on Captain Anika Wilson, the defense attorney?"

"Same. No one saw Hudson because he didn't leave his house until it was time to catch his flight, but this situation leaves him with no alibi. I'm working on tracking the whereabouts of Anika instead. She started her morning with yoga, but then I lost her. The only thing out of the ordinary so far is the corner of a Jeep across from the studio, but I couldn't get the license plate. I'm still working on it."

"At least it's something. Keep digging and I'll be in touch."

"Are you in place?" Lola asked.

"Yeah."

"Stay safe and say hi to them for me," Lola said, and then giggled.

Mac loved how she found fun in almost anything. "Will do. Talk soon."

CHAPTER
FIFTY

SERGEANT THOTA LIVED on the outskirts of Alamogordo, close to her hotel. Mac hadn't called ahead because she didn't want to give him a chance to disappear. If she needed him to help her identify the woman, she'd have a great place to start. Even if the mystery woman wasn't responsible for Daniels' murder, maybe she would be a key witness for Hudson's case.

She walked up to the small one-story stucco house and knocked on the door. At first, no one answered, so she knocked again. A man's voice from the inside said, "Just a sec." When the door flung open, it wasn't Thota. Instead, Technical Sergeant Sommers stood in front of her with a scowl on his face.

"What the hell are you doing here?" Mac blurted out in surprise.

"I fucking live here, and you're the last person I want to see. I thought I'd seen the last of you."

"Well, I'm back. I thought you lived with your girlfriend on base. Weren't you two supposed to get married or something?"

"Yeah, until you came along and had to drop an atomic bomb on my relationship. You couldn't leave well enough alone. You had to open your big mouth."

"I said nothing," Mac said, flailing her arms in frustration. "I've never met your girlfriend."

"Ex-girlfriend, thanks to you. Once she found out about you, she decided I was the devil. She took it upon herself to drain my account and throw all my stuff out onto the front lawn. I may have been out of line, but did you have to destroy me over it?"

"Out of line? You've got to be kidding me. We were at the gym in a public place. I thought you were my friend. A good sparring partner, someone who would have my back, but no, you had to take it too far. You shouldn't have pinned me down and tried to assault me." Mac turned to leave. Before she could react, he grabbed her by the arm, propelling her body inside. It didn't register when he slipped the door shut behind her as she caught her balance until it was too late. His fist swung hard, nailing her in the ear. Her skull rocked to the side and stars materialized in front of her eyes. Grabbing ahold of the wall, she stepped back, trying to steady herself.

"Assault you? I didn't assault you, you arrogant bitch. I tried to kiss you. Now you're going to find out what an assault is like." He lunged forward, but this time Mac was ready. Stepping to the side, taking advantage of his forward momentum, she slammed her knee into his chin, knocking him to the floor.

A skilled fighter in his own right, he rolled to the side and was back on his feet, wiping blood from the corner of his mouth. His meaty arms reached out for her, but she dodged to the side, dropping low and coming up on the other side. She pivoted and swung her leg in a practiced roundhouse kick to the side of his head when he grabbed her leg mid-air and flung her into the wall. Her back cracked as she hit, compounding the bruise that was already there.

Lying still while she regained her bearings, she waited for him to approach. When he did, she reached up between his legs, grabbed onto his family jewels, and squeezed. He dropped his thick body forward, afraid to move. "Stop this shit or I'll rip them off," Mac growled through clenched teeth. Her head was still buzzing from the impact.

He held up both hands. "I give," he said in a pleading voice. She released her hand and got back to her feet when he punched her hard, making her cheek explode in pain. "You don't know when to quit, do you?" he said, throwing her to the floor and pushing his weight on top of her. His entire two-hundred-plus pounds sank into her stomach with his enormous arms holding her in place. His strong cologne and sweat assaulted her nose as he pressed his body down on hers, pinning her to the floor. Twisting from back and forth, she tried to pull free, but it was no use. He was at least sixty pounds heavier than her and twice as muscular.

Forcing her mind to calm, she stopped moving.

"There you go. That's my girl. If you'd let me have my way the first time, it wouldn't have come to this. It's your fault. When a man has needs, you comply. Do you understand?" He pushed forward and licked the side of her jawline.

It took every ounce of her control not to pull away. Regulating her breathing, she relaxed her hands and stopped pressing against his as she sank her body into the floor. "You win," she said, rolling her head to the side. "Do what you want."

A sickly smile crawled across his face as he wrapped one hand around both her wrists, trying to keep her pinned in place, and started working his sweatpants down around his knees. She waited while he exposed himself, dropping his pants and boxers down around his ankles. When he shifted his weight, his grip released on her wrists when he tried to shimmy her pants down. She allowed him to grab hold of the side of her leggings. When she sensed he was off balance, she twisted hard, slamming her full weight into his body and knocking him off her. He rolled with his pants still around his ankles, his small penis going soft at the assault.

He scrambled to his feet, trying to pull his pants up when she balled up her fist, thrusting an uppercut into the soft cartilage of his nose. He screamed out in pain as the door flung open.

A tall, thin blond man stood in the doorway, taking in the scene. Mac assumed it was Sergeant Thota. At first, she thought he'd defend his roommate, but instead, Thota looked at Sommers and shook his head. "You are such a colossal asshole," he told his roommate. Thota stepped into the house and shut the door, pressing his hand out in front of him. "Who might you be?" he asked, pulling Mac behind him and placing himself between her and Sommers.

"I'm Master Sergeant McGregor," she said, still catching her breath.

"The McGregor?" Thota asked, and turned to Sommers. "You have to be the stupidest man alive. Do you have any idea who she is?"

Sommers looked from Thota to Mac and back again. "Yeah, I used to work with this bitch," he said, still seething and holding his nose.

"Well dumbass, you not only assaulted a higher-ranked non-commissioned officer, which violates at least three articles of the Uniform Code of Military Justice, but on top of that she's taken down three to four serial killers and has friends in high places. You're destroyed if she presses charges against you. Guess what, asshole? I'm not going to bail you out this time. You've crossed too many lines."

"But—" Sommers said.

"But nothing," Thota responded. "Pull your fucking pants up and get out before I call the cops." He turned to Mac. "That is, unless you want me to make the call. Then I'm happy too," Thota said.

Sommers looked at her with wide eyes.

"Another time," she said, and Sommers relaxed. "Right now, I need a bag of ice, some Tylenol, and a little of your time." She faced Sommers pinning him with her eyes until he hiked up his pants, grabbed his keys and wallet off the table and walked out.

"Anything," Thota said, walking toward the kitchen. Mac followed, beginning to relax now that Sommers was out of the house. Once in the kitchen, he walked to the freezer, fished out a bag of peas, and handed it to her along with a glass of water and some Motrin. "Sorry, all I have is vitamin M. They give this stuff out like candy at the base clinic."

"It'll do the trick. Thank you."

Sommers stomped around the house but avoided the kitchen. The front door slammed shut, and Mac relaxed.

"So, what can I do for you?" Thota asked.

Mac gave him a quick rundown of the events and asked him to kindly keep her visit to himself. The fewer people who knew, the better. She suspected Sommers would keep his mouth shut without her having to ask. "One of my contacts tells me you had a conversation with the same woman who was last seen with Daniels. Can you tell me anything about her?"

"I can't be involved. I'm sorry," he began.

Mac held her hand up. "I'll keep your name out of this. I need to identify her in case she's witnessed something. Someone set my fiancé up for murder, and I need to find something to clear him." She sounded desperate to her own ears, but she didn't care. "I want to start a family with this man. He's innocent. I need to prove it."

Thota paused for a moment. "I would do anything for my wife, which is why I can't be involved. But I will tell you what little I know as long as you promise to keep my name out of it."

"You have my word," Mac said.

"I'm not sure if it'll help since it later came back. Her information belonged to someone else. A dead woman. When I entered it into the system, it didn't flag her information. She gave me the proper address and everything," Thota recalled.

"You help hundreds of clients each week. Is there anything that stood out about this woman? Anything at all that can help me track her down."

"She was the most beautiful woman I'd seen in person. She had this dark chestnut hair and chocolate-brown eyes, high cheekbones, and well…" he said, looking down. "I don't mean for this to be creepy and well, I'd never think of cheating on my wife, but she was the type of woman most guys would give their right nut to be with. I mean, she exuded sexual energy like no other woman I've come across. Something was exciting about her, but off. I don't know how else to describe it."

"What do you mean, off? Like she was crazy or something?" Mac asked.

"Not crazy like the guy downtown who talks to paintings and other inanimate objects. More like dangerous. Almost like a captivating black panther a person would be drawn to watch and maybe reach out to touch—until the elegant creature turned to attack. I have no way to describe her other than enchanting and breathtaking."

"Do you have any reason to believe her natural hair and eye color weren't brown?" Mac asked, thinking of the only person she had ever met who fit the description.

"Why do you ask?"

"A hunch."

"Could have been. I mean, she looked a lot like you, except for the porcelain skin."

CHAPTER
FIFTY-ONE

SHE'D CHECKED EVERYWHERE. There was no sign of Mac, and it had been over forty-eight hours. Gennavie stalked the living room, trying to figure out her next move. She put out quiet feelers to everyone she thought might have intel. Hudson was still sitting in military confinement. The plan had been to shake things up and have him transferred back to the downtown jail, but what was the point if she couldn't watch Mac suffer? Only one person could tell her where she was, and it was about time she paid her a visit.

The next evening, she drove into Texas and checked into her hotel room near the Beaumont Federal Penitentiary. She would have flown but didn't want to leave a trace. If anyone discovered what she was up to, things would go wrong. As long as her alias for the prison worked, then she would have some answers and make sure the deal was still on.

Early the next morning, Gennavie waited in line and showed her fake credentials. As a blond, she was quite fetching, but also quite unrecognizable. It took an hour to process through security. One guard offered to pat her down on the way through, and she declined. When she walked into the visitors' room of the prison, she watched Mac's mother come out in handcuffs and sit at a table. Gennavie had never met her in person, but the pictures she'd looked at were not what stood in front of her. Prison had not been kind to this woman.

"It's about time you came to visit," Reina said.

"Things have been busy and not as smooth as we'd hoped."

"Are you any closer to bringing my daughter back to me so she can take the throne? I can't let my empire sink into a black hole while I'm in here," Reina complained.

"I am quite sure your empire would be fine with or without me, but I can deliver Mac as long as you keep your end of the bargain."

"You have nothing to worry about, my dear. How is Vincent doing these days?"

Gennavie dropped her voice and recounted what she knew about Vincent's condition. "I'm not sure if he can last. We have to get him out now," Gennavie said.

"I'll do no such thing until you convince Evelyn to agree to our terms. She has to be willing, otherwise it won't work. Is Hudson in place?"

"Who's Evelyn?" Gennavie asked with a confused look on her face.

"My daughter, you idiot. She lives in some fantasy world where her given name just isn't good enough. Now tell me about Hudson," Reina said.

"Of course. It took a little doing after he got himself released, but he's back in military confinement for now. When I return, I plan to have him thrown back into the much more violent civilian facility."

"You do that and stop screwing around. This is taking too long. The sooner Evelyn takes over, the sooner they can release me from this hell-hole and I'll be back where I belong."

"I need Vincent protected until we can pull him out of prison," Gennavie said, crossing her thin arms over her chest.

"It wasn't part of the deal. I agreed to make sure they release him if you convince my daughter to do what I want."

"Deal's change. I need to know Vincent is going to be safe and operational when he gets out before I make so much as another move."

"What is it with you and that little good-for-nothing? A woman with your looks could do so much better. Why don't you take Hudson for yourself once this is all over? He'd be your plaything and is much nicer to look at," Reina said.

"You may not understand, but Vincent does it for me. He's the only man I've ever met who gives me the power and control I crave." She slammed her hand down on the table. "Agree to protect him and make sure he gets the best medical care possible, and I'll convince Mac to beg you to let her do whatever you want her to."

The two women stared at each other for a long moment until Reina said, "Very well. But if you don't deliver, I will have Vincent executed."

Gennavie walked away from the meeting wondering if Reina was the reason, they had attacked Vincent, and why he was now in the infirmary. She wouldn't put it past the only woman who was more brutal than she. It was time to figure out what Mac is up to in New Mexico and get her to cooperate.

CHAPTER
FIFTY-TWO

MAC HUNG UP THE PHONE. She craved the sound of Hudson's voice but was afraid to call the confinement facility where he was being held. They recorded all calls going in and out of Security Forces, and she wasn't sure how connected her stalker was. All afternoon she'd been thinking of the description Thota provided. The description he gave only fit one person in her past.

Gennavie had natural red hair, but aside from that, she fit the description. She was also the most ruthless woman Mac had ever met, aside from her own mother. If Gennavie was after her, then she did, in fact, have a lot to worry about. Her mind was still cloudy surrounding the assault in temporary housing, but every time she closed her eyes, she sensed Gennavie. She wasn't one hundred percent sure because the same short, heavy-set man played somewhere in her memories. The drugs in her system came back as GHB, a popular date-rape drug having the inconvenient side effect of temporary amnesia. No matter how hard she tried, she couldn't remember what happened that night. It was just a lingering sensation tickling her subconscious that Gennavie was there.

How on earth had she gotten on base? Gennavie had warrants out for her arrest in connection with several murders in and around the Seattle area. Vincent, her boy toy, was facing the death penalty for some things they had done. The two left a long list of dead in their wake, one of which Mac was quite fond of. When she was working on the case, Vincent had murdered Alice. The young woman came forward to help Mac solve the case after Gennavie and Vincent had killed Alice's fiancé. Mac would never forget the promise she made to Alice's uncle Don. It was her first time notifying a family member of a death and she'd promised to take down the person or people responsible. She believed she would until Gennavie disappeared, never to be heard from again, until now.

She had just discussed the cases and what little she found out with Hudson's defense attorney, Aeddan Bartz. She liked him and was confident he would do everything to help Hudson out of this mess. As talented as Bartz was, the mounting evidence was hard to argue with. She sat down and made a list of what she had so far and what she still needed to figure out.

Lt. Col. Daniels' Case: Knife found with Hudson's prints. Planted behind a bush next to Daniels' house. No solid alibi for Hudson. Time of death window too wide. Discuss with medical examiner. A mysterious dark-haired woman with Daniels around the time of death. Matches the description of Gennavie minus hair and eye color. Interview neighbors to see if the local police have missed anything. Obtain leverage from Dad and Uncle. Flimsy motive of jealousy.

Capt. Anika Wilson's Case: Killed while Hudson's flight was delayed. No alibi. He stayed home. Had time to make it to Anika's house and back to the airport prior to the flight. Evidence planted under Hudson's bed. A pink thong, panty and hair belonging to Anika was confirmed through DNA. Possible break-in. Anonymous tip. Follow up with Joe Romero to see if any of the neighbors saw anything. No motive to kill.

Assault of Sgt. Landry/Me and Drug Charges: GHB in Landry's system and in mine. Inconclusive in Hudson's. Medical reported–large enough it may have left his system faster. Only remains in blood for up to eight hours. Tested six hours after arrest. They found a small bag of cocaine in Hudson's front pocket. Hudson's belt wrapped around Landry's neck. Fingerprints on the belt and inside the Humvee. Hudson admitted to going into the vehicle to check on Landry and loosened the belt to allow him to breathe. Hudson's prints were all over me and the bed we shared after earlier activity. They found no other prints, hair, or skin. They found a small silhouette in dust under the bed. Too small to be Hudson.

Mac reviewed the information again, making sure she missed nothing. If Gennavie was behind this, it wouldn't be long before permanent damage was done. Mac had to stop her and find out who her accomplice was. She needed to find what the Alamogordo police had against Hudson, other than the prints on the knife. That couldn't be it. They had to have more than that to charge him, didn't they? The planted evidence was damming.

She picked up her burner phone again and dialed her uncle.

"Hello," Uncle Lu bellowed into the phone.

"Hi Uncle Lu, it's Mac. How are you?"

"Hey young lady, I didn't recognize your number. How the hell are you? It's been awful quiet around here since you went back to Washington."

"I'm on a burner and I'm back in town on some unfortunate business. Is Dad still in town with you?"

"Yeah, the good-for-nothing stays in hiding for years and now he won't leave. He's moved in with me. Can you believe that?" Uncle Lu said, chuckling into the phone.

"That's great news. Would the two of you have time to meet? I need to stay under the radar. Someplace quiet."

"Are you okay?" Uncle Lu asked with concern in his voice.

"No, but as soon as I figure all this out I'll be doing well."

"You know your pops and I will do anything for you. How soon can you meet?"

"In about two hours. Can we hit up the place outside El Paso? You know, the one with the good burgers?"

"Sure, I'll grab your dad and meet you at 1700 hours. Be safe," he said and hung up the phone.

It took forever to make the long drive into El Paso. Her guard was up after the last time a crooked cop pulled her over. Uncle Lu had dealt with him, but she still wasn't sure how far her mother's reach went into his department. She had to keep a low profile, and a ticket giving away her location would not do her any good.

When she walked into the small café on the outskirts of town, she had to smile at the two men waiting for her. They both got up at the same time and sandwiched her into a warm hug. "It's good to see you too," she said, unable to wipe the smile from her face. It had only been a few short months since, but it felt like so much had happened since then.

They released her from their bear hugs and sat. "All right, young lady, spill it," her dad said. "What have you gotten yourself into this time?"

"It's not what I've gotten myself into. It's what's coming for us." She gave them a rundown of everything and her game plan to help Hudson.

"Well, holy shit, do you ever just have a dull moment?" Uncle Lu asked.

"I wish," she said, smiling. "I was looking forward to some quiet time with my new fiancé to plan the wedding."

"Wait a minute, when did that happen and why didn't he ask first?" Her dad looked hurt.

"This isn't the Dark Ages, Dad, and I'm a grown-ass woman. Did he need to ask for my hand?"

"I suppose not, but at least you could've told us," her dad argued.

"I would have, but they arrested him right after he proposed, and a lot happened since then," Mac said louder. They weren't hearing her. "Look, there will not be a wedding if we can't figure out how to release Hudson from prison. If he goes away for murder, you won't have to worry about knowing. Everything will go to shit." Mac hadn't meant to lash out. It wasn't their fault, but frustration and anger coursed through her.

"Okay, okay," Uncle Lu said. "Let's get some food in us and come up with a game plan."

CHAPTER
FIFTY-THREE

AFTER HER MEETING with Uncle Lu and her dad, she felt better. They had resolved nothing, but at least the two men agreed to help her. The next morning, she waited outside the Alamogordo police station for her dad and uncle to show up. They were running behind and she hoped it wouldn't anger the man they were meeting with. Another forty minutes passed before they pulled up in Uncle Lu's large Chevy truck. "What happened?" she asked, getting out as a way of greeting.

"Nice to see you too," her dad said, pulling her into a hug. "This guy," he said, pointing at Uncle Lu, "got a flat tire on our way over."

"Yeah, it took us forever to change it," Uncle Lu confirmed, showing his dirty hands.

"I appreciate you guys coming. Sorry you ran into trouble. Let's go find out if your friend is still willing to talk to us."

The McGregor clan walked through the doors into the small police station.

"Well, as I live and breathe, the McGregor brothers. I never thought I'd run into the two of you again." A woman with cropped blond hair who looked around Mac's dad and uncle's age came out from behind the plexiglass and gave them both a hug. She was in good shape for her age and much smaller than the two men.

"You too, Judi. How have you been?" Uncle Lu asked.

"Oh good, just working and hanging out with my grandbabies on the weekends," she said, and turned to Mac. "And who might this be?"

"This is Evelyn, my daughter," her dad said.

"No, can't be," Judi said. "I remember when she was just a little squirt. My my, haven't you grown into a beauty?"

Mac blushed at the compliment. "Thank you."

"So, what can I do you for?" Judi asked.

"We had a meeting with Steve, but I had a flat and we're way behind. Is he still available?" Uncle Lu asked.

"For the three of you, I'll make him available," she said, turning on her heels, heading back behind the plexiglass, and leaving them in the waiting room.

A few quick minutes later, a man with dark salt-and-pepper hair came out to retrieve them. But he looked much less happy about it. "Let's make this clear. I'm only seeing you because it's a professional courtesy."

"Oh, come on Steve, you can't still be mad," Uncle Lu said, extending his hand.

"After what your sorry ass did to my sister, you should be happy you're still breathing," Steve said, crossing his large arms over his chest.

"We were just kids. It was a lifetime ago," Lu argued.

"That may be, but you still broke her heart, and she never recovered."

Lu had dated Steve's sister when they were kids. Steve had been against it. He knew his sister was what most people would call fragile, and Lu was a bit of a wild card.

"She can't still be upset after all this time."

"You said you were going to marry her, you asshole. Now, what do I have the displeasure of helping you with today?"

Lu's shoulders dropped, relaxing at the change in subject. "We're here about a case under your jurisdiction. What can you tell us about the Daniels case?"

"I can't talk about an open investigation with a civilian," Steve said, nodding his head toward Mac and her father.

"I can vouch for them. They're helping with a related case I'm working on. What do you have?" Lu said.

"Fine, but if there's blowback, it won't be pretty for you. Come with me," Steve said, leading them back to his office. It was a small room with boxes stacked along all the walls. Mac wondered how he would find anything in here. Steve went behind his desk, opened one box, and pulled out a tan file. "It looks like we had a lead on a witness. A dark-haired woman was last seen with the deceased. We traced her back to the base legal office, but because of attorney-client privilege, we couldn't nail down any additional information on her." He flipped to the next page of the report. "According to this, my guys traced the last number Daniels called prior to his death, but it went straight to a disconnected burner phone. That's when we caught a break."

"What break?" Mac asked. "Did you find the woman?"

"Nope, we found the smoking gun. More to the point, the knife used to stab him. It had this guy's prints all over it. This Air Force guy had a beef with Daniels over some girl," Steve said.

"Who told you the motive was jealousy?" Mac asked.

Steve looked over at Lu, and Lu nodded his head. "We received an anonymous tip about the location of the knife. The lady that left the tip said she heard about how obsessive this Hudson guy was over his girl, and he killed Daniels because he thought Daniels was hitting on her."

"Do you have the name or any information from the person who called in the tip?" Mac asked, astonished.

"Like I said, anonymous. So, no, I have no information about her," Steve said, taking a defensive stance.

"Did it ever occur to you, the same woman last seen with Daniels was also the same woman who left the tip and planted the knife?" Mac said, raising her voice.

"Now listen here, young lady. You don't come into my police station telling me how to do my job," Steve said, raising his voice to match hers.

"Now, everybody calm down," Lu said. "Steve, is there anything else you can tell us about the case? Once you had the murder weapon, did your guys look any further?"

"Nope, no need. We had the Hudson fella dead to rights, and the judge agreed with us. The damn FBI got involved because he crossed state lines. So, don't go accusing me of not dotting my I's and crossing my T's. I did my damn job. Now what's this all about?" Steve asked, his face turning red.

Lu placed his hand on Mac's shoulder so she wouldn't respond. "We believe someone planted the knife. Similar evidence may have been planted in your suspect's home in Washington. We're chasing down leads."

"Well, I can't imagine how that's possible, but if anything surfaces, will you notify me? I'm not in the habit of sending the wrong man to prison," Steve said.

"No, you're not," Lu said. "We'll keep you posted."

MAC PARTED ways with her family. They headed back to El Paso. She appreciated their help, but the visit hadn't given her anything new except for a sinking sensation that all the investigative agencies involved weren't willing to look deeper to figure out what happened. Putting away a man who had no prior record and a stellar military career seemed to satisfy all parties. There had to be something more to work with.

Before she knew where she was going, she pulled up to Daniels' house. It sat unmoving and vacant, like someone had sucked the life right out. She'd been here in the past for Christmas parties and other events, when Daniels and his wife were still together. The house had been so full of life with his kids running about and everyone they worked with chatting about things. The memory brought a smile to her face, remembering how kind and supportive Daniels had been. He didn't deserve this, and she hated it if he'd died because of someone who was after her.

Pulling her tired body out of the car, she went to talk to the neighbors in case they had any information the cops didn't already have. The first house she came to was a stucco two-story that sat to the left of Daniels' house. If the person were home, they would have had the perfect view. She knocked on the door and stepped back so she didn't appear threatening. The door slung open to reveal a woman with tight pink curlers in her bright-red hair and her plump, short body in an oversized bathrobe. "What the hell do you want?"

"Um," Mac said, taking another step back. "Would you have a moment for me to ask you a few questions?"

"Are you one of them?"

"One of who?" Mac said, with a confused look on her face.

"One of his sluts. Are you here to collect his things? You can have him and his stupid stuff," she said, lunging forward.

Mac took another step back and held up her hands. "I'm not here about your husband. I don't know who you're talking about. I'd like to ask questions about the man who used to live across the street."

"I don't got nothing. I already told the cops that. Who the hell do you think you are coming here and messing with my morning? Damn cops are such an invasive species. They can't just leave well enough alone. Where were you when he hit me? You couldn't give me the time of day, but some high-level military guy gets whacked, and you guys are all over it like stink on shit."

"Ma'am, I'm sorry for what you've been through, but I'm not a cop and…" The woman scrunched her face into a strange expression, stepped back, and slammed the door in her face. It was one of the weirdest encounters she'd ever had.

Backing off the woman's porch, she took a different approach. Taking in the neighborhood, she spotted an elderly man on his front porch, rocking back and forth in a beautifully crafted rocking chair. Mac waved, and he waved back. *That's a good sign*, she thought and headed toward him.

"Good afternoon, sir. Do you have a few minutes?"

"Oh well, yes, I have all the time in the world. It's the gift called retirement. Come have a seat."

"My name is Mac. Can I ask you a few questions?"

"Sure, Mac. I must say, that's a strange name for a pretty lady, but who am I to judge? My grandson told me the other day one of his schoolmates wants to be an otter. The strangest things are going on these days."

"Interesting," Mac said. "My name is Evelyn, but everyone calls me Mac in the military. They like to give nicknames."

"How did you get yours?" he asked, scrunching up his wrinkles into what appeared to be a lopsided grin.

"My last name is McGregor, so after basic training I became Mac," she explained. "What's your name?"

"Oh, I'm George. No nickname, just George."

"It's nice to meet you, George," Mac said, settling into the comfortable rocker. "These are nice."

"Yeah, my son makes them from scratch. He's a woodworker. You went toe to toe with old Beatrice. I hope she wasn't too vicious. You'll have to excuse her behavior; she's been through a lot with that worthless husband of hers."

"Nothing I can't handle. How long have you lived here?"

"Oh, let me think. The wife and I moved here about twenty…" He stopped to think for a moment. "Goodness, it's been twenty-eight years now."

"Did you know Daniels? His house sits across the street and two doors down," she said, pointing to the one.

"Yes, he was a nice man. Such a shame what happened to him. The cops said it was some kind of jealousy thing. Never understood that one with all the fish in the sea."

"It may not have been that simple. Were you here on the day Daniels was murdered?"

"Yup, sure was. I like to keep an eye on things. This used to be a nice, safe neighborhood, but as of late there have been thugs coming around. Porch pirates steal things off people's front doors. Can you believe it? How ballsy or stupid do you have to be to come up to someone's house and steal their property?"

"I would have to say it's pretty stupid. Did you happen to see anyone coming or going in October before Daniels died?" Mac asked.

"Sure did, told the cops all about it but they didn't take down the information. All they wanted to know was whether I'd seen some big fella lurking around. I saw no such thing, but they kept trying to convince me I had like I'm some kind of senile old fool." He pressed his hand on Mac's arm. "Lots of other things on this old body are going, but my mind isn't one of them."

"I'm glad to hear it. Can you tell me what you saw?"

"Sure can. A woman coming and going at all hours, if you know what I mean. On the night they say Daniels died, that same lady was at his place. She stayed a long time. I know because I had finished dinner when she arrived. The nine o'clock news ended and at least an hour passed before she left. It had to be at least eleven or so."

"Did she do anything strange when she was coming or going?"

"Not when she was coming, but when she was leaving she had gloves on her hands. They were black. They stood out because we don't wear gloves here. In October, it's still pretty warm. No need for them."

"Did she have anything in her hands?" Mac asked, with a little prickle of excitement. Something to work with.

"Yup, she was carrying a white grocery bag. The disposable kind they give you from the store. I thought nothing of it at the time, but she went around the side of the house with it. I thought she was going to drop it in the garbage but then realized they always kept the Daniels garbage cans in his garage. Nothing on that side of the house except for some shrubs. I'm not sure what she did, but she came back out with the bag but nothing was in it."

"How could you tell?"

"When she was heading to the side of the house, it was dangling from her fingers and pulled tight like something was sitting in the bag's bottom. When she came back out, the bag fluttered in the breeze. Nothing holding it down or in place. Empty."

"You're perceptive, George. What did you do before you retired?" Mac asked.

"Oh, it was great fun. I used to work as a private investigator. People do some of the wildest things to each other and will pay a nice chunk of money to find out what their partner is up to. I've seen some craziness in my time."

"I'm sure you have. Do you think you could pick her out of a lineup if it came to it?"

"Sure, it was dark, but her face was clear as day when she went under his outdoor lights."

"Could you describe her to me?"

"Long, dark hair. Petite, maybe a hundred twenty or thirty. Something like that. She dressed like she'd been at a business meeting or something when she went in, but on her way out, she'd changed."

"What was she wearing on her way out?"

"She'd put on all black. Head to toe, pants, boots, shirt, the whole nine. All black."

"Can you describe her face to me?"

"Like I said, lots of things going out on this old body, but my mind and my eyes aren't one of them. Light skin, with kind of a..." He thought for a moment. "European look, with high cheekbones and chiseled features."

"That's helpful. Thank you. When she left, did she take anything with her?"

"Yup, she went back into the house after she did her thing on the side of the house. She refilled her plastic bag and headed to the car."

"Any idea what was in the bag?" Mac asked.

"If I were a guessing man, it was her clothes from earlier."

Mac got up and extended her hand to George. "You have been a tremendous help. Here's my card if you think of anything else. My cell phone is on the back. It's the best way to reach me."

"Will do, young lady. Good luck figuring this thing out. Daniels was a good man, and I'd like to see whoever did that to him answer for what they did."

"I'll do my best, George. Thank you."

MAC SETTLED back into her little hotel room and called Lola.

"Hey, Trouble. How are things coming along?" her sister asked.

"Still in place, trying to figure things out. Anything new?" Mac asked, being vague about her location in case someone had the ability to listen.

"So, your little friend is a slick one. I was able to dig up some pictures of her around the base, at the legal office, and around Daniels' neighborhood," Lola said, sounding proud of herself.

Mac still had no idea how she would hack into the footage on base, and she wasn't sure she wanted the information. Likely the less she was aware of, the better. "Do we have a positive ID? Is it Gennavie for sure?"

"That's where the slick part comes in. In every frame I found with her on camera, she was always either looking away or she was wearing a large hat masking most of her features. The jawline is right, height and weight are spot on, but I can't give you a positive ID. Nothing you can take to the authorities. It might help throw a shadow of reasonable doubt on Hudson's case, but there's no crime against seeing a man after hours."

Mac blew out a long breath. "Did you get any footage showing her at the house on the night of Daniels' death?"

"Sure did, but I only glimpsed one of the neighbor's cameras and you can make out minor details, but it's not Hudson. The figure in the picture isn't big enough. At a minimum, Hudson's attorney should be able to use it to their advantage."

"Thanks, Lola, that'll help. Do you think she's smart enough to scope out where all the cameras are prior to going places? In today's environment, thousands of cameras can catch you. I'm a little worried about that while I'm here. If it's Gennavie that's after me, no telling what resources the woman has. She has been living off the radar for months now and the FBI hasn't been able to track her down. It tells me she has the ability to stay off the grid. Any ideas about how we can flush her out?"

"Only one I can think of, but you won't like it, and neither do I."

"Lay it on me."

Lola remained quiet for a moment. "We can use you as bait and set a trap."

"That's not a half bad idea."

"Last resort," Lola said. "Look, I gotta go, but there has to be a way to flush her out."

"I'll talk to you soon. Stanton's calling in," Mac said. She disconnected with Lola and switched over to Stanton. "Hi boss, how is everything going? You and your family are safe, right?" she asked with concern laced through her voice.

"Yup, still kicking and in one piece. Nothing's happened since you left town," he said.

"Well, then, it was the right decision. I just got off the phone with Lola," she said, filling him in on what she found.

"That's good news, but we have bigger problems. I had lunch with Bartz, and he told me the FBI wants jurisdiction over the murder charges, the assaults on base, and the drug charges. They figure if they can stack everything, there's no way a jury won't convict in a federal court."

"They're right. It's no different from the Air Force. They don't go to court without something that has teeth, even if it's a minor dereliction of duty charge or a failure to go. They want a conviction, so they make sure something on the charge sheet will stick," Mac agreed.

"Well, it's a good thing Bartz is good at what he does and has experience in the federal system. So far, he's kept him on base and is drafting a motion now to keep the drug and assault charges under military jurisdiction. He's confident the judge will at least hear him out and he has enough reasonable doubt to at least have a chance. Those pictures of a woman at Daniels' house on the night of his death might help."

"I found a witness, too. He's an old guy who likes to sit out on his porch and keep an eye on the neighborhood." She told him about Lola's idea of using her as bait to flush out the people hunting her. If the woman was Gennavie, then she'd been impulsive in the past and Mac may be able to use it to her advantage.

"I hate the idea," Stanton said. "If Gennavie is the one after you, who's the other guy? We don't know who we're up against. It's too dangerous. Finish up out there and get home so we can attack this head-on."

"I'm not sure what else I can do here, but I'm not coming back. Not yet."

"Why not? We can protect you," Stanton tried to argue.

"I'm not willing to put you or your beautiful family in danger. I need you guys to stay on base and stay safe until this is over."

"There's something else you should know," he said, not arguing further. "Bartz may lose the battle surrounding Hudson staying in the Security Forces confinement facility. He's their first sergeant and in the direct chain of command of most of the military members who are supposed to be guarding him and keeping him confined. They all like him and keep trying to do special favors for Hudson that are against regulations. Their intentions are good, but it's making it difficult for Hudson's commander to keep him on base. We need to figure this out soon before they transfer him back downtown. Any ideas?"

"If Bartz loses the argument and Hudson has to be transferred, push for them to put him in a pre-trial cell where he belongs. If we can keep him out of the general population, then he may be okay. Keep me posted," Mac said, anxiety pulling at her emotions as she hung up. There had to be a way to stop this before Hudson paid the ultimate price. If he went back to downtown confinement, he might not make it back out. Getting into her backpack, she pulled out her notebook and reviewed what she had so far. The list seemed unbearably long. It seemed impossible to clear him of everything. Stanton may be right—the Feds only needed to make one thing stick. If Hudson ended up with a federal conviction it would ruin his military career and everything he'd been working so hard for.

MAC LAID her head back on the bed and clicked on the old box television that sat to the left on the broken stand. When she first arrived at this place, she smiled when they referred to the room as "luxury accommodations." That was not what she would call it. She was happy it looked clean, or as clean as a hotel with rotating guests could be. She clicked through the channels and almost clicked past the news until she saw the judge who was overseeing Hudson's case plastered on her screen.

A tall, dark-haired woman with large chocolate eyes looked back at her from the screen. *"In breaking news, they have found the body of the Honorable Judge Teresa Keys in her upscale condo. Her death rocked the judicial system to its core. People in the legal community held the judge in high regard and considered her to be fair. Her passing will cause a significant backlog in the processing of cases with over a hundred on her pending docket. One of which is Master Sergeant Gavin Hudson, the decorated military member facing charges of murder, assault, and drug possession. Hudson remains in custody on base, but sources have indicated the possibility of moving him back to the downtown confinement facility."*

Mac knew of the judge prior to Hudson's case being assigned to her. Judge Keys was the same judge who presided over Vincent's case. The judge struck Mac as wise and caring. She remembered her blondish-gray hair pulled into a tight bun with large spectacles perched on her nose. Mac had testified at his trial about her involvement and investigation surrounding the case. The judge had been kind and respectful toward Mac and praised her in open court for her work in bringing Vincent to justice once they found him guilty.

She had often wondered whether his testimony was part of why Vincent got the death penalty. His defense team argued against it, but Vincent insisted on testifying on his own behalf. The testimony sealed the deal. He came across as cold and calculating, with little emotion for his victims. Captain Anika Wilson was part of the defense team. She was brilliant and made some compelling arguments. It was never a good idea for the accused to testify unless he or she was not guilty, which almost never happened. Still, if they weren't guilty of what they were being charged with, it opened the door to any other misconduct the accused may have been involved with.

Her attention went back to the television when she heard her name. *"Master Sergeant Hudson was in confinement at the time of the judge's murder, but they want to question Master Sergeant Evelyn McGregor, also known as Mac, in connection with the judge's murder investigation. Hudson and Mac got engaged to be married right before Hudson's arrest. No one has seen in over seventy-two hours. If you have any information about Sergeant McGregor's whereabouts, please contact the Spokane Police Department."*

Mac's jaw dropped open; she couldn't believe what she'd heard. How could they think she was involved? Did they think she was AWOL? She wanted to call Stanton or Hudson's commander, but she wasn't sure who to turn to. The commander's position made him a mandatory reporter and he would have no choice but to give up her location if she called him. Stanton didn't fall under the same requirements as a defense attorney, but she still didn't want to put him in that position since he was the only one who knew where she was. At least Hudson was in the clear for this one.

She dialed Lola.

"Hey, twice in the same day. You might be smothering me. We used to go months without talking."

Mac tried to laugh, but it came out strangled. "Lola, it's bad and I need your help yet again."

"Come on Mac, what else can happen now?"

She gave her all the details she had. "Will you look at the case file? They don't have much yet, but at least the investigator should have put preliminary notes in the system. I need to know what I'm up against and why they think I'm involved."

"Stay put. I'll call you as soon as I have it."

Mac got up and paced around the tiny room, racking her brain. Why on earth would they think she had anything to do with the judge's murder?

Only seven minutes had passed when her phone rang.

"That was quick."

"That's what you love about me. My wicked hacking skills."

"It's so much more than that. So…" Mac said, anxiety crawling through her.

"Okay, don't freak out," Lola said, hearing the panic in her sister's voice. "So far, it's only wild allegations. Joe isn't on the case file. It's some guy named Malone. His theory is that you killed the judge to prove Hudson's innocence. Her murder was exactly the same as Anika Wilson's, down to the same ligature marks on her wrists, ankles, and neck. The killer was thorough and had hit the judge in the head in the same place where Wilson had a contusion."

"That makes little sense. Yeah, it might throw reasonable doubt about the Wilson case, but would do nothing to clear him for the Daniels murder or the assault and drug charges."

"Yeah, but if Gennavie is trying to destroy you, her plans are only going so-so. Hudson isn't withering away in a prison the way she wanted. It might trigger her to want you to suffer in other ways," Lola speculated.

"That's a pretty far-fetched theory, even for Gennavie."

"I'm trying to get in her head. What do you want to do with this new info?" Lola asked.

"Not sure, but at least we have reasonable doubt on the Daniels case even if we can't make out her face. His defense attorney can prove another person was at his house on the day he died. I'll visit the ME that did Daniels's autopsy, in case I can narrow down why the doctor put the time of death window so large."

"I can answer that one for you. The responding ME was in training, but the report now shows the time of death between eleven p.m. and three a.m. on the fifteenth and sixteenth of October."

Mac thought this over for a moment. "It fits the timeline of the neighbor who watched her leave the house after eleven. But it only puts a Band-Aid on the mounting evidence against him. Sure, we can show he might not have killed Daniels, but I've got nothing on the other cases so far. Except now, we can point to the undeniable fact that he was in confinement on base during the latest murder. I'm not sure it's going to be enough. Do you think I should turn myself in? At least if I'm in confinement, then additional charges can't materialize. Maybe if there's no one to play with, she'll go away." Mac sounded desperate to her own ears.

Lola huffed into the phone. "Come on Mac, that's not the woman I know. You will not bow down to this woman and give in to what she wants. Pull your big-girl panties up and figure this thing out. I'll dig further into the judge's case, but in the meantime, focus and figure out a different angle."

"Thanks for the pep talk. I need it."

She hung up and sat back on the bed. The exhaustion from the last several days made her body ache.

CHAPTER
FIFTY-SEVEN

HUDSON WALKED BACK into the confinement facility with his head down. Dread filled his body. He could handle himself, but after the way he left things with Gorilla and his crew, it would not be pretty. His attorney told him they should put him in pre-trial confinement, but things weren't always that easy. From what he saw, Gorilla carried a lot of weight in the facility and would reach out and touch him in pre-trial or anywhere else. Maybe he would get himself thrown into solitary. He'd read once that solitary was terrible for an inmate's mental health, but at least he would relax and not wonder when the next assault would happen.

It didn't take long for them to process him, and he walked down a long row of cells far away from the pre-trial confinement area. "Ooh, sweet cheeks is back, fellas," Gorilla said behind him. "I sure missed you until they told me you're a pig."

Hudson stopped walking and turned to face his opponent. Gorilla was still locked in his cell but was baring his teeth at Hudson, trying to get a rise out of him. "I'm not a cop," Hudson said, trying his best to stay calm.

"Come on, move along," the guard behind him said.

Hudson continued to his cell, but this wasn't good. Cops got killed in prison. If he was a cop, then they should have segregated him. He wasn't, and whoever was running this place didn't give a shit what happened to him. By morning the entire facility was in an uproar, thinking he was part of the police. The rumors were spreading like wildfire that he was some kind of undercover informant out to testify against them.

"This is going to be fun," Hudson mumbled to Billy, who had somehow survived while Hudson wasn't there to protect him. He hadn't asked, but only assumed Billy had been smart enough to give Reina back her money to stay alive.

"What did you do?" the small man in glasses asked, looking up at his cellmate.

"On base, I work in the Security Forces. I'm part of their leadership, but I'm not a cop. It doesn't matter because everyone in here thinks I am."

"Oh," Billy said. "Can I help?"

"If I were you, I would stay clear of me." Hudson stepped out of their cell and got in line with the rest of the inmates, bracing himself.

Billy filed in right behind him, not listening to the warning. They were almost at the cafeteria before it started.

Behind him, Hudson heard Billy screech, "Watch out."

Hudson ducked on instinct, but the metal cafeteria tray still grazed the top of his head, leaving a long scrape. It would have been much worse without the maneuver. A little trickle of blood worked its way past Hudson's right eye. He swung around, blocking the next blow. Billy stepped back and looked like he shrank himself as small as possible into the corner of the opposite wall. Surrounding Hudson on every side, the inmates were chanting, "Kill the pig. Make him pay. Kill the pig, make him pay," with Gorilla leading the charge. He had both meaty hands in the air, pounding his fists, getting his followers more riled up.

There was no use in arguing with them. It didn't matter to these men; they only needed the slightest reason for violence. Many of them were in for years if not life, and didn't care whether they would make it out. Every few seconds, the circle of men would move closer until he and Gorilla were face to face.

"You don't want to do this," Hudson said.

"I never fucked me a pig," Gorilla said, slamming his fist into Hudson's chest. Hudson backed up enough to deflect the blow and not take the man's powerful impact head-on. As he pivoted, he spun back around, slamming his balled fist into Gorilla's ear, sending the man off balance. Gorilla shook his head back and forth and the circle widened. Everyone wanted a show. Hudson slammed the heel of his foot into the back of Gorilla's knee, sending him to the ground. He screamed out.

"You signed your death warrant, little piggy," Gorilla said. "You're going to pay for that."

Gorilla was fast for a man his size. He spun back to his feet, grabbing Hudson from behind and holding on like his life depended on it. The man's death grip tightened around Hudson's chest, making it hard to breathe. He twisted from the right to the left, trying to find leverage, but Gorilla wrapped his hands like a vise grip and wasn't about to let go. Until Hudson slammed the thick part of his skull into Gorilla's nose. The sickening crunch let him know he'd re-broken it. Gorilla let go, allowing Hudson to spin around.

"Get him," Gorilla spit through the blood running across his swollen mouth.

"Shit," Hudson mumbled.

Within seconds, the entire circle of Gorilla's men started in. Hudson counted eight. It would be difficult, but not impossible.

The first one rushed him, lowering his head for momentum, allowing Hudson to grab the back of his head and slam it into his knee. He dropped like a sack and didn't move again. The next man came at him, grabbing him from behind. Hudson kicked his feet in the air, catapulting himself off a nearby wall and causing the man holding him to fly into his buddies behind him. They pushed him back into play in time for Hudson to swing around and slam his fist into the man's face. Blood sprayed across the wall, and the shouting increased. Hudson didn't have time to think about where the hell the guards were. He slammed his right leg into the man's midsection, who was coming next, pivoting and delivering an uppercut into the jaw of the guy coming in on his left. He used the momentum to grab onto the man's body and slam him against the wall.

Three down, five to go. Hudson kicked one man in the back and grabbed his hair, slamming his head into the concrete wall. Only three left. All three large men rushed him at the same time. He grabbed two of their heads and slammed them together. The third man smashed his fist into Hudson's head, throwing him off balance. He hit the floor hard.

The last man standing started toward him. Hudson wiped the blood from the side of his mouth, pushing his enormous arms behind him, launching his body into an upright position like a practiced fighter. He threw his entire weight into the man, throwing him off balance and back to the ground. His adrenaline was pumping through his system so fast he didn't realize the man had stopped moving. He kept hitting him until a guard pulled him off.

"Inmate Hudson!" the guard screamed in his ear, making Hudson stop.

He went limp and put his hands behind his back so the guard wouldn't hit him. He wanted no more violence. The guard led him away while the other guards called for help to get the other nine men, including Gorilla, lying in a bloody mess, to the infirmary.

The guard who took him down the hall shook his head. "Buddy, you're either one lucky son of a bitch or just that good. Few could have walked away from that."

"Thanks, I think," Hudson murmured.

"You'll be happy to know you've earned a stay in our luxury solitary confinement facility. The warden wants to meet with you."

They stopped by the infirmary, where the nurse put a bandage on Hudson's head and cleaned up his scrapes. All things considered, he was in good shape compared to the others.

The guard took Hudson down a long hall until they came to a vacant row with only one cell at the end. The man opened the solid steel door, took off Hudson's cuffs, and slid the door closed. It was one of the nicest sounds.

CHAPTER
FIFTY-EIGHT

"MAC, I HAVE SOME BAD NEWS," Stanton said into the phone.

"That can't be good. What happened?"

"They took Hudson back to the downtown confinement facility. Someone leaked that he's a cop, which isn't true, but they didn't care."

"Is he okay?" Mac's stomach tightened into an uncomfortable knot. She couldn't handle it if she lost him. Please make him okay.

"He took on nine guys," Stanton said, sounding impressed. "One of them was a guy named Gorilla."

"Dammit, Stanton," she began, and then remembered she was talking to her boss. "I mean sir. Is he okay?"

"Yes, he's fine. He has a few scrapes and bruises, but overall he's good. He single-handedly took down nine guys. They jumped him in the cafeteria. The warden called Bartz to tell him his client would be in solitary confinement until they could figure something else out. That's the good news."

"If that's the good news, I'm not sure I want the bad," Mac said.

"You know about the judge's murder, right?"

"Yeah, I caught it on the news."

"Well, he's going to be sitting for a while until they can reassign her docket to another judge. It sounds simple, but I guess the system is so backed up it can take six months or more before his case is in front of a new judge. I'm not sure if Hudson can survive that long. He's one of the good guys and now that they think he's a cop, he'll have a target on his back. Even after today, they might still come for him."

"What do you think I should do?" Mac said, sounding desperate.

"No idea, but we'd better come up with something quick before something bad happens to him that he can't handle on his own."

"I'm doing what I can here. I have one other lead to follow. Did you give Bartz the photos of the woman seen at Daniels' house on the day of his murder?"

"I did, but no one is listening. They all have their sights on Hudson. One of the key investigators said it was possible you doctored the photos and the timestamp to match in order to get him off the hook."

Stanton took the phone away from his ear as Mac screamed out in frustration. "What in the hell do they want me to do? Hand-deliver the woman to them in cuffs?"

"It would be helpful," he said. "Now relax, this is bad, but we'll work it out. There has to be an answer to all of this. I need you to remain calm and use your beautiful brain to help Bartz and me come up with something. With the judge being murdered, it only makes sense you're next on this psycho's chopping block. I need you to stay in hiding and keep a low profile," Stanton advised.

"If I stay in hiding, won't it make the authorities think I'm guilty?" Mac asked.

"That's possible, but if you come out of hiding, you might be dead. I can vouch for you and make sure they know I put you someplace safe, and I'm not willing to give up your location until I'm convinced it's okay for you to come. In the meantime, make sure you stay that way. I'll be in touch," he said, and hung up the phone.

Mac's world was closing in on her. The mounting evidence against Hudson was impossible. Each time she chiseled away at a little piece of it, the authorities would dismiss her, or additional evidence would surface. Everyone had already concluded without looking into the case. She thought about her gentle giant locked away in solitary confinement. It couldn't be good for him, and she hoped he was keeping his spirits up. But deep down, she was terrified for him. No one, even Hudson, as strong as he was, could face this much without fear in his heart.

The thought of their wedding slipped through her mind, and she had to wonder if she could ever walk down the aisle with him. It was unlikely at this point, but she still allowed herself to daydream about that day for a moment. She pictured her handsome soon-to-be husband standing at the front of the beautiful outdoor venue in a tailored black tux hugging his massive body, showing off his broad, sexy shoulders and trim waistline. Closing her eyes, she allowed herself to picture her dress. It was long and flowing, with elegant lines hugging her Latino figure in all the right places. She never let herself dream about her wedding day before Hudson came along, but now she pictured the stunning backless gown draped over her olive skin. In her mind, everyone was there. Her entire family and Hudson's, which wasn't a ton of people. The ceremony was small and intimate, the way she always wanted it.

Deep in her heart, she knew the day wasn't coming. She had no reservations about waiting for him to be released from prison, but they would both be old unless the worst happened. With the charges against him, it was possible for him to receive the death penalty in a federal court. There was no way she could face that reality. The thought of watching Hudson, the only man she had ever loved, strapped down and injected with a lethal concoction was something she didn't want to think about. As the image came into her mind, she forced it back out.

That was not how this was going to end. She was sure of it.

CHAPTER
FIFTY-NINE

MAC WAS RUNNING out of options and only had one place left to turn. The one place she swore to herself she wouldn't go. It took her the better part of the day to drive to her destination. The entire drive she went back and forth, trying to figure out if she was doing the right thing, but she saw no other way. At the least, her trip would bring some information. A huge fence with three rows of barbed wire surrounded the mammoth facility. One at the top, one in the middle, and one at the bottom. The towering, dirty tan buildings greeted her as she drove past the watchtower to check in.

Her stomach tightened into knots as she got out of the car and walked into the facility.

Behind the plexiglass stood a rail-thin black woman. "Who you here to visit?" she asked, peering above her spectacles.

"Reina," Mac said.

The woman raised her left eyebrow. "Now why'd you want to do that, honey?" she said with a deep Southern drawl.

Mac cleared her throat. "She's my mother."

"Oh. Well, I sure am sorry. Nasty woman, that one." She cocked her head to the side, looking Mac up and down. "Well, yeah, I guess now that you say so, I can see the resemblance. Tell you what honey, you fill out this paperwork and tell me if you need me to pull you out of there.

I'm Litia, but everyone around here calls me Lit. Tell the guards Lit needs you, and I'll pull you right on out."

Mac smiled, trying to make her stomach stop rolling. "That's kind of you, Litia. I mean Lit. But she doesn't want to hurt me. If I know my mother, she has something else in mind."

"Well, you tell me if you need my help. People never cease to amaze me. Capable of all kinds of nastiness."

"Thank you," Mac said, taking a seat with her clipboard and filling it out.

Forty-five minutes later, she sat in the visiting area waiting for her mother to be led in. She sat in the booth on one side of the plexiglass and watched her mother come in and be cuffed to the other side. The once elegant and powerful Reina sat in front of her, looking battered and a little broken. In the orange jumpsuit with no makeup on, she looked much older than she had. Her once pristinely kept appearance was fraying around the edges with her dark hair pulled back, high-lighting the gray growing in.

Reina picked up the phone and sat across from her daughter without missing a beat. "Hello Evelyn, it is so good you're here. Thank you for coming to visit me. I didn't think you would," she said before Mac got a word in.

"I hadn't planned to, but I had no choice," Mac said, indicating this was not a friendly visit.

"Well, I forgive you for putting me in here as long as you'll agree to my terms," Reina smiled.

"What kind of evil do you have planned?" Mac asked. Every instinct in her body told her to leave.

"Why do you always think the worst of me?"

"Because I find it's the best place to start. Otherwise, I'll end up disappointed. What do you want?"

"Well, my darling daughter, you owe me after all the trouble you caused. But, if you cooperate, I can make it all go away."

"Make all what go away?" Mac asked.

"Hudson," was all she said.

"What can you do for Hudson?" Mac asked. She couldn't believe what she was hearing, but she had to admit that she wasn't surprised.

"I can make the charges go away. He would be a free man in a matter of hours if you would do what I want you to."

"And what is that?"

"I need you to take over my business until I'm released. As long as you help me, then I'll leave Hudson alone. He will be get out of that nasty solitary confinement and breathe free air."

"How in hell do you know he's in solitary?" Mac seethed. "Who's been feeding you information?"

"Not so fast. You think you still have leverage, but you don't. The only choice you have is to comply. Do what you're told and take over my empire. Run it like it's supposed to be run and get me the hell out of this place. That is the only way Hudson will survive this. If you refuse, I'll make sure Gennavie has him killed and sends you pieces of your handsome man. She'll hand-deliver a new piece each week."

"You wouldn't," Mac said, her eyes wide. She had a hunch her mother had her hands in it, but she didn't know Reina and Gennavie had teamed up to take her down. Mac took several deep breaths and remained silent while she processed the information. "So, what you're telling me is Gennavie has evidence to exonerate Hudson and she'll use it to release Hudson if I agree?"

"It's what I'm telling you. You could take lessons from Gennavie. She's a crafty woman and knows how to get things done."

Mac couldn't believe her ears. Her mother wasn't only teaming up with Gennavie, she was telling her to be more like the deranged woman.

"Tell me, Mother, what do you plan to do with me if I comply?"

Reina laid out the entire plan. What she intended to do if Mac agreed, and what she planned to do if she didn't. It went much deeper than Mac could have thought.

Mac sat and listened, not making a sound. She let out the breath she'd been holding. "Well," Mac said, getting to her feet. "You have given me a great deal to think about. I'll be in touch."

CHAPTER
SIXTY

ON MAC'S way back from the prison, she felt deflated. Things were going to be a lot worse before they got better. The question was how to keep things from spiraling. If she sacrificed herself to save Hudson, then they would never be together again, and her life would not be her own. She would belong to her mother, which was the exact thing she had been running from her entire life. There was little she wanted except to be married and settle down with Hudson. Maybe have a couple of kids. The image of their children together crossed through her mind. A little boy who was stocky like his dad, and a precious little girl with delicate features and dark hair.

If she couldn't stop this nightmare, she would never meet her future children, let alone be married to the man she loved, but she couldn't see a way out. She would do anything for Hudson. The love she felt for him was something she never thought she would be able to find. He was her other half. She always thought it was silly and a fairy-tale. True love didn't exist. There was no right person for everyone, but boy was she wrong. Hudson was her exact match. When they were together, everything worked. No matter what they were up against, it was good. The thought of him in her arms was something she craved, and anything happening to him was unacceptable. There had to be another way.

After stopping at a hotel for the night, she made the rest of the drive back to Alamogordo. Before she realized where she was, she had pulled up to Daniels' house. There had to be something she could point to. If she got him out of the murder charges here, then maybe the prosecuting attorney would listen to what she had to say about him being set up. The pictures were a start, but the attorney had a point. Photographic evidence wasn't what it used to be. Now, so many tools could manipulate evidence. If there was a way she could find actual, tangible evidence, then maybe she would have a chance at creating more cracks in the foundation of Hudson's case. There had to be a different way than giving up her life and becoming her mother's property. Not that she was unwilling to sacrifice herself to save Hudson. She couldn't imagine going through the rest of her life without him. It was more than she could bear.

Getting out of her car, she placed a pair of gloves over her hands. The neighbor's words slipped through her mind. "The gloves stuck out because no one wears them here." Maybe there was something to it. Why would she be wearing black gloves and how would it help with the case? Mac walked around the property, looking at each bush. Nothing was in the bushes except for some disturbed dirt where she assumed the police had collected evidence. Making her way to the back of the house, she checked around the back porch, under the porch, and around the outdoor furniture. So far, nothing. Looking at the back door, she contemplated going in. Under the circumstances, a breaking-and-entering charge would be the least of her worries, but it would muddy the waters if they arrested her for something she was actually guilty of.

It was worth the risk. If she kept playing inside the law while Gennavie did whatever she wanted, she would lose.

She picked the lock, looking around the yard to make sure no one was around. It was one of the many skills her dear old mother had taught her growing up, and this one was easy to open. Walking into the large kitchen, she stopped and listened. It was too quiet. She made her way through the kitchen, finding nothing of note until she came into the bedroom. On the bed, they'd left everything the way it was at the time of the murder.

The king-size comforter on the large poster bed still had an excessive amount of blood soaked into it. Now looking brownish-red and dried, she wondered why they hadn't sent a forensic cleaning crew. Daniels' wife had to be still reeling from the news and hadn't thought about what to do with the house after telling her children. The trauma it had to bring was going to take some time. His widow's mind was likely focused on how to help her family heal, not what the house would go for once cleaned. Mac hoped the lack of a cleanup crew would give her the evidence she needed.

She went around the bed looking for something that would lead to the killer. Not who the killer was, because she was certain she already knew. She needed to find unequivocal evidence of Gennavie's involvement, and that she had committed the murder. Once she did that, she would have to figure out how to convince the police to pay attention to the crime scene and do another sweep before the cleaners came. She remembered a guy she had dealt with in El Paso who did crime scene clean-up and wondered if he also provided services in this area. Under the circumstances, she hoped they wouldn't come soon. Making her way through the bedroom, she found a black hair tucked between the comforter and the mattress. It was synthetic and came from a wig, but it was something.

Going back to the kitchen, she found plastic bags in one drawer and placed the hair inside. Remembering a trick Lola taught her, she rummaged through the bathroom until she found some leftover powdered makeup his ex-wife had left behind, along with a makeup brush. She went around the bed looking for any place where there wasn't already fingerprint powder. While brushing the powder over the nightstand, she came across an undusted print. Getting her phone out of her back pocket, she snapped an up-close picture of the print, hoping they would run it for her. It was only circumstantial evidence, but it painted a picture along with the photos Lola had retrieved. It had to amount to reasonable doubt.

SHE MOVED into the bathroom and got down on her hands and knees, looking under the sink for anything they might have missed. She stuck her head inside with her flashlight lit up, trying to find something the police had overlooked.

She thought she heard a sound. Before she could react, her hair was yanked back hard and she was flung onto her back. Mac found herself looking up into the barrel of a gun. The long, slender arms led to the beautiful green eyes and stunning red hair that belonged to none other than Gennavie.

"You," Mac said.

"Yes, me. Who else did you expect to come for you?" Gennavie stepped back, aiming her gun at Mac. "Get up."

Mac did as she instructed. "Why are you here?"

"Why do you think, dumbass? I'm here to make sure you don't ruin our plans." Her lips curled into a wicked grin.

"Yeah, about that. What are you planning to do once you help my mother with what she wants?"

"I'm going to be rich and powerful so I can do whatever I desire." Gennavie stalked back and forth.

"What has she promised you?"

"Everything I want, as long as I convince you to do her bidding. So, tell me, my little puppet. What will it take to make you comply so I can get my Vincent back?"

"So that's what this is about. She's promised to spring Vincent for you. Why on earth do you need him when you can take over the empire yourself? You should replace me and run the place better than I ever would."

"Nice try." Gennavie faced Mac, training the gun back on her. "I won't stop until Hudson is dead, or you help me get Vincent back. I don't want to run Reina's company. I want my partner in crime, so we can go play together like we used to before you came along and ruined everything."

"Vincent put himself in prison, not me," Mac said, paying close attention to Gennavie's patterns as she moved back and forth. *A little closer*, she willed her.

"We had been playing for years before you came along. Couldn't you have left well enough alone? Stayed in Spokane and let us play in Seattle. Instead, you had to stick your nose where it didn't belong and take Vincent from me."

"You're a powerful woman in your own right. Why on earth do you need Vincent? He's not much to look at. You can do so much better."

"I need you to agree to Reina's plan so I can have my life back. It is as simple as that. You give me what I want and Hudson goes free. Otherwise, you will both pay the ultimate price," Gennavie snarled launching forward to slap her across the face.

Mac slipped her head to the side, opening up the opportunity she needed to throw Gennavie's weight forward. Mac launched herself off the edge of the tub and grabbed the gun.

The two women grappled for control. Mac thrust her knee into Gennavie's stomach, making her lose her grip on the gun as it slid across the tiled floor. Gennavie recovered, throwing her weight on top of Mac as she rolled, going for the gun. Mac felt sharp, claw-like nails run down her arm. She flipped over to defend herself grabbing onto Gennavie's black wig and ripping it from her head causing her red hair to cascade from the cap holding it in place.

Gennavie looked like she was losing control. Her eyes went dark around the edges and Mac saw the wild, uncontrolled animal that lived there. Gennavie dropped her full weight, straddling Mac's body. At first, Mac held her arms away, but Gennavie pulled loose, smashing the side of her head. Before Mac regained control, Gennavie pushed her hands over Mac's neck and squeezed. She pulled at her fingers, trying to make Gennavie loosen her grip, but it was no use. The more she fought, the tighter her fingers squeezed until blackness crept into Mac's vision. She tried to breathe in air but there was precious little until her foot found the wall, giving her leverage to thrust her hips up, launching Gennavie forward.

Mac scrambled to her feet, backing away for a moment, letting the sweet air fill her lungs. Gennavie was crawling on all fours toward the gun and almost got her hands on it when Mac wrapped her hands around her ankle and pulled hard. Gennavie's body slid away from the gun while Mac catapulted herself across the room and grabbed the butt of the gun in her hand. When she spun around, she spotted Gennavie's back as she ran at full speed. She sprinted after her, but by the time she got around the corner, she was out the door. Mac watched as she spun the tires of her compact rental car, tearing ass out of the subdivision.

She leaned against the door, catching her breath. It was time to leave before someone reported the commotion. Gathering her evidence, including Gennavie's red hair still wrapped around her fingers, she headed out the back the way she came.

She climbed back into her own car. It was a relief to meet the myth, the legend—the one the newspapers had dubbed the princess of death. It was about time. A face-to-face with Gennavie. The woman was everything Mac thought she would be, and more stunning in person. The pictures she'd seen of her during her investigation were nothing in comparison. The familiar feel crossed through her mind that she was the woman who had assaulted her in base housing. It wasn't a surprise people remembered her when they met her. It might be her undoing.

CHAPTER
SIXTY-TWO

ON HER WAY back to her small room, Mac called Uncle Lu. She needed to get rid of the gun and didn't want to leave it somewhere a kid would come across it. But she also couldn't risk being caught with it. With no idea of the history of the gun, the last thing she needed was to be apprehended with it. Now, to figure out how she was going to make the police pay attention to the little evidence she had.

Mac met her uncle and dad, hoping they would come up with something to help her. They met back outside the Alamogordo police department with the evidence she'd collected.

"Hey young lady, how are things looking?" her dad asked, looking at his daughter. She looked a mess with her hair unkempt and long red lines down her arm where Gennavie had scratched her. Not to mention the red mark on her neck that would turn into a bruise soon.

"Not good. I have some additional evidence, but I don't have the proper chain of custody and I'm not sure if it's enough to make them listen." She told him everything she had, which wasn't much. A fingerprint, some hair samples, and the photos might do it, but she didn't feel confident since every time she gave them another piece, they shut her down.

Both men listened, but neither one of them gave her a hopeful look.

"All we can do is present what we have. I'll handle the chain of custody. Give it all to me," Uncle Lu said, walking toward the front door of the building. They all walked in to find the front of the office empty. The kind lady that greeted them before was nowhere to be found. It didn't stop Lu as he pounded his fist on the door.

Someone in the back hollered, "Just a sec." The Alamogordo police chief, Steve Watson, came out of his office in the back. "What the hell do the three of you want now?"

"We have additional evidence we want to turn in for your consideration in the Daniels' case. I think it's compelling and might change your mind about things."

"Okay," Steve said, buzzing the door. "Whatcha got?"

Mac and her dad stayed silent while Lu explained how they'd gone together to interview the neighbor and witnessed Gennavie break into Daniels' house. The suspect fled, but they were able to discover photos on the night of the murder, hair from a synthetic black wig, and red hairs from the assailant that should provide a positive identification.

"So, what do you think?" he asked when he finished.

"I think you're out of your jurisdiction, and you had no business stomping all over my crime scene," Steve said, his face a strange color of red.

"You released the scene, and we're trying to show you there's more to this case than you're seeing," Lu said, raising his voice.

"I don't care if you bring me a smoking fucking gun. You broke protocol and stomped all over the evidence. You have a personal connection here that will be torn to pieces in court."

Mac's dad stepped forward, keeping his voice low. "Look Steve, this is important. We know it's a lot to ask. We're asking you to run the hair sample and see if you get a DNA match on the woman in his house."

"What the hell would it prove? That he was getting a little poon-tang from some sweet thing? It doesn't get close to pointing to murder," Steve argued.

"It proves someone else was in the house on the day of Daniels' murder. Doesn't it give you pause? Plus, she pulled a gun on my niece and planned to kill her," Lu said, thrusting the gun at him in frustration.

"How do I know this woman wasn't defending herself because you guys are trying to frame her or something?" Steve argued.

"Are you kidding me?" Mac said. She'd had enough. "This woman came after me, threatening to kill me and Hudson unless we help get her husband out of prison. She admitted to her involvement, and you don't give two rats' asses what happened. All you want to do is keep your conviction rate up. We're asking you to do your fucking job and all you're doing is giving us the runaround." She lunged at him, losing her cool.

Steve stepped back, and her dad grabbed her by the waist, pulling her kicking and screaming out of the police station.

Once they were outside, she calmed.

"If I let go, are you going to be okay?" her dad asked.

"Yeah, I'm calm, but he wasn't listening," Mac said, on the verge of tears.

Lu walked out of the building, shaking his head. It was over, and Mac knew it. "Don't lose hope, honey," he said. "We'll figure something out."

Mac took several deep breaths, trying to gain full control of her emotions. "Thank you for all your help. You've been more supportive than I have a right to ask for. I need to go back to Washington and check on Hudson. He's stuck in solitary confinement, and I'm not sure how long he can stand it without personal contact."

"Why don't you turn in the rental car and come back with us? You can stay at our place until you fly out tomorrow."

"Thanks, but my rental is from the El Paso Airport and I need some time alone. I need to wrap my head around my new reality," she said, blowing out a breath. Giving them both a hug, she said goodbye and climbed back into her car. She knew where she had to go, but she wasn't looking forward to the drive or the visit.

They had stacked too much evidence against Hudson. She pulled out her notebook and stared at the list. If she didn't know Hudson and only saw the evidence, she would consider convicting him too. That was the problem. It was hard to argue with everything stacked against him.

SIXTY-THREE

IT TOOK a little time to pack up her things, change her flight, and head down the road. After driving for most of the night, she pulled off the road to catch a little sleep before hitting visitors' hours first thing in the morning. She looked rough, but she couldn't care less at this point.

Lit greeted her as she walked in but stopped mid-sentence. "Hon, what in the world happened to you?"

"It's a long story. Can I visit my mom?" Mac said, not making eye contact. She was trying to make peace with being beaten.

"Sure hon, but are you sure you want to expose yourself to that woman twice in one week? I sure wouldn't."

"Can't be helped. Can you get me in there? It's important."

"No problem. You wait here for a second. Make yourself a little coffee and I'll be right back. You sure look like you could use it."

"Thanks, Lit," Mac said, sinking into her chair. Another thirty minutes passed, and Mac drifted off to sleep. She jerked awake when a hand landed on her shoulder and gave it a shake.

"You sure you want to go? Why don't you grab a little sleep and come back tomorrow?"

"No, thanks. Is she ready?"

"Yeah." The kind woman must have sensed something wasn't right by the way Mac looked at her when she made eye contact. She delivered Mac to her mother without saying another word.

Mac sat across from her mother, picking up the phone. "You win," she said in a whisper.

"What did you say, dear?" Reina said, a grin curling at the edge of her dry, cracked lips.

"I said you win. You can have what you want. Make this stop and I'll do it. Whatever that is."

"It's about time," she said with a smug look on her face.

"What happens now?" Mac's stomach twisted. She was afraid to ask, but what choice did she have? The thing that hurt the worst was not being able to be with Hudson. If she kept fighting, he might die. At least he would be safe. Maybe she could check on him from whatever hell hole her mother had in mind.

"Now that you're ready to cooperate, things become quite civil," she said, grinning bigger. "I will notify Gennavie you are ready to play ball. Once you go back to Washington, she will contact you," Reina said.

"Why would you send me back to Washington? I thought I was giving up my freedom for Hudson's safety," Mac said, confusion crossing her face. In her mind, she thought the worst-case scenario would be a quick flight to Mexico to take care of her mother's place and then on to whatever devious plan she had.

"You need to button things up so no one comes looking for you," Reina said, watching her daughter. "For starters, I need you to quit your job."

"The military doesn't work that way," Mac interrupted. "You can't quit. I have another year and a half until my enlistment is up. If I walk away now, I'll be AWOL. It's impossible to break the contract without a ton of work and approval from the higher-ups. Trust me, I've had plenty of clients try with no success."

"Okay, then I guess you'll have to be in that AWOL status for a while. What does it do to you? Will you have warrants against you or something?" Reina looked intrigued, and Mac realized this was a business decision for her. She was weighing the pros and cons of the situation and whether bringing Mac in was going to cost her more than Mac was worth.

"If they can't find me right away, they'll flag my identity and put me into a national database. If any of the government agencies scans my identity, then they'll notify the Air Force of my location. They'll arrest me, and I'll be taken into custody. A court-martial would follow, and I would likely face prison time along with some other disciplinary consequences." Mac said all of this knowing it was going to be a long road. No one who knew her would ever think she had gone off on her own accord. It wasn't how she operated, and most people would think something was off. They would launch a full investigation for a while, but the more time she stayed away, the more people would realize she wasn't coming back. Knowing her mother, she already had a new identity waiting for her.

"Well, in that case things will be a little difficult, but we'll have to be careful. Keeping you off US soil will be important, but it shouldn't be a problem. We can have my new lackeys take care of any business needed to be done in the States while you run the organization from your post in Mexico."

"I thought your operation in Mexico was off limits," Mac said.

"Yes, thanks to you. We can't go back. You'll have to pay your dues for many years before I'll trust you after the little stunt. It cost me a ton to relocate and get my new place up and running," Reina said, anger flashing in her eyes.

"But you've been here the entire time. I've checked. No way you set up a new base of operations that fast."

"My dear Evelyn, you underestimate my capabilities. I have a whole new crew in a new place. It is being set up as we speak. I need you to go there and help the rest of the operation move forward so we can start transporting the product and making a profit fast. Your shit stain of a brother Carlos was working a guy who hid my money from me. We had to wait until I convinced my accountant he needed to put it back where it belonged. It took some time to apply the proper motivation, but after a small amount of time, he cooperated."

"Who hid your money?" Mac asked. This whole thing was so foreign to her. She couldn't imagine how her mother lived like this.

Waiting for someone to betray her for leverage or money. It would be a miracle if Reina ever trusted anyone, but maybe that was how she'd stayed the queen for so long. Trust no one, even your own sons.

"Carlos was always ambitious, as you well know. He hired an accountant to manage my finances because it was all getting too large to keep the books myself." She waved her hand in the air like it was a normal thing to have millions spread across multiple accounts. "Carlos got it in his head that I wasn't fit to run my empire and wanted to take me down so he would rule. In his twisted thinking, he used Billy, our new accountant, to hide my money. Billy was smart enough to put an insurance policy in place for himself and didn't give Carlos complete control. Smart boy, that one."

"What happened to the accountant?"

"Funny thing, he's in prison with your honey." Reina paused, letting the information sink in. "I put him there to see what kind of man you were planning on marrying. I'm sure you're not surprised he defended my accountant and kept him from dying, but he made some pretty nasty enemies doing it as I'd hoped. Your boy toy is the reason I have my money back in play. He convinced my accountant to make a deal to save his own skin. I give you credit my dear. He passed all my tests and survived it. Impressive."

It sounded like Hudson. He was always defending the underdog and looking out for the little guy. "Is that why they came after him and put him in the infirmary?"

"Oh, that man of yours is one tough cookie. From what I hear, he took down all my men in prison. One of them is a nasty fellow by the name of Gorilla," Reina explained like it was all so normal. Mac was still having a hard time wrapping her mind around all of it. "Because of Hudson, I'm back in business. If he wasn't such a liability and you two weren't a formidable pair together, I would consider bringing him in. The things I could do with that man."

Mac shivered. She didn't want Hudson anywhere near her mother. "What do you plan on doing to make all the charges disappear for Hudson?"

"Gennavie has everything needed to restore his freedom."

"Like what? I want everything to be returned to the way it was except for, of course, me. His career, his home, his life, everything. You agree, you and your people will not go near him for the rest of your days. I will do anything you want me to with no resistance if you make him whole again. Otherwise, no deal."

"Ooh, you will do everything I want you to. Down to the last little detail, and the reason you will is that otherwise, I won't only take your freedom," she said, baring her teeth. "I'll make it my life's mission to not only destroy you, but I'll take down everyone you've ever cared about. Hudson will be the icing on the cake. Once I'm done with him, I'll move on to your uncle, father, and sister, and then maybe I'll start in on your boss. He sure has some cute kids and a pretty little wife."

Mac said nothing for almost a full minute. "There's no need for any of that. I told you I surrender. Tell me what I need to do, and I'll do it. Leave my people alone." Mac tried not to be surprised that Reina had not only thrown her ex-husband in, but her own daughter. It made her wonder if her mother had a heart made of pure ice. She would never have the privilege and the joy of having her own children now, but she couldn't imagine causing them harm. Reina had single-handedly destroyed and killed or ordered the murder of three out of the five of her children, and wouldn't hesitate to take down both her daughters if it meant she would have freedom and power.

CHAPTER
SIXTY-FOUR

THE NEXT DAY, Mac turned in her rental car. The man behind the counter raised his eyebrows. "Wow, that's a lot of miles. Where did you go?"

"The rental was unlimited, right?" she asked.

"Well, yeah, but I've never seen that much put on a rental in such a short amount of time. You'd have to drive nonstop to do it."

"I had lots to do," was all she said as she signed the document and walked toward the shuttle, which whisked her off to her flight.

Dread hadn't left her the entire drive back to El Paso, and the more time passed, the more the depression and anxiety surrounding what her future held enveloped her like a weighted blanket. Every time she thought about the things she had to do, she couldn't breathe. Anxiety would crawl through her body, and she would have to choke back the nausea climbing up her throat. No other answer materialized, no matter how many times she flipped it around in her brain. If she couldn't pull it off, it would be too high of a price to pay. Her loved ones had always been there for her. The few she allowed close to her were precious. If anything happened to them, she wouldn't be able to survive.

When she landed at Spokane airport and gathered her things, she was in a piss-poor mood. Not paying attention to her surroundings, she didn't register the arm reaching out to grab hold of her shoulder. She spun around with wide eyes, ready to fight, when she saw Momma Hudson standing with a surprised look on her face.

"Hi, sweetie."

"Momma Hudson, what are you doing here? I thought you were going to stay put until we figured this out."

"Well, I'm not sure if my boy told you, but I am not a patient woman. I've been talking with your daddy. He is the nicest man." Something mischievous flashed through Momma Hudson's eyes. "He told me you would fly in today. Your uncle checked the flights and made sure when you were coming. We almost mixed it up since you changed plans."

Mac stared at her, wide-eyed. The last thing she needed was to take care of Momma Hudson for a visit. The things she was about to do didn't require any witnesses, and she would never forgive herself if Hudson's mother got hurt somehow along the way.

Mac got her voice to work again. "Um, it's great to see you. But now is not a good time. Let me buy you some dinner and then we'll talk about getting you back home."

Momma Hudson waved her hands in the air. "None of that, young lady. I haven't been to visit my boy yet. They say he's in a solitary confinement place and can't have visitors, and you're going to tell me why that is. You look like hell, honey," she said with a smile on her lips. "I think you're the one who's going to need a good meal, some sleep, and then we'll figure this thing out."

Mac didn't know what else to say. Her eyes kept scanning the airport for Gennavie. Reina hadn't given her an exact timeline to take care of business and go to Mexico, but if she knew her mother, she didn't have much time. Reina couldn't expect her to fly around the US, destroy her life, and board another plane to Mexico without food or rest. Or could she? Mac wasn't sure, but what she was sure of was Gennavie would come for her if she took too long. "Okay Momma Hudson, let's get you to my place and eat some food."

"Oh honey, you have no food, but we can stop on the way and pick something up."

"How do you know I don't have any food?" she asked, with a

perplexed look on her face.

"I'm a logical old lady at my age. From what your daddy told me, you've been all over God and country trying to figure out a way to help my boy, and for that I am grateful. But it also tells me you have no food in your house, at least nothing worth eating." Momma Hudson pulled Mac into a hug. "Now stop giving me crap and let's get going."

Mac couldn't help but smile. What she was going to do with Momma Hudson only put another layer on the situation. It solidified how much she liked her. Most people complained about their in-laws, but Mac thought she was lucky to have someone like Momma Hudson in her life. Then she reminded herself that she couldn't marry Hudson. She'd made a deal, and she had every intention of seeing it through.

"I need you to know everything is going to be okay," Mac said, squeezing Momma Hudson's hand. "You need to trust me. Your son is going to be fine."

The next morning, Mac rose before dawn. It was going to be a long day, and she needed her energy. Looking in the mirror, the woman who stared back at her looked foreign, with enormous bags under her normally bright and alive eyes. This was the hardest thing she'd ever had to do. Two hours later, she pulled up to the prison. She'd called in several favors and convinced the warden to allow her to visit Hudson in person. It was nice to have contacts with leverage. Captain Boom had a working relationship with Warden Juliana and convinced him it was necessary. Mac was grateful when Boom didn't ask too many questions.

Her heart pounded in her chest as she walked into the prison and began the process. It took over forty-five minutes before she got in. They led her to a small room and told her to wait. When she saw Hudson being led in, she almost lost her cool. Blinking back tears, she took several deep breaths as she watched the guard secure him to the table with his cuffs. He had some new bruises and a cut along his cheek, but overall, he looked pretty good.

A huge smile crept across his face. "It's so good to see you," he said before he took his seat. "This is like the never-ending nightmare."

"It's going to be okay now," she said, taking a deep breath in and letting it out. "I need to tell you something, and I need you to let me say this or I might not be able to."

"You can tell me anything. We'll get through this and make it work. Have some faith," he said, trying to inch closer to her until his cuffed hands strained against his wrists. "Anything new that can help us?"

"Yes, the nightmare is going to be over soon," she said, as a single tear slipped down her left cheek.

"That's great news. I never doubted you."

"I'm sorry," she began, but had to stop.

"What are you sorry for? None of this is your fault."

"I'm sorry because I can't marry you. Forget about me and move on," she said, trying not to look at the pain she was causing him.

His eyes looked back at her, pleading. "What are you talking about?" he asked, slumping his enormous frame into the chair. To her, it looked like all the life had drained from his body. She hated to do this to him, but the other way was not an option.

"Don't you understand? I don't want to marry you. I can't be with someone like you. If I don't distance myself from you, then I'll lose all my work. Don't you get it? We're toxic together and I'm done." Tears were flowing now. She choked on the words as she placed her engagement ring in his hand. "I never want to see you again." She sobbed, getting up and knocking on the door for the guard to let her out.

As he slid it open, she looked back one last time at the pain she caused the man she loved so much. If there was any way she could take it back, she would. He looked devastated as she hurried past the guard and out of the room.

As soon as she was back outside the prison and could force herself to control her voice, she dialed Momma Hudson. "Hi, it's Mac."

"I know who it is, honey. How are you this morning? Did you get some sleep?"

"A little," she said, taking another deep breath. "I was able to pull some strings and work it out so you can come visit your son in about an hour."

"What wonderful news. I'll be right over. Thank you for everything, Mac. You are so good for my boy. He's lucky to have you."

Mac hung up the phone without saying another word. If she did, her voice would betray her. At least his mom would be by his side to help him through.

CHAPTER
SIXTY-FIVE

MAC LOOKED around the parking lot. At first, there was no sign of her. Then, on the far side of the lot, a redhead came around the corner. Gennavie pulled up to the side of the prison, avoiding the cameras fastened to the front. Mac opened the door, not sure what to expect.

"Get in," Gennavie said.

Mac climbed in and they drove out of the parking lot. Mac figured she was taking it slow so they wouldn't draw any attention. The last thing Reina would want was a paper trail of any kind.

"Hand me your phone."

Mac handed it over without asking questions as they drove away from her future and into a world she never wanted to go to again.

Less than ten minutes later, Gennavie pulled over to the side of the road. Before she got out, she grabbed Mac's arm and slapped handcuffs on one side, clasping the other side to the steering wheel so she couldn't go anywhere.

Gennavie got out of the car, looking elegant and in control. Mac watched as she tossed the phone into the Spokane River and watched it sink.

The two remained silent on the drive until they pulled up to an old house sitting back off the road, looking a little broken with its peeling blue paint. It looked no bigger than Mac's first one-bedroom apartment from the outside.

Gennavie pulled around the back and got out. "Come on, my pet."

Mac hoisted her body out of the car. Gennavie and Reina had planned it well so far. Driving a Toyota Corolla with no stickers in a bland beige color that no one would pay attention to was a start. She wondered if the plates on it were real, but she guessed they weren't.

This little house was a perfect place to hide. No one would think to look for her here. If neighbors saw them coming and going, no one would notify the police. This was the type of neighborhood where they avoided the cops instead of welcoming them in. The small house had no visible cameras and sat outside town. Mac wondered how long they would stay.

"What's the plan?" Mac asked.

"Now that you're cooperating, we're going to prepare for your brief trip and wait."

"What are we waiting for?" Mac asked as she followed Gennavie into the small, dingy home at gunpoint.

"I took the liberty of packing your things."

A small bag Mac recognized from her house sat on a couch that looked like it had been through a war zone. The dirty green fabric sagged in the middle like an elephant had sat on it.

Mac's shoulders tightened at the violation of Gennavie coming into her home and taking her things, but she'd have to get used to it. Her life didn't belong to her anymore.

"You didn't answer my question. What are we waiting for?"

"We're waiting for what we want," Gennavie said, pulling the door closed and pulling off the gray hoodie she had been wearing.

"And what is that?" Mac asked.

"As soon as we receive word they released Hudson and Vincent, then we'll deliver you and I'll go play. Everyone gets what they want," she said with an evil grin playing at the corners of her full lips.

"This is never what I wanted," Mac said, crossing her arms.

"Oh, stop whining. You take over a huge drug empire and rule next to your own mother. How bad could it be? I mean, all the luxury and money. Who could ask for more?"

"That stuff was never important to me. If it was, I would have stayed and grown up in the house putting up with that psychotic bitch," Mac spat. She was angry and didn't have anywhere to send the anger except in Gennavie's direction.

"Sit your ass down so we can start."

"Start with what?"

"Sit your ass down and stop being difficult. If you play along, things will go fine." Gennavie trained her gun on Mac. "I said sit, my little puppet. We need to start. Once they release Vincent, I want this to be buttoned up nicely. No extra things for me to take care of. I'll take my money, pick up my man, and be gone. Never to see your ugly mug again."

"What are you going to do to me?" Mac asked, keeping an eye on Gennavie's finger playing with the trigger of the gun in her hand. This woman couldn't care less if she lived or died as long as she got what she wanted. Mac was a tool to her and nothing more.

"Fucking sit," she said, sweeping the barrel of the gun from Mac to the chair that sat by itself in the middle of the room.

Mac did, letting Gennavie strap her arms and legs to the cold metal surface. The uncomfortable metal seat sank into her flesh as the casters on the bottom moved. It was going to be hard to keep the circulation from cutting off if she sat too long.

"Now sit still or it won't turn out right."

"What are you talking about?"

"Your transformation. The all-new you will be ready before long."

Mac watched in horror as Gennavie walked over and grabbed a small trash can, some scissors, and a brush. She could only sit and watch as Gennavie brushed her long, beautiful, thick, dark hair out. Mac kept reminding herself that hair grew back, and it didn't matter. Without Hudson around, did it matter if she looked or felt pretty? It was best she got used to this new identity. Mac's breath caught in her throat when Gennavie grabbed the back of her silky dark hair like a ponytail and cut it off, dropping a sizeable chunk onto the floor.

"Oh, don't be so emotional. It's only hair. If you're a good girl, maybe your mommy will let you grow it back."

Mac took several breaths and closed her eyes. If she didn't look, maybe it wouldn't be so bad. Gennavie worked around her head. Cutting and snipping had Mac melting into the uncomfortable seat like a floaty losing all its air.

Her eyes shot open when Gennavie grabbed the back of her chair and pulled her toward the sink in the kitchen. Once the wheels hit the gold-speckled linoleum, the chair rolled. Gennavie adjusted the chair so it moved up and in line with the sink and forced Mac's head back. Mac flinched when she bent forward and kissed her cheek.

"Maybe we can have a little fun before I turn you over."

Mac forced herself not to react. She wouldn't give Gennavie the satisfaction. She laid her head back into the sink and closed her eyes.

CHAPTER
SIXTY-SIX

"SO, WHAT DO YOU THINK?" Gennavie handed Mac a small mirror. Staring back at her was a woman she didn't recognize. Her platinum-blond hair looked foreign on her head since Gennavie had left her eyebrows her normal chestnut-brown color. The combination left her looking washed out and drained, which matched how she felt on the inside. If she survived this ordeal, maybe one day she would make it back to real life. And, if she was lucky, she would be with Hudson again—if he hadn't given up on her by then. She willed herself to keep some hope in the back of her mind, otherwise she wouldn't be able to make it through this. First, find out if they had released Hudson.

"Oh, come now my little pet, I think you kinda look hot as a blond," Gennavie said, with a nasty smile creeping across her face.

"Now what?" was all Mac said.

"We have an appointment for the next step in about an hour. In the meantime, I thought we might have a little fun."

Mac was pretty sure she wanted nothing to do with Gennavie's idea of fun. She blew the air out of her lungs as Gennavie ran her long fingernail along Mac's jawline, down her neck, and around her breast. She did everything not to shrink away from the woman but couldn't help it when Gennavie grabbed hold of her left nipple through her bra and tugged hard.

"Look, as much as playing with you sounds like fun," Mac said, "I haven't eaten since yesterday. We don't want me passing out, do we?"

Gennavie let go of Mac's nipple and tapped her on the cheek. "I suppose not, my pet. I need you looking good for our appointment today." Gennavie circled her, grabbing the back of her hair and wrenching her head back. "But when we're done, we'll have plenty of time."

"What's the appointment for?" Mac asked again.

"The next step to your new life. It should excite you to become the woman you were always supposed to be instead of slaving away for the government. They don't care about you. You're only another number in uniform who they can order around. They would have used you until they were done with you and either kicked you out or forced you into retirement. Under Reina's rule, you live in luxury."

It was the one thing that was most important to Gennavie. Luxury was ugly under these circumstances. The thought of poisoning millions with her mother's products—all for money—was vile to Mac. Her mother had no problem selling to children. There was a rumor that Reina had a team in the States who worked toward targeting middle school children because they were easier to sell to if they were from affluent families. The thought of poisoning children made her sick. To her mother, it was a business decision. Like the decision to sell Tia, her oldest sister. Tia died because her mother tried to trade her to her drug supplier's son. Business, with no love for her daughter. Mac was not at all sorry she'd killed the man who drove her sister to suicide. Tia had killed not only herself, but her unborn child. Their mother put Tia in a situation where death was a better option than fighting.

Mac squared her shoulders; she couldn't allow herself the same fate. It would be hard to survive, but she had already been through so much. Maybe if she played her cards right, one day she would infiltrate deep enough into her mother's business to dismantle it. A problem for another day, she reminded herself.

"Come on," Gennavie said, removing the rope from around her

ankles and wrists. "Let's grab some food and move on to the next thing." Mac thought she saw disappointment in Gennavie's eyes.

An hour later, with a full stomach, Gennavie led Mac down a stone staircase into a basement in downtown Spokane. It sat underneath a restaurant Mac frequented. She didn't know the shop was there. Gennavie stayed behind her the entire time with the gun trained on her back. Mac had no intention of fleeing. It was too important for Hudson to be released. She would wait until he had his life back and then, maybe. "You two are late," a tattooed man said. He looked like a decorated bean pole with every inch of his skin covered in colorful art. His head was topped off with bright-green hair falling into his eyes.

"Yeah, this one had to eat," Gennavie said.

"Now we're going to have to be quick. I have another appointment at the top of the hour." He walked up to Mac without greeting her, looking her up and down. "Nice. The camera is going to like you. Go sit," he said, pointing to a makeshift photo studio with enormous lights and a white backdrop. Sitting on the small circular chair in the middle of the equipment, Mac stared at the wall. "Okay, now turn to the side. A little to the left." He came over and adjusted her. "Now tilt your head up. Good, good. Now smile." Mac's mouth smiled, but her eyes did not. Dread grew in the pit of her stomach. He turned to Gennavie. "Go pick out two or three outfits that will work." Gennavie walked over to a long row of clothes hanging from a metal rack and picked out a few blues, green, and tan tops she thought would photograph well.

An hour later, she was looking at three new passports and government driver's licenses with different names. In each one, she was wearing something different and had a different name, date of birth, and address. The woman in the photos only kind of resembled the woman she had been only yesterday. The new documents were quite impressive and looked identical to the real ones issued by the government. When she was little, her dad put together some fake documents for her and her sister, but she never saw them or had to use them. She had been too young to worry about any of it. When she became an adult, her dad made sure she had everything she needed to enlist in the military. After, she never looked back. She had to admit, she wasn't sure if her current documents, as Evelyn McGregor, were one hundred percent authentic.

Once they finished with the session, Gennavie put her back in the car and took her back to the house to wait.

CHAPTER
SIXTY-SEVEN

THE NEXT MORNING Mac woke with Gennavie untying her from the uncomfortable bed she was trying to sleep in. At first, she thought Gennavie was going to violate her in a way she would have to live with for the rest of her life. "What are you doing?" Mac said in a whisper.

"Relax, it's time to move. We're getting ready to transport tomorrow and need to be close to our exit as soon as we receive word."

Mac sensed there was more. Gennavie was angry and a little off her game. The woman who was always in control wouldn't make eye contact with Mac. "Did something go wrong?"

"Your fucking mother is changing the agreement. Now, she wants me to go with you to keep an eye on things and you in line until they release her from prison," Gennavie said, making quotation marks with her fingers. "It's going to take more time to bust Vincent out than she thought it would."

"What about Hudson?" she asked as her left hand released. Rubbing her wrists, she watched as Gennavie stalked around the room.

"Of course Hudson is being released this afternoon because I can keep my word and do my fucking job. I fed all the documents to that damn defense attorney of his yesterday. I did my part, but now your mother is stalling. Going to Mexico was not part of my plan."

"Maybe it's a good thing. You can come with me to my mother's home and help Vincent from there. Plus, if I know Reina, it will be one hell of a palace."

"Are you fucking delusional?" Gennavie said, launching the back of her hand across Mac's face. Mac moved back out of the way before she made contact. "We aren't friends. I hate your fucking guts. You're the reason I'm in this mess. If I destroyed you right here and now, I wouldn't think twice. Now I have to spend time with you. What the hell is wrong with that woman?" Mac sat back on the thin mattress, watching Gennavie. As she paced, she calmed down. Reina was the only woman Mac had ever met who could get under someone's skin like that. "You may have a point. Reina's fortune is substantial. Maybe a piece of that pie will be worth my time. Since you came along, I've had to deplete a lot of my funds because I can't work. Reina's fortune would come in handy when starting my new life with Vincent."

"Did she say how long she thought it would be before she got Vincent out?"

"No, something about him being on death row. I mean, come on, she's one of the most powerful women I've ever come in contact with. Breaking a guy out of prison should be simple for her."

"What about her? How long do you think it will take for her to be released? They have a lot of evidence against her. I'm not sure how she's going to pull it off with so many states and the federal government trying to prosecute her."

"I'm sure she'll come up with something. Why the hell do you care? Your only job is to run the place until she gets back. It can't be too hard."

"It might be news to you, but I've never run a drug cartel and I have no idea what I'm doing, nor do I have any interest in the business. Your mind is perfect for running her empire. You're fueled by the same things she is. You coming with me helps me out." *Plus, you're a substantial source of intel*, she thought to herself.

"It can't be helped. Change your clothes so we can move to the next location."

Mac didn't argue. Thirty minutes later, they were getting into the little Toyota. "It sure will be nice to ride around in Reina's Bentley," Mac commented.

"Yes, it will." Gennavie looked at Mac, tilting her head to the side. "Why are you trying to be nice to me?"

"I figured it would be easier to work together if we learned to communicate a little. Sounds like this thing won't be over soon. No telling how long it will take Reina to spring herself from prison, let alone Vincent. At least they haven't prosecuted her yet. If she can find her way back to Mexico before that happens, the extradition treaty will be in her favor. Vincent is already a felon. It will be harder to get him out and then out of the country."

Gennavie looked at her, unsure for a moment. "You don't think she would double-cross me once you're in place, do you?"

"No idea. She hasn't hesitated in the past to destroy her own children and you're not even blood, so I have no idea what she might do with you."

"Well, we'll have to see about that. For now, I'm looking forward to coming out of the shadows. This shit where I'm a ghost and can't play is bullshit. I've been in hiding far too long. At the very least, I can look forward to getting back to my glorious self."

Mac marveled at how large this woman's ego was. Maybe she could use it to her advantage. "True, there's that. As long as you remain useful to Reina, you'll be fine." Mac reached with her hand that wasn't cuffed to the door and patted her on her arm.

They pulled up to the next rental property. It was only a stone's throw from the airport. As they got out, Mac watched a plane fly overhead. "We fly out tomorrow. Now that I'm being forced to accompany you, we had to wait another day."

"Interesting," Mac said, raising an eyebrow. "You're saying she could get you on the same flight as me with less than twenty-four hours? Sounds to me like she had this planned all along."

"What the hell do you know? As long as I have you, she won't cross me." Gennavie bared her teeth.

"It sounds like she already has. I'm her daughter and I've been on the receiving end of this."

"I have it under control. Now go inside before someone spots you." Gennavie pointed her gun at Mac.

Mac raised and dropped her shoulders. "I'm saying you should watch your back with that woman."

"As soon as Vincent meets me in Mexico, I'll be gone and won't have anything else to worry about."

"If you say so," Mac said, walking into the house. This one was nicer than the last. It had fresh paint on the walls and leather couches. A welcome sign hung on the wall and a sign-in book on a little table sat to the left as they walked in. Mac sat on the couch, waiting.

CHAPTER
SIXTY-EIGHT

HUDSON SAT IN SOLITARY CONFINEMENT, trying to figure out what went wrong. Mac wouldn't go from wanting to be his wife to never wanting to be with him again. None of it made any sense. And then he remembered the year before when they accused her of selling drugs. He had just met her, but he'd still turned his back on her. It hadn't taken him long to come to his senses, but he was trying to understand. How could they go from being everything to each other and having a future together, to her wanting nothing to do with him? Staying in solitary would only make it worse. It gave him too much time to speculate and obsess about it. Was his mind playing tricks on him? he wondered. It was possible. He'd read plenty of articles about how inmates who sat in solitary for too long developed mental health issues. He wasn't delusional about Mac's visit that morning. The woman of his dreams wouldn't desert him at a time like this. At first, he hadn't registered the guard until the man rapped his baton on the metal door. "Inmate Hudson, get your ass up. It's your lucky day."

"What's going on? Is Mac okay?"

The man's moon-shaped face cocked to the side. "Son, I don't know what you're talking about or who this Mac fella is, but you're being released."

Hudson looked at him, not sure what to say. "You mean I made bail again?"

"No sir, they've dropped all charges. From what I understand, someone provided all kinds of stuff to your defense attorney that cleared you. You're one of the few sorry assholes who receive a second chance at life. When folks come in here, it's like the roach motel. People get in, but they almost never go back out. At least not for long. Once they're institutionalized, they keep coming back for more. Something's wrong with the system. I keep telling them, but they never listen. You're one of the lucky ones. Your momma is waiting to pick you up."

"My mom's here?" Hudson looked at the man like he was crazy. "How?"

"No idea, not my department, but if you'd like to stay with us, I'm sure we can arrange it."

"Uh, no, I'm good," Hudson said.

"Now push your hands through. Regulation says I have to escort you out in cuffs, but once we clear the inner walls, I can take them off."

Hudson pressed his hands through the hole and waited for the guard to snap the cuffs in place. The guard walked him through the prison and past Gorilla's cell.

"Hey sunshine, you're a dead man walking after what you did."

"Don't mind him,' the guard said behind him. "He's pissy because he's never going to breathe free air again. Don't come back and you'll never have to deal with him again."

"You can count on it," Hudson said over his shoulder.

The guard led him out of the prison and as promised, the cuffs unlatched from his wrists as soon as the steel door separating the inmates from the outside world slid shut. He hoped to never hear the sound again. They gave him the opportunity to change into his civilian clothes and returned his belongings. After signing some documents, the guard led him to a waiting room he hadn't been in before where his mom was waiting. What surprised him was the man with her. He wondered why Mac's dad had his arm around his mom. Mac's dad stepped to the side as Hudson walked out.

His mom ran forward at the sight of her boy. "Oh honey, Mac said I can visit you today, but I didn't know you were going to be released until we got here."

It reminded him of the only other time they released him from prison. His mom had been waiting for him then, too. To this day, he wasn't sure if his mom thought he had done it or not.

They found the drug dealer who fed his brother the poison leading to his death, mutilated in a back alley. Hudson was the primary suspect during the investigation. An eyewitness said they saw Hudson leaving the location before the cops arrived. They held Hudson for several weeks pending trial. His defense attorney discredited the witness during the pre-trial hearing and got the case thrown out since no other evidence tied him to the murder. It was the beginning of Hudson's career back then. They convinced him his days in the military, and as a free man, were over. Once they released him, he swore never to step foot in another prison. He hoped this time he would keep that promise to himself.

He engulfed her in a gentle bear hug. "It's good to see you too, Mom, and it's even better to be out." He pulled away from his mom and addressed Mac's dad. "It's good to see you again." They shook hands. "What are you both doing here? Is Mac okay?"

"Why wouldn't she be?" his mom asked. "I talked to her this morning. She said she called in a favor for me to come visit you." The worry in her son's eyes was unmistakable. "What happened?"

"She came to the prison this morning and told me she doesn't want to marry me."

Before Hudson finished getting the words out, Mac's dad had taken out his phone and started dialing. "Nothing," Mac's dad said. "I think it's dead or disabled."

Hudson started talking on his phone. "Thanks. I was just released." Pause. "Have you talked to Mac?" Pause. "What do you mean you haven't heard from her? When was the last time you talked to her?" He paused again. "Well shit, apparently the last anyone saw her. Any idea where she would go?" Hudson paused again. "Okay, thanks. Call me if there's any news." He turned to face the two people who were staring at him. "Her boss Captain Stanton received a message from her this morning saying she was going back into hiding and not to worry."

"That can't be good," Mac's dad said, worry lines creasing the sides of his eyes. Hudson noticed when his mom slipped her hand into his and gave it a gentle squeeze, making him wonder for the second time what was going on. "Okay, before we jump to conclusions, let's go to her place."

CHAPTER
SIXTY-NINE

THIRTY-FIVE MINUTES LATER, they pulled in front of Mac's small house. It always reminded Hudson of a little cottage out in the woods where you might find pixie fairies. As if to solidify his thoughts, a young deer lifted her head as they approached and gave him an inquisitive look. There was no movement on the inside. As soon as his mom put her rental car in park, he pushed the door open, taking long strides to the front door.

"Gavin," Mac's dad called from behind him. Hudson turned around, and he placed latex gloves into Hudson's hands. "In case we need to dust for prints. We just got you out of prison. We don't need anyone thinking you did something wrong here."

"Good call," he said, twisting the doorknob in his hand. It was an old-school setup with a round handle versus one you would push down on. Hudson's stomach twisted when it opened. Mac would never leave her home unlocked after a killer broke in and trashed the place. Even before then, she was careful about her personal security. "That's not right," he mumbled, more to himself than the people stacked close behind him.

They split up, making their way through each room, and came back out empty-handed.

"It looks like someone threw a bag together. Her room is in disarray, with things scattered everywhere and her uniforms left behind. Everything related to the military is still here," Mac's dad said.

"It makes sense if she's going into hiding. She wouldn't need her military gear," Mom commented. "Would she have gone to your place, hon?"

"I guess it's possible. It couldn't hurt to check." Hudson pulled the door shut and locked it with his key as they filed out and into the car. Hudson's mom drove faster than she should have. Twice Hudson grabbed hold of the oh-shit bar above his shoulder. "Ma, if you kill us on the way, we won't be able to help Mac."

"Yeah hon, but she's supposed to be my new daughter-in-law. That makes her family, and well…before you met her, I was pretty worried. That worthless ex-wife of yours left you in shambles after she cheated her way through half the base."

His mom was getting too worked up. "I'm sure it'll be fine. We may need to call in some help, but we will find her," he said as they walked up to his house. His door, unlike hers, remained locked tight. He let them in and walked around the house, looking for any evidence of where Mac might have gone.

Walking into the bedroom, he stopped dead. Bullet holes had turned the entire room into Swiss cheese. She'd told him someone had taken shots at her, but he didn't know it was this bad.

There was a note on the shredded pillow—his pillow. *Don't try to find me. This is for the best. It's the only way you will remain safe and free. All my love, Mac.*

Relief and worry washed over him. She still loved him, but where was she? His gut turned, thinking she'd done something stupid to save him.

The other two gathered around him, and he lowered the note so they could read. Mac's dad growled. "Shit, this can only mean one thing."

"What?" Hudson's mom said.

"She made a deal with the devil, would be my guess. My bull-headed daughter."

"What on earth are you talking about, David? What devil and who did she make a deal with?"

"He's talking about Mac's mother," Hudson said. "She's not the friendly type like you."

She smiled at him. "But I still don't understand. If she's with her mother, then she's safe, no matter how rough around the edges. A mother would never hurt her babies."

Mac's dad smiled. "In your world they wouldn't, but in her world, if it advances her career, then anything is on the table. If Mac is working with Reina and Gennavie then her life is in danger."

"We need help." Hudson dialed Joe's number.

"Hey buddy, they told me you got sprung this afternoon, Joe said. "I can't tell you how happy I am for you. When can we celebrate?"

"That's going to have to wait. Mac is missing and we think she might have made a deal for my release. Do you know anything about it?"

"Nothing," Joe said. "She was moving heaven and earth to get you out and clear your name. She must have hit a brick wall and figured it was the only way."

"That's our guess too," Hudson said.

"Our guess?" Joe asked.

"My mom and Mac's dad are here. They came to help, but they don't have any more information than I do."

"Where are you guys now?"

Hudson brought him up to speed on the note and what they'd found so far, which was little.

"Let me make some phone calls and I'll call you back. In the meantime, don't do anything stupid to get yourself back in trouble."

None of it mattered now. He had a couple of people who would help. He needed them to work some serious magic. Doing something stupid to save Mac was what he had in mind. He hoped he would reach her fast enough. "Lola, hey, it's Hudson. Yeah, I'm out and things are better on my end. Have you talked to your sister?"

"No. Should I?" Lola asked, concern laced through her voice.

Hudson brought her up to speed. "Do you still have access to facial recognition software?"

"Does a bear shit in the woods?"

"I'm guessing that means yes."

"Yeah, where is her last location?"

"That's the problem," Hudson said, running his hand through his hair as he paced around his living room. "I have no idea. They still had me locked up the last time I saw her. It was almost twenty-four hours ago. Can you run a scan over most of Spokane? Assuming she's still here, and they haven't already sent her to Mexico."

"You think she would be dumb enough to work with our mother on this?"

"Dumb, no, desperate, yes. If it'd get me my life back, I do. It's part of her charm—selfless acts of valor."

"Yeah, that's my sis alright. Okay, let me run some new software I got my hands on. Once I find her, we're going to need to move. I'll scan the entire city—airports, bus stations, and any other exit plan I can think of. I'll call as soon as I have something. Tell my dad I said hi."

"How did you know he was here? Never mind, I'm not sure I want the answer to that," Hudson said, hanging up and continuing to pace while he tried to figure out the next best move. He walked into his room, started rummaging through his military gear, and pulled out a flack vest from his time in the field. When he walked out, he found Mac's dad on the phone.

"Agent Bardot, please. Yes, I'll hold."

CHAPTER
SEVENTY

THE MORE TIME THAT PASSED, the more uptight Gennavie became. Mac was on her own but took comfort in knowing they had released Hudson. The paranoia surrounding Gennavie was palatable. She wouldn't let Mac go to the bathroom by herself. The plan was falling apart. The plane they should have been on left early in the day.

"What's going on?" Mac asked.

"Your fucking mother is what's going on," Gennavie shot back, growling at Mac as she passed. Gennavie stalked around the room like a caged animal while Mac sat strapped to the chair.

"Why haven't we gotten on our flight? Weren't we going to leave this morning?" She had been in Gennavie's custody for over forty-eight hours now. The woman kept checking the windows. "Maybe Reina has another plan. Have you thought of that?"

"What the hell are you talking about? The woman is incarcerated. No other plan exists."

"Then why hasn't she called?"

"I have no idea, but I'm going to find out." Mac watched as Gennavie set up a tripod in the center of the room. She pulled Mac out of the way and into the corner. Mac's hands had gone numb as the ropes cut in. Running was not on Mac's mind. She needed a way out of this. A solution that didn't involve putting Hudson in danger again. If she ran, the nightmare would only begin again. Her mother wasn't one to take things lying down.

Gennavie grunted behind her, and Mac craned her neck to the side, trying to figure out what she was doing. In the middle of the room, pointed at the door, Gennavie was setting up an M240 automatic machine gun perched on top of the sturdy black tripod.

"What the hell is that thing for?" Mac asked, getting concerned.

"I'm not taking any chances. We may have no choice but to sit here and wait, but I'm not about to be surprised by any visitors," she said as she laced what looked like fishing wire from the trigger to the door. Mac prayed an unsuspecting neighbor wouldn't come by uninvited. More to the point, no one she cared about would come looking for her. Mac was confident that given enough time, her friends and family would find her, but it wouldn't fix the current problem. Gennavie would still be after them, they would still be in danger, and her mother would still pull strings from her prison cell. Worse yet, if they came, they might not survive. Enough bullets stuck out of the gun to take down a small army, let alone one or two people.

"She'll get rid of you if she's done playing with you or if she has someone else to do her bidding," Mac said. It wasn't a great idea to get this woman riled up any further, but if the opportunity presented itself, maybe she could overtake her. No way Mac would run without making sure Gennavie wasn't waiting in the shadows.

CHAPTER
SEVENTY-ONE

IT WAS UNREAL. One minute, Hudson's life was flipped upside down, and the next minute, they returned everything to normal. They expected him to report back to duty and receive a full briefing on his status that afternoon. At first, he tried to argue with his commander's assistant, but he gave in. There wasn't much he could do until Lola got him a firm location. Trying to be patient, he dialed Joe.

"Hey man, anything new?" Hudson said into the phone.

"Nothing yet, but there sure are a lot of people up in arms about how this thing went down."

"Yeah, I talked to Bartz, my defense attorney. He and the FBI received conclusive video footage of me with Mac at the time of Daniels' murder, along with photos of a mysterious woman leaving his house with blood on her hands. Lola was able to add to it by tracking my whereabouts in Seattle and clearing my name for Captain Anika Wilson. And, to put the cherry on top, a nice anonymous letter said they planted the drugs on me and injected them into my system. It cast enough reasonable doubt to make them drop the charges, especially once they leaked the letter to the press."

"The young sergeant stationed outside your temporary housing confessed to the hazy memory of a desirable woman seducing him right before he lost consciousness. His statement says he thought it was all a dream because the woman looked like someone out of a porn magazine, not an actual living woman. She had to be part of his fantasy. Women in his world didn't look like that, and with the drugs in his system, it couldn't have happened that way."

"Yeah, I'm betting not everyone thinks I'm innocent. I've gotten a couple of sly comments, but nothing I can't handle. What worries me the most is that the woman has Mac. No other explanation I can come up with explains where Mac is. Mac's dad talked to Agent Bardot, who confirmed two visitors to Reina in the last thirty days. One was Mac and the other was a woman named Veronica Smith."

"Who the hell is Veronica Smith?" Joe asked.

"Bardot thinks it's Gennavie using an alias, but we won't know for sure until the warden gets back to her with confirmation. If it is Gennavie then we have confirmation they've been working together."

"How does that help us out?" Joe asked.

"Bardot is working the angle. She's trying to set up an interrogation with Reina to get to the bottom of it. In the meantime, Reina is being held in solitary confinement, so she can't cause any more trouble.

"At least there's that. Look, Hudson, I gotta go, but as soon as I have something, I'll call. Everyone on the force has Mac's picture and is looking for her."

"Thanks, Joe."

An hour later, Hudson stood outside his commander's door waiting to be called in. He hadn't eaten since the day before, and his stomach turned every time he thought of what was happening to Mac right at that moment.

"Come in, Sergeant Hudson," Lieutenant Colonel Dixon said from the other side of the door. "How are you holding up?"

"As well as can be expected, sir."

"I can only imagine. Take a seat."

Hudson didn't sit, but squared his shoulders and faced his commander. "With all due respect, sir. I'd like to continue my search for Mac right now."

"I can respect your wishes, but I need to go over a few things with you that can't wait. I need you to understand some complications you will face in the near future."

"None of it matters unless I save Mac." Hudson sank into the chair across from his boss and let out a long breath.

"I'm going to do everything I can to help you, but first we have to address your status before things spiral out of hand. During your time in confinement, they put you in a status that stripped you of all your pay and benefits. What is your current financial position?"

"Sir, is this necessary right now?"

"Hudson, listen to me. If we don't get this under control, it will spiral. When you find Mac, do you want to be homeless?"

"No, sir."

"The other issue is returning your good name. Several people still think you're guilty and are out because someone pulled some strings for you. We need to have a press conference to clear you. I can set it up for this afternoon."

"Sir, you don't seem to understand. You don't want me in front of a camera right now or in front of anyone, for that matter. I'm not focusing on anything else until we have Mac back. I don't think I could if I wanted to."

"Hudson, I'm trying to be understanding, but I need you to put your big boy pants on and take care of this shit before it gets out of hand. My boss, the installation commander, isn't asking. Do you understand?"

"Yes sir," Hudson said, getting up from his chair as his stomach twisted into knots.

"Now go to your office and put your blues on so we can get this thing over with and focus on what's important," Dixon said.

Two hours later, Hudson checked his phone for the hundredth time. Still nothing back from Lola or Joe on Mac's location. He was useless standing next to his commander, waiting to go on camera while Mac was in danger. Would she do the same thing? Wait around for other people to find him if he were the one being held? Hell no, she would investigate and turn over every rock.

And then it came to him. Maybe he could use this to his advantage.

They walked in and took their places in front of the sea of reporters. He wondered if this was how Mac felt when she had to stand before the same people.

"Good afternoon, everyone. I'm Lieutenant Colonel Dixon, and most of you know who Master Sergeant Hudson is."

The entire room went quiet as they waited to find out all the juicy details.

Mac sat strapped to her chair and stared at the small television. Gennavie left her secured to the tiny chair in the middle of the room and went out. She'd left the television on loud to drown out any efforts Mac may have made to call for help. The house sat back off the street with no neighbors close by. Mac wouldn't dare call anyone with the gun pointed at the front door. She wasn't prepared to sacrifice another person for her own release.

On the television stood the most wonderful man she had ever met. He looked handsome in his blues uniform with his shoulders pressed back. His eyes looked tired and worried, lacking sleep and food. A large man like him shouldn't go long without either, but he didn't take care of himself when he worried. She hoped he would move past this and her one day and move on. The thought of him being with another woman made her stomach turn, but she couldn't help it. They'd both be destroyed if she didn't let him go.

He stepped forward to the podium, and she remembered her experience in the same spotlight not long ago. It amazed her. It had only been a few short weeks. So much had changed since then. One minute she was going to be his wife and the next she was agreeing to a life of imprisonment in her mother's compound. Hudson's voice flowed out of the television, and she closed her eyes, picturing herself with him. He explained why they'd incarcerated him and his theory on why someone had set him up. The facts weren't spot on, but he was pretty close. His commander explained the enormous complications Hudson would face to bring his life back. His mother had to take a second mortgage out on her home for bail, and all of it was now being reversed. Once the commander finished, Hudson stepped forward again.

"This is where I need your help." He waited while the room went quiet. "My future wife and the woman I love is being held by the same people who set me up for crimes I didn't commit. If you receive any intel about the whereabouts of Master Seargent Evelyn McGregor, please call Officer Joe Romero at the Spokane Police Department. Do not engage with her captor. She is likely armed and dangerous."

The room exploded then with questions about Mac's disappearance.

CHAPTER
SEVENTY-TWO

GENNAVIE WALKED in through the back of the house to find Mac still secured to the chair after the newscast ended. The reporter on the screen was talking about the rising problems with drugs in the community. Mac breathed out a sigh that she hadn't come in minutes earlier and prayed some good-intentioned person wouldn't try to come in and help her. She twisted her body around to look at what Gennavie was doing. The woman was humming.

"What are you so chipper about?" Mac asked, with an edge laced in her voice.

"Things are coming together. I was getting worried your mother wasn't a woman of her word, but boy was I wrong."

"What are you talking about?"

"Well, my little plaything in Seattle called to tell me Vincent is making a full recovery from his injuries."

Mac wrinkled her brow. "What injuries?"

"Well, my man," she said, placing her hands on her hips, looking proud, "shoved a pipe up some guy's ass."

She couldn't help but let her mouth fall open. *What the hell is wrong with these people?* Mac wondered. "Why would he do that?"

"To become the alpha, silly. I'm sure your little boy toy did some pretty vicious things to get the upper hand while in the can." Hudson wasn't capable of it. Killing in self-defense was about the closest he came to violence. "They scheduled a new trial because the silly little bitch of a judge got what was coming to her. Some of the witnesses against my husband have changed their story. He might walk free."

"Why would people change their story after testifying?" Mac asked, but already had a good idea.

"Oh, nothing a little persuasion couldn't fix. His new defense attorney is much better than that little bitch, Anika. She had no idea what she was doing. If things keep going in this direction, there will be enough reasonable doubt in his case to reverse his conviction and they'll release him from death row."

"Where does my mother come into play?"

"She's the one who helped me set it all up. Of course, I had to do the dirty work because she's still sitting in the can, but I'm not sure I can pull it off without Reina's help."

"What happens now?"

"Well, it looks like we're going to be here for a little while. I still haven't got our flight plans, but your mother is doing a great job getting everything else taken care of. I'm willing to wait, and you're going to be a good girl and wait with me. Do not give me a lick of trouble."

CHAPTER
SEVENTY-THREE

AS HUDSON WAS LEAVING the press conference with his commander, his phone rang. He excused himself and stepped away. "Hey Lola, news?"

"Hey, yup, I found the man who set her up with a fake ID. You might get a bead on her location."

"Got it. Text me the address. I'll call as soon as I have anything. Thanks," Hudson said, hanging up the phone and dialing Joe. "Hey, got a location on a guy who may have gotten Mac a fake ID. Can you meet me?"

Hudson took enough time to go to his office to change back into civilian clothes and grab his own truck. He met Joe outside the small restaurant less than an hour after receiving the call from Lola.

"Stay behind me. No cowboy shit, understand? You've got no jurisdiction here." Joe said.

Hudson wanted nothing more than to tear this guy apart, but things didn't work that way. The last thing he wanted to do was get Joe in trouble.

"Fine, promise," Hudson said and followed him down the stairs into the basement. He felt naked with no weapon, but Joe insisted he would come unarmed.

When they came to the landing, a strange-looking stick of a man turned with surprised eyes. "What the hell?" he said, and tried to take off in the opposite direction. A door led to the back of the small space where the man made a beeline for the back of the room.

"Freeze," Joe yelled, pushing his gun out in front of him. Hudson crossed the small space before the green-haired man disappeared through it and yanked him hard by the back of the shirt, listening to the thin fabric tear in his hand. He didn't weigh much, and Hudson had no problems slamming him onto the concrete floor.

"He said freeze. That means you fucking freeze," Hudson growled.

"Okay, okay, calm down, man. What the hell do you want?"

"I want you to tell me about a visitor you had yesterday. It would have been two women, one brunette and one redhead," Hudson said, staring down at the man. Joe had his gun trained on him.

"I don't know what you're talking about," he said, as Hudson slammed his foot into the man's ribs.

"I think you do." Hudson reached down, grabbed his green hair, and hoisted him into a sitting position, listening to him scream out and wriggle beneath his fingers. "I think you're going to tell me everything."

"Now, why would I do that?"

Joe stepped forward, placing his hand on Hudson's arm. "You have the right to remain silent and a right to an attorney, or you can help reduce the charges against you and cooperate."

"What charges?" His eyes grew wide and defiant.

"Everything I can fucking think of to put you behind bars for the better part of your natural life, and from the looks of this place, there's plenty of evidence or…" Joe let the words hang in the air.

"Fine, what do you want? And can you tell your muscle here to let me go?"

Joe nodded his head and Hudson released his hair, grabbed his arm, and hoisted him into the same chair where Mac had sat. "Spill it, asshole. What did you do to Mac?"

"I have no idea who Mac is." Hudson reached over and smacked the man on the back of the head. "Dammit, stop that," he said, rubbing the back of his head. "I don't know Mac, but the two women who were in here yesterday were hot, but no brunette or redhead. They were both blond."

"Blond? What did you give them?"

"The works. The one in charge paid for a full package for the other lady. I still have pictures of her. I can show you." He slipped past Hudson and walked over to his computer and turned the screen around. Hudson's breath caught in his throat. Staring back at him was Mac, but as a blond. All her beautiful chestnut hair was gone, now cropped above her shoulders. She still looked stunning, but different. Hudson couldn't stop staring at the picture.

Joe cleared his throat. "Did they say where they were staying? Any indication of where they would be?"

"Nah man, just said they needed the full package. The passport I gave her says they might be traveling, but I don't have any idea where or any of that."

"Fine, get up," Joe said.

"Oh, come on, you said the charges would be gone if I talked."

"No, shit for brains. They might be reduced, and they will, but you're still under arrest. Now come with me or I'll let my friend here take a turn on you before we go in." He held his hands up, then with quiet resolve placed them behind his back and turned around. Joe took him upstairs and placed him in the back of his cruiser. "At least we have the name she'll be traveling under."

"Yeah, maybe it will give Lola something to work with. She'll be able to track any flights leaving Spokane with her on it."

"Keep me posted. I'm going to deliver this guy to lock-up, but I'm free after if you find any leads."

Hudson climbed into his truck to head back to base, his phone ringed and he pulled to the side of the road. "Yeah," he said without looking at the caller ID.

"I might have something," Lola said. "An eyewitness reported to the Spokane police tip line. She thinks the woman they're all looking for is held up in a small house on the outskirts of town."

"Where is it at?"

"I'll text you the address. It might be the break we're looking for. The house is owned by a shell company, but I've been able to trace it to another company owned by none other than Gennavie's uncle Frank. He's the high-powered defense attorney out in California. If he's funding her, then it explains how she's been able to stay off the grid for so long and not run out of money. I've got the FBI looking into it. If everything lines up, they might freeze his assets."

"Great work, Lola." His phone beeped as the text came through. "I'll call you back as soon as I have something."

HUDSON'S TIRES squealed as he pulled a U-turn, heading toward the address Lola gave him. He dialed Joe on his way and told him what he had. "K, I'm on my way. No going in half-cocked without backup," Joe said, trying to sound stern but coming across as worried.

"I'll wait until you pull up. We have no idea what we're walking into." The last thing Hudson wanted to do was excite Gennavie and make her do something stupid to Mac when she panicked. He pulled up in front of the house. It looked deserted, but that meant nothing. The blinds were pulled closed, and he didn't have a clear view inside. He wanted to run through the door like a human battering ram, but it wasn't a good idea, so he waited. It took a long time before Joe pulled up behind his truck with the same green-haired man still locked in the back. "I thought you were getting rid of him."

"Didn't have time, so he'll have to wait." Joe opened the passenger side door, secured his passenger with handcuffs, and locked his hands behind him.

"I thought they couldn't get out once locked in the back."

"They're not supposed to, but I've seen some perps do some pretty creative things. I'd rather not take any chances."

The two men approached the house. Joe was in the lead with his gun out, and Hudson stepped behind him. Joe pushed his body to the side of the doorjamb and cracked his knuckles on the solid wood. "Police, open the door." No answer. They waited another minute without a sound coming from the inside, so Joe tried again. When he turned around, Hudson was gone. "Shit."

Sounds came from the back of the house. Joe sprinted around as Hudson was letting himself in. "Dammit, I told you to wait. I don't have probable cause and I'm not about to add breaking and entering to the things I do today."

"Wait here. I need to check." Before Joe said another word, Hudson disappeared into the house. He was careful not to touch anything as he walked from room to room. The tiny place only took him a few minutes to clear. He poked his head back out. "They're not here, but they were."

"How do you know?"

"Blond dye in the kitchen sink and the clothes Mac was wearing the last time I saw her." The memory flashed through his mind of Mac in tears, telling him the one thing he never wanted to hear. He took a deep breath, taking comfort in knowing that she was trying to protect him. Hudson took the corner of his t-shirt, wiped the doorknob, and pulled it closed behind him. "You should be able to secure a warrant with the information Lola is sending you now. We're getting close. I can feel it," he said more to himself than to Joe. He was trying to convince himself it was all going to work out okay.

"Okay, I'll put in for the warrant, but no more of this shit where you go off without me."

"Got it." He watched Joe pull away for the second time and called Lola. "Hey, not here, but they were at one time."

"Perfect. I'll work with Agent Bardot to convince a judge to sign off on Frank's financials. It might throw Gennavie off her game if she doesn't have any operating money. We need her to make a mistake."

"What's Reina's status?"

"Last I heard she was sitting in solitary, but I don't think it's going to last. Our theory has little evidence, and it's a bit of a stretch. If the warden confirms Gennavie's identity as one of Reina's visitors, then we may have more of a leg to stand on. Gennavie still has an active warrant out for her arrest."

"Keep me posted," he said and hung up, letting his head fall back as he closed his eyes.

CHAPTER
SEVENTY-FIVE

MAC WOKE THE NEXT MORNING. She was getting tired of being dragged all over Spokane by a crazy woman. Gennavie was becoming more erratic as the days passed, and she still hadn't talked to Reina about flight plans. She had to know that the more time they stayed in Spokane, the bigger the risk of being caught. Mac had no idea if Gennavie had caught wind of Hudson's press conference.

As the sleep cleared from her groggy mind, she realized something was wrong. She'd slept well, which couldn't be right. When she tried to move, she couldn't twist her head. Something around her neck pulled tight against her skin. Not tight enough to cut off her air supply, but the leather was cutting into the soft skin under her chin.

"What the hell?" she said into the quiet room. As she sat up, there was no sign of her captor. Her head was swimming, and her balance was off as she tried to stand and made it into the bathroom. The woman staring back at her looked foreign. Severe bags were under her swollen eyes and her face looked gaunt from lack of food and water. Around her neck was a thick leather strap. Grabbing hold of it, she tried to pull, but it held without a clasp to release it. A tiny lock held the thing together. Mac slid the door shut when the motel room door opened. She struggled with the collar to get it off. *What is she going to use it for?* As the thought crossed her mind, the door flung open.

"You're a fucking bitch," Gennavie growled. The woman was coming unhinged. She had a small remote in her hand that looked a lot like a garage door opener, but Mac had a good idea it was something else.

"What are you talking about? I didn't do anything."

"Yes, you did," Gennavie screamed and hit the button, sending Mac to the floor, convulsing as the shock collar sent waves of electricity through her system. Gennavie released the button and Mac's body became still. The smell of burned flesh assaulted Mac's nose as she regained her bearings and attempted to sit up as Gennavie's hand clamped down on the remote again.

"Wait," she said, holding up her hand. "I've been here with you the entire time. What did I do to you?"

Gennavie spit out the next words. "Because of you, we're all over the news. It's all your fault. Your only job was to make sure no one came looking for you. Do you know what that means?"

"Relax," Mac tried, but Gennavie wasn't listening. The electricity pulsed through her. At first she tried to fight it, but within seconds darkness engulfed her brain.

Mac cracked her eyes open, trying to lie still so the collar around her neck didn't dig further into the burn marks. Gennavie was stalking back and forth around the room with the phone on speaker. Mac lay still and listened, not wanting Gennavie to press the button still sitting in her hand. The scratchy comforter brushed against the skin on her arms, and she wondered how Gennavie had moved her. The woman was a lot stronger than Mac gave her credit for.

Mac listened to the two women argue about her fate. It was clear they wanted different things out of the situation. "I don't care if you make her suffer," Reina's voice came out of the phone in Gennavie's hand.

"I don't want to make her suffer. I want her to have to watch me kill Hudson."

"It's too risky. Hudson is an enormous man and can easily over-power you. There's no reason to take the risk. Listen to me. Be patient and I'll have you two out soon enough. Some asshole shoved me in solitary, but now that I'm out, I'll be back to work."

"How can I trust you?" Gennavie growled into the phone.

"Don't let my beautiful daughter fuck with your head. I'm going to keep my word. You have nothing to worry about. I'll make sure they take care of Vincent, and you get what you need to start a whole new life."

"Why don't I kill the little bitch and I'll take over things for you? At least with me at the helm, I'll do it right."

"You'll not kill my daughter. Do you understand?" Reina remained silent, waiting for a response. "Do you understand?" she said again.

"Yeah, I understand, but she's the reason Vincent…"

Reina cut her off. "Let me be very clear. If you don't do what I say, you will not make it out of this arrangement alive. I don't care who you think you are, but I'm done arguing with you. I'm out of time. Can I trust you to be patient and keep Evelyn in one piece until I can make arrangements?"

"Yes."

The line disconnected. Gennavie stomped around the room like a young child throwing a fit. Mac watched, not making a sound. She knew help wasn't coming and she'd have to figure things out on her own. It was clear Gennavie wasn't playing by the rules and her nerves were fraying at the edges.

"Why don't you run?" Mac said in a whisper. "Thousands of men are as twisted as Vincent. They'll do your bidding and make you happy. Walk away and forget all about Reina and her plan."

"I can't, thanks to you. My source of income dried up, and they plastered our faces everywhere. Someone froze my uncle's assets and now I don't have any money. So, I'm stuck with you. Vincent is back in the infirmary, but at least his case is moving forward. As soon as your mother comes through, then maybe we'll get the hell out of here. If your mother keeps her word, she said I would have part of her fortune so long as I bring you in alive."

Gennavie's mind processed everything behind her beautiful green eyes. Mac hoped the other woman would decide money was more important than exacting revenge and hurting her or, worse yet, following through with her threat to kill Hudson in front of her.

CHAPTER
SEVENTY-SIX

LOLA DIALED HUDSON'S NUMBER. They were getting so close. "Hey, how're you holding up?"

"People keep asking me that. I only want to find her."

"Yeah, me too. My sister is one of the toughest women I've ever met. If anyone can survive our mother and Gennavie, it's Mac. Plus, I might have something."

"Lay it on me. I sure can use some good news about now."

"The authorities froze Gennavie's uncle's assets. Until now, she's been working in cash. I'm tracking all her cards. According to Frank's bank records, they withdrew three thousand from one of his accounts at several ATMs in the area. The last transaction was over two weeks ago. She has to be running out of funds and resources. And you'll love this," Lola said. "They let Reina out of solitary, and she made a phone call to none other than Gennavie. Voice recognition software confirmed her identity. She also made a direct threat on your life, and the Feds aren't taking it sitting down. Bardot wants you into protective custody. They believe Gennavie has been working with a couple of prison guards. One of which they found mutilated and barely alive in his own bed."

"I'll worry about myself later. We need to find her before they put me on lockdown."

"Give me a little more time and I'll have her," Lola said and hung up.

Hudson didn't know what to do with himself. It took everything he had not to drive around town looking. He had no way of knowing where Gennavie was holding Mac at this point. The thought of losing her forever was unacceptable. The only way he would have a future and move forward would be to bring her back to him. If something happened to her, he didn't think he would survive it. He took a long sip of whisky. The burn slid down his throat. Not enough for it to affect him, but enough to relax. He lay back on his bed, placing his head on the pillow where Mac had slept.

Closing his eyes, he saw her with her dark chestnut hair piled high on her head with little pearls holding it in place. She wore the most elegant gown as she floated down the aisle toward him. He couldn't believe she'd agreed to be his. He had to be the luckiest man who ever lived. There was no other way to look at it.

His mind jumped forward to the wedding night. Her soft skin was under his large hands, his mouth nibbling on her ear and down her neck. The scent of honey and vanilla overwhelmed his senses as he slid down her neck and engulfed her nipple in his warm mouth. Hearing her moan under him made him feel powerful. Her strong back arched into him as he pulled and played with her, sliding down her flat stomach and kissing her soft skin until he found himself between her legs. Teasing at first, he played with the soft inside of her thighs until his mouth found her wet heat. She wrapped her legs around his massive shoulders and pulled him closer. "More," she begged. "Please," she whispered. He'd never deny his beautiful bride as he brought her to an explosion, and in one swift move climbed on her body and inch by inch entered her.

Noise in the background interrupted his dream. He cracked an eye open, not realizing he'd drifted off. When he saw it was Lola calling, he sat up, losing the dream altogether. "What do you have?"

"I found her. I'm sending you the address now. Be careful," Lola said. "Call me as soon as you have her."

"You got it." Hudson grabbed his keys and sprinted out to his truck at full speed, sending Joe a text with the location.

CHAPTER
SEVENTY-SEVEN

GENNAVIE WAS BOUNCING on the balls of her feet. She kept checking the long rifle perched on the tripod, still in the center of the room, pointed at the front door. Mac sat watching her. Gennavie had a huge smile pasted on her face, and Mac was afraid to ask. She came over to the bed and sat next to Mac. "Nope, that won't do." She cocked her head to the side and leaned forward. "No way you'll have a good view from this angle."

"Do I even want to know what you're talking about?" Mac asked with resolve in her voice.

"Hudson's on his way. He'll be coming through that door." She looked down at her watch. "Should be in about five minutes."

"No," Mac gasped. "I said I'd do whatever you wanted me to as long as he stayed safe."

"Well, he ruined that now, didn't he? I can't let him run around causing me all kinds of trouble, can I?" She set the remote for the shock collar on the nightstand, pushed her gun against the side of Mac's head as she released the handcuff securing her to the bed. She pulled Mac's hands together and clasped the cuffs back in place. "Now come with me. I'd hate for you to miss the show."

Mac stood and let Gennavie move her into the family room. Her heart pounding against her rib cage like it would explode from her chest at any moment. Gennavie pushed her onto the couch and leveled the gun at her head. Mac tried to control her breathing and clear her mind. She had to figure out a way to stop Gennavie from hurting Hudson. Gennavie walked over to the rifle to check it for the fifth time. Mac rolled off the couch knowing the shock collar remote was no longer within Gennavie's reach. A chunk of the stuffing exploded near Mac's head.

"Where do you think you're going?" Gennavie asked, padding her pocket. "Where the hell is the remote?" Gennavie followed with the barrel of her gun pressed forward.

Mac pulled her body around the corner as another bullet exploded onto the tile floor where her leg had been. She crawled forward into the kitchen, looking for anything. And then she saw it. Calmness washed over Mac as she realized she wouldn't hesitate to die for Hudson. If this was her last day on earth, then so be it.

Mac pushed off with her legs and clasped her hands around the handle of the long kitchen knife. She twisted as Gennavie walked through the door. Mac thrust the blade forward with both her hands and held tight, the handle slipped in her sweaty hands as the cuffs bit into her wrists. She threw her body forward, plunging the knife into Gennavie's shoulder thinking only of stopping Hudson from walking through that door. Slipping on the floor, she regained her footing and sprinted through the open kitchen door.

A shot exploded in the small space. Mac looked down. Blood spread over the side of her blue shirt. At first, it didn't register until the pain washed over her like a vicious wave crashing through her system. She spun around to see Gennavie pointing the gun at her.

Mac flew at Gennavie, launching her body into Gennavie's watching her fall to the floor with the knife sticking at a weird angle from her left shoulder. Mac tried to push the gun away, but Gennavie grabbed it with her right hand. Mac slipped on the bloody floor and let the entire weight of her body fall on top of Gennavie. The air rushed from Gennavie's lungs as Gennavie deflated and the gun went spinning forward on the slick floor. She twisted her body under Mac, crawling on her stomach, she reached out for the gun. Mac wrapped her cuffed hands around Gennavie's throat and pulled hard with all her weight. Everything in Mac's body screamed at her as she wrenched herself back and the hole in her side stretched open like a gaping mouth.

Gennavie squirmed, pulling hard against Mac's arms. She dug her long nails deep into Mac's hands, making her scream out in pain, but she held fast. Repositioning her feet so her butt was planted into the small part of Gennavie's back, she thrust herself backward until Gennavie's body went slack.

Little trickles of blood dripped down her wrists when she released and pulled herself off Gennavie. Relief washed over her. She hoisted the woman over and onto her back. Digging her hands deep in Gennavie's front pockets, she came back with the little key to her handcuffs. Standing on wobbly legs, she leaned against the speckled yellow laminate counter for support and released the cuffs, binding her wrists.

They made a loud clank as they hit the floor, echoing through the room. Mac sprinted for the gun at the front of the door. *Hudson* was all she could think of. Pushing off the counter and toward the front door, her left leg stopped in midair, and she went crashing into the door separating the kitchen from the family room. Her head slammed into the wood, making a sickening thud. The world went off balance.

When she opened her eyes, Gennavie had climbed on her with the gun drawn. *Stupid,* was all she thought. How could she be so stupid to leave the gun on the floor?

In the background, a vehicle pulled up out front.

"Please no," Mac whispered. She thrust her arms into Gennavie's outstretched hands. The gun erupted next to her ear, leaving an incessant ringing sound in its wake.

Grabbing hold of the stunned woman's delicate wrists, Mac wrenched them back into an unnatural angle. Gennavie's grip loosened on the gun. Mac twisted it in her hand and pointed it at the woman's chest. Her finger reached the trigger as Gennavie pressed back against her cuffed hands. Adrenaline fueled her brain as she pushed forward, arching her hand enough to pull the trigger.

Gennavie's beautiful green eyes widened in surprise when her blood splattered across Mac's face.

CHAPTER
SEVENTY-EIGHT

MAC ROLLED TO THE SIDE, pushing Gennavie's limp body off her. Warm blood—hers and Gennavie's—was already smeared across her own chest. Scrambling to her feet, she lunged for the kitchen door, making it to the family room in time to hear Hudson's voice on the other side. "No, stop!" she screamed at the top of her lungs, hurling her body at the gun. Everything slowed as her body glided through the air.

The front door was flung open. The last thing she saw as her body hit the tripod holding the machine gun was the man she loved being peppered with bullets. His body hit the concrete steps, and blood sprayed across his chest.

This couldn't be how it ended.

The gun stopped, but she couldn't breathe. Her body was stuck in place from the loss of blood. Her front was soaked. Forcing herself to inch forward but afraid to look, she crawled on all fours through the door. She grabbed his motionless body and pulled herself the rest of the way, feeling her bullet wound tear open further. He didn't move, and she couldn't tell if he was breathing. If he was dead, she would have no choice but to lay down next to him and die. She couldn't imagine a future without him.

She pulled her body the last few inches until she was next to him.

His body was warm yet motionless and covered in blood. "No, no, no," she screamed. This couldn't be right. Blood had sprayed across his chest. Laying her head on his large chest, she wanted to give up until her cheek pressed into a hard surface. She ripped open the front of his gray button-down to reveal the one thing she never expected. "Thank God."

Mac did everything she could to regain her ability to breathe. Underneath, she saw the most wonderful thing she could ever imagine. His Kevlar vest had caught most of the damage. The material had several slugs embedded inside, but they hadn't penetrated all the way through. A hole in his shoulder oozed blood. She hoped it was a through-and-through.

"Hudson, can you hear me?"

At first he didn't answer, so she slapped him on the cheek, but nothing happened. She pulled her hand back and was about to slap the shit out of him until he moaned and took a deep breath. Wrapping her body around him, she squeezed.

"Ouch," he breathed out, wrapping her tighter in a hug.

"I thought you were dead," was all she managed as the entire block lit up with police cars.

Joe came running at them at full speed, with several other officers trailing right behind him. He pushed his gun out in front of him.

Mac lifted her head, looking up at Joe and smiling. "She's in there, but I'm pretty sure she's dead." Not wanting to move, she laid her head back on Hudson's chest. The adrenaline ran out of her body, leaving fatigue in its place.

Joe and his team checked and were back out within seconds as the paramedics surrounded Mac and Hudson, still lying in a heap on the front steps. "Ma'am, I'm going to move you now." She didn't resist and wasn't sure she could. "Where are you hurt?"

Hudson pulled his body forward to take a good look at Mac. His chest hurt like hell, and he realized not all the bullets had hit his vest. He had been so happy she was alive and in his arms, he hadn't thought any further. "You're covered in blood." Panic filled his voice. "What the hell's on your neck?"

"Not mine," she managed, closing her eyes. "At least not all of it."

"Can someone grab me the bolt cutters?" the paramedic shouted. "Okay ma'am, I need you to stay still." He craned his neck around. "Does anyone have the remote?"

"I have it," Joe said from behind him.

Relief washed over her as the sharp blades cut through the leather holding the shock collar in place. It would be a long time before she would wear anything around her neck again. "Sit still," the paramedic instructed. "You've both suffered gunshot wounds."

Hudson looked over at his beautiful bride right before they hoisted her onto the waiting stretcher. "I'm forever in love with you," he said as four men struggled to hoist him onto the next gurney.

CHAPTER
SEVENTY-NINE

AT THE HOSPITAL, Joe, Mac's dad, and Hudson's mom all waited for the news. Mac had lost a lot of blood. Hudson took a bullet to the shoulder and was in surgery.

Hudson's mom was pacing around the room like a worried mama bear when the doctor appeared. "News," she shot at the doctor without mincing words.

"Are you Gavin Hudson's mother?"

"Yes, is he okay?"

"He's going to be fine. He'll be sore for a while but should make a full recovery. The bullet wound closed with what appears to be no nerve damage presenting, but we'll have to wait to be sure."

"Thank you, Doctor," Momma Hudson said, clasping his hand.

"What about my daughter?" Mac's dad asked, worry spread through his eyes.

"She was a bit more difficult, but we're hoping for a full recovery in her case. Thanks to the blood you donated, we repaired most of the damage. The bullet in her side went all the way through and missed any major organs. The burn on her neck will take some time to heal and she'll have a nasty scar, but if she can rest, she'll be okay. She's a lucky lady," the doctor said.

"Can we see them?" Joe asked.

"Yes, but make it quick. They both need their rest."

All three filed into the small room. Mac looked small in her bed next to Hudson. They'd brought in an extra-large bed to make him more comfortable.

Mac smiled when they walked in and tried to lift her head, but laid it back down as her brain swam. "Hi," was all she managed.

"We're so happy you two are okay." Momma Hudson came over and hugged Mac and then wrapped her boy in a hug.

"Takes more than that to get rid of us," Mac said, smiling as she noticed her dad and Hudson's mom holding hands, but she let it go for now.

"Toughest woman I know," Hudson said.

Joe cleared his throat. "I'm glad you guys are both okay. Once you're up to it, Mac, I'm going to need your official statement."

"Is she dead?" Mac asked.

"Yeah, she died on the way to the hospital, but you shouldn't have anything to worry about. It looks to everyone like a clear case of self-defense, since we found you with that nasty shock collar around your neck. We confirmed Gennavie was working with Reina."

"What'll happen to my mother now?" Mac asked.

"They'll prosecute her as planned, with additional murder charges against her for the judge and Captain Anika Wilson. They can't tie her to Lieutenant Colonel Daniels' murder, but they're looking into it. In the meantime, they've limited her communication privileges with the outside world to meeting only with her attorneys."

"What about the prison guards they were working with?" Mac's dad asked.

"That was weird," Joe said. "They were twins, both working for the Department of Corrections on opposite sides of the state. Gennavie was sleeping with both. The brother in Seattle took the brunt of it. She lost it, and he almost didn't survive. Once he recovers, he and his brother will be up on charges. Gennavie's Uncle Frank is under full investigation for aiding and abetting a fugitive."

CHAPTER
EIGHTY

IT TOOK Hudson and Mac a long time to pick up the pieces of their lives. It took over nine months to unscrew Hudson's pay and benefits. People in the military community still somehow thought he'd gotten away with something, even though Captain Boom from Public Affairs ran a series of articles and got a spot on the major news channels covering the entire case.

The federal courts found Reina guilty on multiple charges, and she was serving a life sentence in a maximum-security prison. Uncle Frank made a plea deal and negotiated his sentence down to five years after convincing a judge Gennavie was gaining access to only her trust money, not his funds, and he didn't know what she was up to. The prison guard brothers pled guilty and were both serving ten- and twelve-year sentences. Vincent survived his ordeal in prison but had permanent nerve damage, leaving him in a wheelchair. He was working through his latest appeal to take him off death row, but it wasn't looking promising.

.   .   .

Mac's dad went back to Kentucky with Hudson's mom. They decided life was too short to wait, so they didn't. They had a small ceremony with the immediate family—Lola, Mac, Hudson, and Uncle Lu. Hudson and Mac were happy for them, but it took some getting used to since technically it made Hudson and Mac stepbrother and sister.

After their parents' wedding, Mac and Hudson fell into bed, exhausted. It had been a long road trying to bring everything back to a world of normal. Whatever that meant. She couldn't believe things were coming together. All the planning had been more exhausting than any of the cases she remembered working.

The time flew by. It was just over a year since Hudson had asked her to be his wife and she'd offered her life to save his.

"Are you excited?" Hudson asked, snuggling his large body up against hers.

"I've been waiting for this since the day we met," she said with a soft smile.

He nibbled on the soft spot right below her ear that sent shivers down her spine. "Isn't it bad luck or something, the day before..." she tried to say, but it sounded more like mumbling.

He rolled her over, covering her mouth with his, the heat of anticipation growing. "No more bad luck for us," he whispered.

Her soft skin under his large hands—the way she responded to his touch, pressing her body toward his—made him want her more than ever. His excitement came from watching her let her guard down and releasing her inhibitions.

Spending the rest of his life bringing her pleasure was the only way he wanted to spend his future. He ran his lips down her neck, kissing and nibbling as he went until he slipped her hard nipple into his mouth. Her body arched up in anticipation as she let out a soft moan.

Replacing his mouth with his hands, he rolled her nipples between his fingers, kissing as he worked his way down her flat stomach. When he reached the soft spot between her legs, she opened and let him in. Her orgasm came fast and violent. Before she had the chance to recover, he pulled his body up on hers and entered, mounting excitement pulsing through his body as he thrust into her.

Her body tightened around him as his excitement mounted. He pulled her legs up on his large shoulders, driving deeper and faster until her body began to shake under his. The explosion came fast and hard for both of them as he emptied himself.

He collapsed, rolling to her side, careful not to crush her. Their bodies were covered in a sheen of sweat. He had never been so happy and satisfied. He couldn't believe she was going to be his. He knew every day he would work to bring her pleasure, happiness, and if they were truly lucky, a few beautiful children that looked like her.

CHAPTER
EIGHTY-ONE

"HOW ARE YOU HOLDING UP?" Lola said as she came into the small room.

"A little nervous, but okay I guess."

"Oh, come on, you look stunning. It's almost time. Let me help you with that." Lola walked over and adjusted Mac's hair, spraying it all in place. It was back to its normal chestnut and had begun to grow back out. Lola slid the silk choker over the scar around Mac's neck. It was healing, but Mac didn't want the reminder in any of her wedding photos.

Little Olive popped her head through the door. "Annie Mac, it's time," she said in her sing-song voice. She was dressed head to toe in the cutest little white dress with tulle draped around her ankles. She'd been complaining about what she called "socks pants" the entire morning, but she looked adorable.

Mac smiled. "Are you ready?"

"Yup," Olive said, coming in to grab her mother's hand. The two walked out, leaving Mac alone for a moment.

She'd never thought this day would come. It was unreal.

She dabbled in a little extra makeup over the scar and made sure the choker covered it. It was a constant reminder of how precious life was. Adjusting her veil one last time, she walked out into the church with the train of her stunning backless wedding gown trailing behind her. Excitement buzzed in the air as she took her place at the back. Everyone she cared about was present. Ali stood next to her sister while Momma Hudson sat in the front row with Ali and Joe's baby boy. Joe stood next to Hudson and smiled.

Hudson stood at the front of the church with his strong shoulders back, smiling as she walked toward him. It was time for her to have a normal life with the man she loved more than anyone else. She couldn't stop beaming as she took her place next to him. This was where she belonged.

THANK YOU FOR READING MY BOOK!

Please leave a review, so other readers will give my book a chance. I appreciate your feedback, and I love hearing what you have to say.

I need your input to make the next book and my future books better. Please leave me an honest review letting me know what you like and don't like so I can keep the good stuff and get rid of the not-so-good.

If you found mistakes, typos, or there is a way I can make this novel better, please e-mail me at julie@sjpublishing96.com.

RECEIVE A FREE SHORT STORY

Join Julie Bergman's newsletter and get your free short story, updates about future books and get to know the author only at: https://juliebergman-author.com/my-books.

ACKNOWLEDGMENTS

A special thanks to my editor and mentor Shavonne Clarke who has openly answered all my questions and concerns along the way. Without her help and support, I would not be here. She is simply amazing. Thank you to all the fans who have taken a chance on my new book to help me launch my career as a writer.

ABOUT THE AUTHOR

Julie Bergman is a retired military veteran who served her country for over 20 years. She lives in beautiful Spokane, Washington with her supportive husband, four wonderful children, and a slobbery Olde English Bulldog with attitude. After over 17 years in the JAG Corp and a master's degree in forensic psychology, her fascination with crime and the dark side of humanity has spilled into a military-based serial killer series that you won't be able to put down.